W9-BJF-010

ACCLAIM FOR JAMES PATTERSON'S WOMEN'S MURDER CLUB THRILLERS

14TH DEADLY SIN

"Patterson and Paetro produce another hit with *14th Deadly Sin*...Each book can be read as a standalone but you'll want to read all fourteen of them. Each story line is full of mystery, intrigue...not a book to be missed."

—FreshFiction.com

"Patterson and Paetro do it again with the latest chapter in the Women's Murder Club series...a classic example of the author's work—it is well written, provocative in just the right ways, and, of course, never dull."

—RT Book Reviews

"Many people consider the Women's Murder Club to be Patterson's best collaborative series. If you haven't yet had the pleasure of sampling the canon, *14th Deadly Sin* is an excellent place to jump on. And while truly a book for all seasons, it may well be the beach read of this summer."

—BookReporter.com

UNLUCKY 13

"*Unlucky 13* moves the reader right along, with Patterson and Paetro keeping the proceedings engrossed and enthralled with situations that more often than are not ripped from real-world headlines. It will give fans and newcomers alike much to love."

—BookReporter.com

"Non-stop action...another great story by Patterson and Paetro."

—FreshFiction.com

"Rapidly paced to its final conclusion... The novel has many twists and turns to keep readers turning pages until the end. *Unlucky 13* is a great addition to this popular series."

—*West Orlando News*

12TH OF NEVER

"As always, Mr. Patterson does not disappoint!... It lived up to all expectations, and of course, leaves you begging for the next book." —BaumanBookReviews.com

"Patterson and Paetro always give readers their money's worth, and *12th of Never* is the gold standard for that proposition... You'll find it moving and compelling from beginning to end and, yes, beyond... Start reading, and you won't stop."

—BookReporter.com

11TH HOUR

"The pages turn at an alarming rate and contain an abundance of thrills and surprises... an impressively high-caliber entry in this enduring series... Patterson and Paetro aim to please—and they've got you in their sights."

—Examiner.com

"Each chapter races by at a fast and furious pace, snatching the very breath from your lungs."

—NightsandWeekends.com

10TH ANNIVERSARY

"Short, pulse-pounding chapters come at you like bullets... a whirlwind of a ride... Don't miss this one."

—NightsandWeekends.com

"Verdict: Patterson and Paetro spin a fast-paced triple mystery that expertly weaves the stories together…Highly recommended." —*Library Journal*

THE 9TH JUDGMENT

"Everything that an outstanding mystery and thriller should be, as it shocks, tantalizes, and teases, right up until the very end." —BookReporter.com

"Another great Patterson/Paetro novel for those of us who can't get enough Patterson—ever!"
—TheReviewBroads.com

THE 8TH CONFESSION

"The ending was so mind-blowing…I immediately wished I had another Patterson novel to pick up." —Bookalicio.us

"Mystery, mayhem, and murder most foul."
—*Publishers Weekly*

"Vintage Patterson…a must-read."
—TheNovelBookworm.com

7TH HEAVEN

"An ideal Patterson read for long-term fans and newcomers to the series." —TheRomanceReadersConnection.com

"A solid, fast-paced read…[with] some truly compelling characters…I can easily understand why it's such a popular series. I want more!" —*Akron Record-Courier* (OH)

THE 6TH TARGET

"Another masterpiece." —1340magbooks.com

"A maddeningly compelling read—the kind that only Patterson can assemble." —EdgeMiami.com

THE 5TH HORSEMAN
"Those who haven't read any of the novels in the Women's Murder Club series are cheating themselves."
—BookReporter.com

"An absolutely tantalizing and spellbinding read…Patterson scores a perfect ten." —NewMysteryReader.com

4TH OF JULY
"Stunning…nail-biting…a great read."
—RebeccasReads.com

"A compelling page-turner that, once you start reading, you can't put down…Grab hold of this one."
—EdgeBoston.com

3RD DEGREE
"Buy this one—you will understand why Mr. Patterson is referred to as 'the most addictive writer at work today.'"
—Bestsellersworld.com

"Incredible…chilling…The suspense is never-ending and the plot is to die for!" —Myshelf.com

2ND CHANCE
"Inspiring heroines…juicy subplots…briskly paced…Patterson chalks up another suspenseful outing for his Women's Murder Club." —*People*

"A fast-paced thriller by the page-turningest author in the game right now."
—*San Francisco Chronicle*

"Prime Patterson: first-rate entertainment…ripples with twists and remarkably strong scenes."
—*Publishers Weekly* (starred review)

1ST TO DIE

"I can't believe how good Patterson is…He's always on the mark."
—Larry King, *USA Today*

"Patterson boils a scene down to the single, telling detail, the element that defines a character or moves a plot along. It's what fires off the movie projector in the reader's mind."
—Michael Connelly, author of *Nine Dragons*

"His clever twists and affecting subplots keep the pages flying."
—*People* (Page-Turner of the Week)

"Delivers a sharp punch."
—*Chicago Tribune*

"That rapid-fire, in-your-face, you'd-better-keep-reading-or-else format will make you finish *1st to Die* in one sitting."
—*Denver Rocky Mountain News*

BOOKS BY JAMES PATTERSON

Featuring The Women's Murder Club

15th Affair (with Maxine Paetro)
14th Deadly Sin (with Maxine Paetro)
Unlucky 13 (with Maxine Paetro)
12th of Never (with Maxine Paetro)
11th Hour (with Maxine Paetro)
10th Anniversary (with Maxine Paetro)
The 9th Judgment (with Maxine Paetro)
The 8th Confession (with Maxine Paetro)
7th Heaven (with Maxine Paetro)
The 6th Target (with Maxine Paetro)
The 5th Horseman (with Maxine Paetro)
4th of July (with Maxine Paetro)
3rd Degree (with Andrew Gross)
2nd Chance (with Andrew Gross)
1st to Die

A complete list of books by James Patterson is at the back of this book. For previews of upcoming books and information about the author, visit JamesPatterson.com, or find him on Facebook or at your app store.

15TH AFFAIR

JAMES PATTERSON
AND MAXINE PAETRO

GRAND CENTRAL
PUBLISHING
New York Boston

The characters and events in this book are fictitious. Any similarity to real persons, living or dead, is coincidental and not intended by the author.

Copyright © 2016 by James Patterson

Hachette Book Group supports the right to free expression and the value of copyright. The purpose of copyright is to encourage writers and artists to produce the creative works that enrich our culture.

The scanning, uploading, and distribution of this book without permission is a theft of the author's intellectual property. If you would like permission to use material from the book (other than for review purposes), please contact permissions@hbgusa.com. Thank you for your support of the author's rights.

Grand Central Publishing
Hachette Book Group
1290 Avenue of the Americas, New York, NY 10104
grandcentralpublishing.com
twitter.com/grandcentralpub

Originally published in hardcover and ebook by Little, Brown and Company in May 2016.
First international mass market edition: November 2016

Grand Central Publishing is a division of Hachette Book Group, Inc.
The Grand Central Publishing name and logo is a trademark of Hachette Book Group, Inc.

Women's Murder Club is a trademark of JBP Business, LLC.

The publisher is not responsible for websites (or their content) that are not owned by the publisher.

The Hachette Speakers Bureau provides a wide range of authors for speaking events. To find out more, go to hachettespeakersbureau.com or call (866) 376-6591.

ISBNs: 978-1-4555-9838-0 (international mass market), 978-1-4555-8527-4 (trade paperback), 978-0-316-29005-0 (ebook)

Printed in the United States of America

OPM

10 9 8 7 6 5 4 3 2 1

ATTENTION CORPORATIONS AND ORGANIZATIONS:
Most Hachette Book Group books are available at quantity discounts with bulk purchase for educational, business, or sales promotional use. For information, please call or write:

Special Markets Department, Hachette Book Group
1290 Avenue of the Americas, New York, NY 10104
Telephone: 1-800-222-6747 Fax: 1-800-477-5925

To friends of the
Women's Murder Club

PART ONE

PART ONE

CHAPTER 1

ALISON MULLER WASNT classically beautiful, but she was striking, with swinging blonde hair and peekaboo bangs brushing the frames of her wraparound shades. Her black leather coat flared above the knees of her skinny jeans, and her purposeful stride was punctuated by the staccato clacking of her high-heeled boots.

That afternoon, as she cut through the golden-hued lobby of San Francisco's Four Seasons Hotel, Ali checked out every man, woman, and child crossing the floor, on the queue at reception, slouched in chairs in front of the fireplace. She noted and labeled the tourists and businesspeople, deflecting the stares of the men who couldn't look away, while on the phone with her husband and their younger daughter, Mitzi.

"I didn't actually forget, Mitz," Ali said to her five-year old. "More like I lost track."

"You *did* forget," her daughter insisted.

"Not completely. I thought your big day was tomorrow."

"Everyone wanted to know where you were," her daughter complained.

"I'll make it up to you, sweetheart," Ali said.

"When? With what?"

Ali's thoughts ran ahead to the man waiting for her in a room on the fourteenth floor.

"Let me speak to Daddy," Ali said.

She passed the stunning exhibition of modern art and reached the elevator bank at the northwest end of the lobby. She stood behind the couple in front of the doors. They were French, discussing their dinner plans, agreeing that they had enough time to shower and change.

Ali thumbed her phone, checked her e-mail and the *Investors Business Daily* headlines and the text from Michael asking if she'd gotten lost. Ali's husband came back on the line.

"I did my best," he said. "She's inconsolable."

"You can handle her, dear. I'm sure you can do it. I'll order her something online when I get home."

"Which will be when?" her husband asked.

God. The questions. The never-ending questions.

"After dinner," Ali said. "I'm sorry. I wouldn't blow you off if it wasn't important."

The elevator doors opened.

"Gotta go."

Her husband said, "Say good-bye to Mitzi."

Shit.

She said, "Hang on a minute. I'm losing reception."

Ali stepped into the elevator and stood with her back to the corner, her jacket parting to reveal the butt of a gun tucked into her waistband. The doors closed and the car rose swiftly and quietly upward.

When Ali got out at the fourteenth floor, she spoke to her daughter as she walked along the plush carpeted hallway.

"Miss Mitzi?"

She reached room 1420 and rapped on the door, and it opened.

Ali said into the phone, "Happy birthday. See you soon. Kiss, kiss. Bye-bye."

She clicked off, stepped inside the room, and kicked the door closed behind her as she went into Michael's arms.

"You're late," he said.

CHAPTER 2

MICHAEL CHAN TOOK off Ali's glasses and sucked in his breath. He couldn't get over this woman—and he had tried. She smiled at him and he put his hands on both sides of her face and kissed the smile right off her.

One kiss ignited a string of them: deep, telling, momentous. Michael lifted Ali and she hooked her legs around his hips and he walked her into the luxurious blue-and-bronze suite backlit by the watercolor sunset over San Francisco.

Chan didn't notice the view. Ali smelled like orchids or some exotic musk, and she had her tongue at his ear.

"Too much," he muttered. "You're too damned much."

She was panting as he lowered her to the bed.

"Wait," she said.

"Of course. I'm a patient man," he said. His blood was surging, narrowing his focus. He put his hands on his hips and watched to see what she would do.

She looked up at him, her warm gaze flicking over his body and his strong features as if she were memorizing him. They met infrequently, but when they did, they pretended they were strangers. It was a game.

"At least tell me your name," she said.

"You first."

He pulled off her boots, tossed them aside. She sat up, shrugged off her coat, and shoved it over the edge of the bed. He plucked the gun from her waistband, looked through the sight, smelled the muzzle, and put it on the nightstand.

"Interesting," he said. "Hand-tooled."

He sat on the bed next to her and told her to lie down, and he lay next to her. He moved her bangs away from her eyes.

"Your name."

She reached down and ran her hand across the front of his pants. He grabbed her wrist.

She said, "Ummmm, I'm Renata."

"Giovanni," he said. "Prince of Gorgonzola."

She laughed. It was a terrific laugh. "Finally, I meet the Prince of Cheese."

Michael kept a straight face. "Correct. And you should never keep royalty waiting."

He stroked her cheek, then dipped his fingers beneath the neckline of her blouse.

"I think I may have met you once before," she said.

He freed the pearl buttons from their loops.

"I don't think so," he said. "I would have remembered."

He ran his hand over the tops of her breasts, then gathered up her hair, wrapped it around his left hand, and pulled her head back.

She moaned and said, "You paid me with three gold coins. I came to your room in the hotel overlooking"—she sighed—"the Trevi Fountain."

"I've never stayed in Rome," he said.

He turned her so that she faced away from him. He stroked the long side of her body down to her haunch and back. He enjoyed the soft sounds coming from her throat as she tried to twist away from him.

"Did you tell your husband?"

"Why would you ask me that?" she said.

"Because I want him to throw you out."

He undid the closure at the waist of her jeans, pulled down the zipper, got to his feet, and removed her jeans and all of his clothes.

He didn't hear the sound at the door.

This was unlike him. He had superior senses, but they were engaged. Ali was looking up at him with—what was that look in her eyes?

She said, "I heard a card in the lock."

A voice called out, "Housekeeping."

Chan said, "I didn't lock the door. You?"

Ali said, "Hell no."

Chan shouted, "Come back later," but the door was already opening and the cart was bumping over the threshold. He grabbed his pants from the floor and, holding them in front of him, he went toward the foyer.

He shouted, *"No! Wait!"*

The three shots were muffled by a suppressor. If Michael Chan had known his killer, it didn't matter now.

Lights out.

Game over.

Michael Chan was gone.

CHAPTER 3

IT HAD BEEN a rough week, and it was only Monday.

My partner, Rich Conklin, and I had just testified against Edward "Ted" Swanson, a cop who had, over time, left eighteen people dead before the shootout with a predatory drug lord called Kingfisher took Swanson out of the game.

All of the SFPD had known Swanson as a great cop. We had liked him. Respected him. So when my partner and I exposed him as a psychopath with a badge, we were stunned and outraged.

During Swanson's lethal crime spree, he had stolen over five million in drugs and money from Kingfisher, and this drug boss with a murderous reputation up and down the West Coast hadn't taken this loss as the cost of doing business.

After the shootout, while Swanson lay comatose in the ICU, Kingfisher figured that his best chance of getting his property back was to turn his death threats on the lead investigator on the case.

That investigator was me.

His phone calls were irrational, untraceable, and absolutely *terrifying*.

Then, about the time Swanson was released from the hospital and indicted on multiple charges of drug trafficking and murder, Kingfisher's phone calls stopped. A week later, Mexican authorities turned up the King's body in a shallow grave in Baja. Was it really over?

Sometimes terrifying events leave aftershocks when you realize how bad things could have become. Kingfisher's threats had embedded themselves inside me on a visceral level, and now that I was free of them, something inside me unclenched.

On the other hand, events that seem innocuous at the time can flip you right over the edge into the dark side.

And that was the case with Swanson.

A dirty cop shakes up everything: friendships, public trust, and belief in your own ability to read people. I thought I had done a good job testifying against Swanson today. I hoped so. Richie had been terrific, for sure, and now the decision as to Swanson's guilt or innocence was up to his jury.

My partner said, "We're done with this, Lindsay. Time to move on."

I was checking out of the Hall of Justice at just after six when my husband texted me to say that he would be home late, and that there was a roasted chicken in the fridge.

Damn.

I was disappointed not to see Joe, but as I stepped outside the gray granite building into a luminous summer evening, I formulated a new plan. Rather than chicken for three, I would have a quiet dinner with my baby daughter, followed by Dreamland in about three hours, tops.

I fired up my old Explorer and had just cleared the rush-hour snarl on Bryant when the boss called me.

Against my better judgment, I picked up.

"Boxer," Brady said, "a bad scene just went down at the Four Seasons. I need you there."

The only scene I wanted to see was my little girl in clean onesies, and me with a glass of Chardonnay in my hand. But Homicide was understaffed, my partner and I had a fresh gap in our caseload, and Brady was a good lieutenant.

I said, "Were you able to catch Conklin?"

"He's on the way," said Brady.

I made a U-turn on Geary, and twenty minutes later, I met up with my partner in the sumptuous lobby of the Four Seasons Hotel. Conklin was as tired as I was, but it looked good on him.

"Overtime pay, Lindsay."

"Yahoo," I said with an appropriate lack of enthusiasm. "What did Brady tell you?"

"To be smart, thorough, and quick."

"Instead of what? Stupid, sloppy, and slow?"

Richie laughed. "He said the Four Seasons wants their hotel back."

We took the elevator to the fourteenth floor, and when the doors opened, we saw that the hallway was cordoned off and law enforcement personnel were standing at the exit doors, leaning against walls, waiting for us.

Conklin and I ducked under the tape and nodded to uniforms we knew, finally pulling up to the open door marked 1420.

The cop at the door signed us into the log, and I asked him, "Who called it in?"

"Hotel's head of security. He responded to complaints of gunshots."

"How bad is it?"

"Bad enough," he said.

"Let's see," I said.

CHAPTER 4

THE FIRST OFFICER stepped aside, revealing a naked male body lying faceup, about fifteen feet inside the deluxe hotel suite. He had been shot once in the forehead, once through the right eye, and had taken another bullet to his chest for good measure.

I said to Conklin, "What do you think? Midthirties? Asian?"

Conklin nodded and said, "That's an expensive watch. He's wearing a wedding ring. We're probably not looking at a robbery."

Someone called my name.

Charlie Clapper, director of San Francisco's forensic unit, came around a corner in the suite. "Boxer," Clapper said. "Conklin. Welcome to the Four Seasons. How can we make your stay here more enjoyable?"

I said, "Tell me you've ID'd the victim and have the shooter in custody. And that by the way, the shooter confessed."

Clapper is a former homicide cop, a pro who knows what he's doing and never has to prove it. He laughed and said, "I guess miracles happen—but not here. Not today."

I peered behind Clapper. Lights had been set up and CSIs were processing the expensively furnished suite, which had soundproof windows and a high city view. There was a lot of blood around and under the victim, but the room behind him looked spotless.

I took in the silvery-blue carpeting and upholstery, the lightly rumpled bed, bedspread still in place. I saw no wine bottles or remains of a room service meal, and the TV was off.

It looked like room 1420 had only been used for a short time before what happened here went down.

Conklin asked Clapper to run what he knew so far.

Clapper said, "To start with, it looks like our victim had company. We found fresh lipstick and a few long blonde hairs on a pillowcase. There's no wallet, no suitcase, no papers, no clothes, no shoes."

"Perfect score," said Conklin.

Clapper went on. "This gentleman checked in under the name Gregory Wang. He used a credit card with that name and the charge went through, but there is no Gregory Wang at the address on the card or anywhere.

"Also notable, the room has been thoroughly wiped down. No prints old or new. Entry was by a key card that was traced to a Maria Silva in housekeeping. Ms. Silva is now off duty, not answering her phone. A patrol car has gone to her address."

"What about *his* prints?" Conklin asked, indicating the victim.

"We ran the victim's prints and came up with nothing. He's not in the system, has never been in the military, or taught grade school, or been arrested. And wait. There's more," said Clapper. "There's a whole other crime scene right next door. Can't be a coincidence, but right now, I don't see the connection."

CHAPTER 5

DR. CLAIRE WASHBURN, chief medical examiner and my best friend, was waiting for the three of us in the room next door to the murder room. She held up her bloody gloves to show me why she wasn't going to give me a hug.

"Take a good fast look," she said. "I'm ready to remove these bodies."

Bodies? Multiple?

This room was smaller but looked in every other way identical to the one we'd just left. Same color scheme, same made-up bed, and same view of the city.

But twice the number of victims.

There were two bodies lying on the pale blue carpet, a young black man and a young white woman; both looked to be in their twenties.

Both were clothed in what you might call middle-of-the-road casual. Girl wearing a pastel plaid cotton shirt and jeans, her red hair fanned out around her head, a look of surprise on her face. Boy wearing black cords and a T-shirt under a blue V-neck sweater. Running shoes.

It looked to me like the male victim had been sitting at the desk, the female in a chair near a coffee table. From the way their bodies had fallen, I thought they'd jumped up when they heard an intruder and had been gunned down, all the shots going into the trunks of their bodies and the chairs they'd been sitting in.

Their blood was spattered on the walls and furnishings, but I saw no spent brass.

I asked Claire, "How long ago did this happen?"

"An hour, maybe."

"Any ID?"

"Nothing in this room but those kids and the clothes they're wearing."

Clapper said, "I ran their prints and got nothing. Their registration info is bogus. Same wiped-down surfaces. I'd venture to say this room is cleaner now than it has ever been."

As Claire and her techs wrapped the two unidentified decedents in sheets and zipped them into body bags, I noticed cords and battery chargers on the floor behind the desk.

I said to my colleagues, "Look at that. These kids had laptops. As I understand it, high-end surveillance equipment is Web-connected. You can activate audio and video plants with an app."

"You think the victims were PIs?" Conklin asked.

"If so, there should be microcameras in the murder room."

Clapper said, "I'm on it."

He left to check and returned a few minutes later with three small bugs: one he'd pulled from a light socket above the bathroom mirror, the second from the desk lamp, and the third from the air duct.

"And just to be totally consistent, no prints on them," said Clapper.

I called Lieutenant Jackson Brady and brought him up to speed. Then I texted Joe, saying I might be pulling an all-nighter. After that, I called Mrs. Rose, a sweetheart of a grandma, who lives in the apartment across the hall from ours and had become our daughter's nanny.

"Can you stay late?" I asked her. "I think dinner might be in the fridge."

"I cooked that chicken for *you*," she said, laughing.

"With spaetzle?"

"Of course."

I promised Mrs. Rose that I'd give her a heads-up when I was on the way home. Then I called and texted Joe again. No answer, no return text.

Where was my husband? Why didn't he call me?

Conklin said to me, "Security needs us, Linds. Urgently."

CHAPTER 6

LIAM DUGAN WAS a stocky man in his fifties, a former sergeant with the LAPD and now the hotel's head of security.

He said to me, "What a living, freaking, blood-curdling nightmare," and walked us down the hall to the fourteenth-floor supply closet. He opened the door, and there, jammed behind the cleaning cart, was the body of housekeeper Maria Silva.

She had short dark hair and was wearing a blue and gold hotel uniform with soaking blood on the shoulder that I could see from where I stood.

Dugan said, "She was a nice woman. Has a husband, two kids. I'm sorry, but I was hoping she was alive. So I touched her. I probably touched the cart and a few other things so I could get in there. Anyway, she took a bullet to the back of her head. Her key card is gone. The girls keep them on cords around their necks."

We taped off the new crime scene, and I met with the cops on the floor, telling them they were on duty until relieved by the night shift.

After that, Conklin and I huddled in room 1418, where

the supposed PIs had been executed. We looked at the blood spatter at the otherwise tidy murder scene and tried on scenarios.

Every way we turned it, it came down to a professional job, all four hits connected. Mr. Wang had been the target and Maria Silva had probably been the first victim.

The woman who had left blonde hair on the pillow could be a witness, the killer, a coconspirator, or a victim. Or she'd walked out before things got sticky and still didn't know what happened. It was possible.

Conklin and I went with Dugan to the hotel security offices and were given a file room with two desks and computers. We sat side by side and cued up the surveillance footage that had been shot over the previous four hours in six key locations.

Dugan said, "Here's a hard copy of the floor plans. I'll keep the footage coming and if there's anything you need, just find me. Nothing's off-limits."

At eight, room service brought us roast beef sandwiches, pickles, chips, and coffee. At ten, I used the ladies' room, washed my face, and looked at myself in the mirror.

My hair was all over the place, not in the sun-kissed beachy blonde tradition. More like my hair hated me. I reset my ponytail while staring deep into the reflection of my red-rimmed eyes. I needed a shower. I'll just leave it there.

I returned to the security department, and as soon as I put my butt in the chair, Conklin pointed to an image on the screen of a man who looked like our male victim in 1420, who had checked in as Gregory Wang.

Wang came through the elevator entrance from Market Street to the hotel lobby, which is on the fifth floor, and crossed through toward reception. He was alone, wearing dark pants and a gray sports jacket, a ball cap shading his face, and he had a computer bag hanging from a strap over his right shoulder. He checked in at the desk, and then we lost him on that tape. Another camera picked him up at the elevator bank for the guest rooms upstairs.

The footage was high-quality. But apart from the spring in Wang's step, there was nothing useful to be gleaned from what we'd just seen. I backed up the tape, watching Wang cross the lobby to the elevators again. Then I watched the lit numbers next to the elevator door rise, make several stops before landing on fourteen, then go back down.

I slid the disc that held the fourteenth-floor footage into the drawer. The time dating read 4:30 p.m. The camera, positioned across from the fourteenth-floor elevator, caught Wang getting out of the car and walking away from the camera, down the hallway. He swiped his key card and opened the door to 1420.

"He didn't knock," I said. "His guest hasn't arrived yet."

We fast-forwarded fourteenth-floor footage and watched people coming and going from their rooms, getting in and out of the elevators. No one raised suspicion. We paused the tape to check out the housekeeping cart; at 5 p.m., Maria Silva was still alive.

At 5:52, a blond-haired woman exited the elevator.

"Well, hello," I said to the screen.

I stopped the video. She was on her phone. Between her haircut, her glasses, and her holding the phone close to her mouth, I couldn't see much of her face. Her overall appearance was stylish, and she seemed self-assured. I started up the video and we watched the woman walk down the hallway and knock on the door of room 1420. The door opened and she went inside.

I kept the video rolling, looking for bad guys to appear,

to put a gun to the housekeeper's head, to go into the room next door and take out the PIs.

Then, when the time code read 6:23—something happened. The screen went gray. The picture was just—gone.

We ran the tape all the way to the end, hoping the video would resume, but there was nothing.

Nothing, nothing, nothing.

All we had were four dead people and no clue as to who had killed them, how they'd done it, or why.

I didn't like this.

I didn't like it at all.

CHAPTER 7

BY THE TIME I got home, it was three in the morning and I had a headache the size of a mushroom cloud.

Martha, our border collie and best furry friend forever, greeted me at the door. She woke up Mrs. Rose, who was sleeping on the couch, but thankfully, Julie slept on. I hugged our lovely sitter, and after she'd gone home, I checked the caller ID log.

Still no call from Joe.

It wasn't the first time I hadn't heard from Joe over the course of a day. He had a consulting job with airport security. He could be in a series of meetings or lost in the details of keeping outbound planes secure.

It was a great job and he loved it—but it was after *three*. He hadn't texted me a single line since noon.

Of course, I was worried. Was Joe OK?

I checked on our little Sleeping Beauty and threw a sigh that relaxed my whole body. I watched her breathe. I rested my hand on her back. I made sure there was no draft, that she was dry and sleeping soundly. I pulled up her blanket, then softly closed her door.

I took an Advil and followed it with the shower I'd been

longing for. After putting on PJs and checking on Julie again, I got into bed and fell asleep, instantly.

Maybe an hour later, my eyes flashed open.

Joe still wasn't home.

I patted the bed and Martha jumped up, circled, and plopped down beside me. I hugged her and thought about the victims at the hotel. I reviewed each of the crime scenes in my mind's eye and hoped that while I slept, answers would come to me.

When I woke up, it was morning.

I had not solved the crimes in my sleep, but Joe was in bed, snoring beside me.

CHAPTER 8

I KISSED MY HUSBAND.

He opened his blue eyes and asked, "What day is it?"

I told him and he fell back asleep.

I woke him up.

"What day is it?" he asked. Again.

"Hey. It's Tuesday, six forty-five a.m. Did you get any phone calls from me, like about six of them?"

"Oh, geez. I'm sorry," he said. "My phone was off."

"You're in the doghouse, buddy."

I swung my legs over the bed. Joe's arm snaked out and he grabbed me and pulled me down next to him.

"Some people on the watch list came up on our passenger manifest," he said. "And that's all I can tell you."

"Fine."

I made another break for the side of the bed, but he didn't let me get up.

"I'm sorry."

"OK. But I worry when I don't hear from you, Joe."

"I know. Same here."

We nuzzled and wrestled around and I relented a little. Then I relented a lot. I shut down the hideous pictures in my mind of dead people, and I even tried to keep from listening for Julie. Martha hung her muzzle on the edge of the bed, and Joe pushed her away without losing a beat.

It was glorious lovemaking. Not fancy, but good wholesome friskiness when I hadn't even thought *kisses* were in order.

I collapsed with my arm over Joe's chest and my head under his chin.

"That was nice," I said.

"Nice? At my age? With no sleep? I'm wondering how I pulled that off at all."

He got me laughing. I said, "It was the best ever, Joe. God. You're amazing."

"Want to go another round?"

"Save something for tonight," I said, laughing again.

I dressed, took Martha for a run along Lake Street, stretched my legs, and watched sunrise and early-morning traffic and other people out for a run with their dogs.

When doggy and I returned, Julie was in her high chair and I smelled pancakes. I went to my sweet girl and kissed and squeezed her a little bit.

"You're sooo cute," I told her. "Did you tell Daddy thank you for the pancakes?"

"Nooooo," she said, slapping her hands on the tray.

"Oh, you like that word too much," I said. So she said it again, laughing and burbling at the same time.

"OK, *I'll* tell him," I said.

I put my arms around my husband's waist and hugged him tight. "I love you so much," I said. "And thank you for making breakfast."

"Uh-huh. Please, sit yourself down."

I pulled up a seat at the table, which was positioned to get a nice bright beam of morning light. Joe dished up the pancakes and crispy bacon, and between bites, I fed cereal to Julie.

It was idyllic. Picture-perfect and framed in gold. We didn't have breakfast table perfection when I was growing up, so I cherished every bit of this. Gloried in it.

Joe said, "I checked my phone and you were phoning me at three this morning."

"I'd just gotten home after working some terrible business at the Four Seasons. The fourteenth floor was like an abattoir."

I told Joe the details, availing myself of his excellent crime-solving mind.

"Among the many mysteries was this woman we saw going into the dead man's room," I said. I described her in full. "She may have been his lover, or lover-by-the-hour, or even his wife. Or I don't know, Joe. All we know is that she's the only living person who can answer our questions."

"The bangs down to her glasses," Joe said. "Not a bad disguise. Even talking on the phone distorts the shape of the mouth. All of that will outwit facial recognition. More coffee?"

"No thanks, honey. I'm going to hit the shower."

I stood under the water and thought about the blond woman with the wraparound shades and how finding her could kick the doors down on all of it.

But in lieu of that, the dead man in 1420 was the beginning of the story.

CHAPTER 9

I FOUND CLAIRE hard at work in her autopsy suite, gowned and gloved up and halfway through the internal exam of the unknown male killed in room 1420. His face had been reflected down over his chin and a Y incision had opened his body down to the pubic bone.

"How's it going?" I asked.

"You know how long I've been ME?" Claire asked me.

"Since I was this tall," I said, putting my hand on top of my head. Actually, we'd been rookies together, back about a dozen years ago.

"And you know how many autopsies I do a year?"

"Why don't you tell me?" I said.

She put a bloody liver on a scale. Bunny Ellis, one of Claire's morgue techs, waggled her fingers hello at me and took Claire's notes.

"One thousand, two hundred bodies more or less pass through these doors annually," Claire said.

"I hear you."

Claire was grumpy. Rare for her.

"What I hate the most—"

"Dead kids. I know."

"And what I hate the second most? Healthy murder victims who could have had full and productive lives. Like Mr. Doe or Wang or whatever his real name is. He was perfect. All his organs are A-plus. He has bones and joints of steel. I don't think this man even got heartburn," she said.

"Tell me more," I said, since this was why I had stopped by this morning.

Claire continued to cut and slice as she talked.

"He has a scar on his knee, probably from falling off a bike when he was six, and that's it."

"What about his stomach contents?"

"BLT on rye with mayo. Green tea."

"You ran his blood?"

"It's waiting to go out. With these."

She showed me a stainless steel bowl with three slugs rattling inside.

"Medium-caliber, like nine-millimeter. Based on that squeaky-clean crime scene, keep your expectations in check," said Claire. "I'll bet you a burger and fries there won't be a record of the murder weapon."

I said, "Who's up next?"

"I only have two hands, Lindsay. Two. I'm not finished with Mr. Wang."

"I'll get out of your way, Butterfly," I said, calling her by her nickname.

As if she hadn't barked at me, she said, "I'll do young Ms. Doe next. That is a clean-looking girl, Lindsay. Skin like milk. She could just barely drive and vote. I'll need backup to get this work done today. Meanwhile…"

"Meanwhile what?"

"Phone keeps ringing. The brass. The mayor. The press. Other bodies from other crimes. If you can break for lunch," Claire said, "the girls want to get together at MacBain's."

By "the girls," she meant herself and me, Cindy, and Yuki, the four of whom Cindy had collectively dubbed the Women's Murder Club.

"I'll try," I said.

I left Claire and loped down the breezeway and through the back door of the Hall of Justice. I showed my badge to the guy at the metal detector, then took the stairs to the homicide squad on the fourth floor. The day shift was drifting in, but a lot of phones were ringing through to voice mail.

Brady was in his office, the ten-foot-square glass cubicle in the back corner of the room. He saw me coming, got up from behind his desk, and opened the door.

Brady is built like a wrestler, blond, taciturn, and as brave as they come. But he's all business, all the time.

"Got anything?" he said.

"Just what I had last night, Lieu. Professional job from start to finish. One ID could blow it open," I said. "We're working on that now."

Before he could say "Keep me in the loop," all his phone lines rang at once.

CHAPTER 10

MACBAIN'S IS THE neighborhood hole-in-the-wall beer-and-burger joint frequented by cops, lawyers, and bail bondsmen who work along the 800 block of Bryant Street. Claire and I stood inside the open doorway and stared at the raucous scene. Customers had parked four deep at the bar, and the tables in front were all taken. Looked to me like a retirement party.

There was time to reverse course and pick another lunch spot, but Sydney, the front room waitress, pointed and mouthed, "They're over here."

Cindy Thomas stood up from behind a table near the jukebox and waved to get our attention. She was wearing her bloodhound clothes: a soft gray hoodie over a T-shirt and jeans. This was how Cindy dressed when she was working a story, and as a top crime reporter for the *San Francisco Chronicle*, she wore bloodhound clothes most of the week.

Sometimes I felt bad for her.

Yes, she was adorable and well employed and happy in love, but her great buddy, me, and her fiancé, my partner, had to keep the red meat to ourselves. Cindy was the press. And historically, the press was not our friend.

Yuki Castellano, the legal arm of the Women's Murder Club, sat wedged between Cindy and the wall with her back to the peanut barrel. She was wearing a knife-sharp black suit, her hair was twisted up, and she had chunky pearls at her neckline. She was dressed for court.

Claire and I waded into the crowd and I stuck close behind her, the pink sweater she'd thrown over her scrubs lighting the way. I wore my usual, rain or shine, at my desk or on the street: blue trousers, white shirt, blue blazer, hair in a ponytail, and my badge hanging from a ball chain around my neck.

I grabbed a seat across from Yuki, Claire sat next to me, and all of our hands shot up at the same time. When Syd arrived, Claire said, "We can order everything right now."

Syd wrote down four burgers—one each of bloody, rare, medium-rare, and charred—with fries all around. Three of us asked for tea and fizzy water, but Yuki ordered rum and Coke, heavy on the rum.

"You're drinking when you're in court?" I asked her.

"Trial was canceled due to circumstances beyond my control," she said.

At that, customers behind us broke into a rowdy drinking song. Folks applauded and stamped in time. So Yuki had to shout her bad story about her college girl client who'd been charged as an accessory to an armed robbery. As Yuki told it, Sandra had been waiting in her boyfriend's car while he went into a store to buy a bottle of booze. Or so he told her. But he'd had a gun, and when the owner set off the alarm, the boyfriend fired his .22 into the owner's chest.

Yuki's eighteen-year-old client had been charged as an accessory and was looking at fifteen to twenty years if the liquor store owner lived. Her bail was set absurdly high and her family couldn't raise a tenth of it.

"I saw Sandra *yesterday,*" Yuki said. "Once again, I told her that I was very connected in the DA's office and that if she'd testify against her gutless boyfriend, I could probably get her sentence reduced—significantly."

"She wouldn't go for it," Cindy guessed.

Yuki shook her head. "Just before court this morning, she ripped up her bedsheet and hanged herself on the bars. *Why?* Why did she do that? Why wouldn't she listen to me? And even if she didn't flip on that rat, there was hope for her. And what about her poor family? God. I am so sick about this."

She covered her eyes with her hands, and we tried to console her. When her drink came, she downed half of it in one gulp. Yuki overestimates her ability to hold her liquor, and I was pretty sure she'd be staggering after lunch.

About then, Claire, already in an uproar, vented about the fresh young bodies piling up in her morgue—without mentioning names and details. Cindy pricked up her ears like a dog who's been asked, "Want to go for a ride in the car?"

"Tell me *something,*" she said to Claire. "I heard there was a shooting at the Four Seasons. Just give me something I can own and work into a story."

I was thinking maybe Cindy could help us. If we couldn't identify the Four Seasons victims, Cindy could run their pictures in the *Chron.* But I wasn't there yet.

I looked around the table and thought how my three girlfriends were all seething with a tension that was only intensified by their having to shout over the retirement festivities around us.

So much was going on, I didn't have to speak.

I was glad. If asked, I would have to say that my life was pretty damned good right now. My little family was healthy, Joe and I were both working, money was coming in, and even staring at a computer screen for the last four hours hadn't stolen the afterglow from my morning romp with my husband.

It didn't occur to me to think how fast things can change. Just like that.

CHAPTER 11

I RETURNED FROM lunch to find Conklin dumping the remains of his Chinese take-out into the wastebasket.

He said, "The security chief sent over lobby footage from before and after the set we've already screened. Maybe those dead kids in fourteen-eighteen came in around lunchtime."

I asked Inspectors Lemke and Samuels to view the eight-thirty-p.m.-to-midnight footage and gave them printouts of the mystery blonde. Then I reset my ponytail, cracked my knuckles, and sat down next to my partner.

"Let's do it," I said.

The video flashed onto my screen.

At time stamp 12:30 p.m., the elegant lobby was humming with guests as well as local businesspeople heading for the entrance to MKT, the hotel's restaurant. Conklin and I sat shoulder-to-shoulder for the next three hours, looking for dead people walking, occasionally shaking out our legs, using the facilities.

By the time the day shift started punching out, my eyes were gritty and my temples were pounding. But I was still watching the video when the time stamp read 3:27 p.m. I hit Pause.

There was a girl hanging around the front desk in jeans

and a quilted jacket, a mile of bulky scarf around her neck. Was she one of the private investigator kids who'd been shot in room 1418? I was about to say "Look at her," when she turned toward the elevator and I saw her face. Damn it. She was not the girl in 1418. Not by a mile.

At that precise moment, Conklin was pointing at a different part of the screen.

"I think I saw this guy on the later footage," he said.

He circled the cursor around a big man who was facing away from the camera, wearing a bulky coat and a knit cap. His body and features were almost entirely obscured—yet he was somehow familiar.

"He reminds me of Dugan," I said, referring to the security chief.

Conklin said, "That's not Dugan. Dugan stoops."

We watched the big man walk away from the cameras, slipping seamlessly between groups of people so that we never had more than a second's glimpse of him.

We reversed the footage, paused, zoomed in, but there was not even a partial view of his face.

"He knows where the cameras are," said Conklin.

"Like he's some kind of pro," I said. "Let's look for him on the later tape."

I booted up the disc we'd already seen a few dozen times, but now we had a new focus. Only a few minutes in, I saw the shadowy male who maneuvered around the surveillance cameras with the dexterity of a rodeo quarter horse. He disappeared into a crowd, reappearing a frame or two later as a charcoal-gray smudge on the move. Then we lost him again, this time for good.

The time stamp read 4:20 when Mr. "Wang" entered the lobby. An hour and twenty-five minutes later, at 5:45, the glamorous blonde made her dramatic entrance.

I knew this part of the footage by heart.

I made screen shots of Wang, the blonde, and the partial angle on the mystery man's back and printed them out. I was thanking Samuels and Lemke for their help when my desk phone rang. It was Brady.

"Valet parking came up with the murdered man's car," said the boss.

"No kidding."

"Subaru Outback registered to a Michael M. Chan. The DMV photo matches his height, weight, eye color. He didn't have a record. He was thirty-two, lived in Palo Alto with his wife, Shirley, and two young kids. Both teach at Stanford. He taught Chinese history. She teaches Mandarin. That's all I've got. I'm texting you the coordinates."

I thanked Brady and told my partner we had a lead. The solid kind.

"Now we're getting somewhere," said Richie.

CHAPTER 12

THE SOFT AFTERNOON sun was lighting the beautiful old homes in the Professorville section of Palo Alto. We took a left turn off University Avenue, and a couple of blocks later, we were on Waverley Street, a lush, tree-lined block in this picture-perfect town.

The Chan residence was on the south side of the street, middle of the block: a sage-green two-story Craftsman home, with a wide shed dormer facing the street and a flower garden bracketing the front walk.

Our well-worn surveillance vehicle, disguised as a suburban minivan with stick-family decals and a GO GIANTS bumper sticker, was positioned directly across the street.

We parked the squad car in the Chans' driveway behind a new Chevy wagon and I called Brady, letting him know we were on the scene. Then Conklin and I took the garden path and the brick steps up to the front door. I rang the bell, and it was opened by an early-thirtyish Asian woman wearing gray sweat pants, a pink Life Is Good T-shirt, a gold cross on a chain around her neck, and designer glasses with purple frames.

I flapped open my jacket to show her my badge and introduced my partner and myself, asking if she was Shirley Chan and if we could come in to speak with her. Fear sparked in her eyes like small black flames. She already knew we weren't selling raffle tickets for the PBA.

"Is this about Michael?" she asked, her hand going to her collarbones. "Is he all right? Please tell me he's all right."

Neither Conklin nor I answered, and in that brief silence, Mrs. Chan switched her focus to Conklin's eyes, back to mine, and back to Conklin.

My partner has magnetic good looks and the nicest way with women of all kinds: meth heads, serial killers, party girls, old ladies lost in parking garages, and in this case, a woman about to learn that her husband had been killed after private time with an attractive, still unidentified bombshell.

Mrs. Chan stepped back into her house, leaving the door open.

We followed her through the foyer and into the many-windowed living room furnished in washed pine and khaki-upholstered love seats, presided over by a fifty-two-inch TV above a fireplace.

Two young children, who looked to be about seven and five, stared up at us. They instantly saw the distress on their mother's face. The little girl clambered up from the floor and, asking, "What's wrong, Mommy?" grabbed her mother around the waist. Mrs. Chan's hands shook and her voice faltered when she told the kids to go to their rooms. They wailed and argued with her until she screamed, "Haley. Brett. *Do what I say.*"

They fled.

We three stood in the homey room, Shirley Chan with her hand over her mouth, refusing to sit down. I pulled out the DMV photo of Michael Chan and showed it to her.

"Is this your husband?" I asked her.

"Oh, my *God*. Was there a car accident?"

Conklin asked her kindly, "When was the last time you saw Michael, Mrs. Chan?"

"Yesterday morning. He called me in the afternoon. But he didn't come home last night. That's not like him at all. Where is he? Where is Michael? What happened to him?"

My partner said, "I'm sorry to have to tell you this, ma'am. Your husband has been shot. He was killed."

CHAPTER 13

CONKLIN WAS AT the wheel of the squad car as we headed back to the city in the dark. Mrs. Chan was crumpled up in the backseat, talking on the phone to her sister in Seattle. Brady called to say that the mayor had threatened to bring in the FBI if we didn't crack the case pronto. The press had gotten tipped and had whipped the story into a frenzy, spraying the stink of fear onto all the hotels in San Francisco. "Tourism dollars are at stake." That was what he told me.

I snapped, "How long is pronto, Brady? Because there are only twenty-four hours in the day, and you know what? We're working twenty-five of them. By ourselves."

"I'll get you some help," he said.

After I hung up, Conklin said to me, "We're going to get our break when Mrs. Chan sees the videotape."

Sure, it was possible. If Mrs. Chan recognized someone who knew her husband walking through the hotel lobby, that might pry open the lid of this big bloody box of I don't know what.

As Conklin took the 101 on-ramp from University Avenue, I listened to the radio: dispatch calling for cars to a drive-by shooting out by the zoo, a bar fight in the Haight, a domestic stabbing in Diamond Heights, all straight-up, call-911 incidents—unlike this.

And then my phone buzzed. It was Joe.

He said, "Hon, I'm stuck out at the airport. I'm sorry. There's nothing I can do."

"Wait. Joe, I'm stuck, too. This is not good."

"I know, Linds. In twenty years, Julie's going to tell her shrink how we neglected her—"

I wasn't amused. I cut him off.

"Did you call Mrs. Rose?"

"Yes. She's already at our place. *Fringe* marathon tonight. She likes our TV."

"Well, that's all right then," I snapped before clicking off.

I was mad at Brady for passing on the mayor's threat and mad at Joe for saying he didn't know when he would be home. I turned to look at Michael Chan's widow. She was leaning against the backseat, staring out the side window at the black of nothing, apparently drowning in the loss of her husband, and the probable devastation of her world.

I was ashamed of myself for snapping at Joe, really ashamed.

I would've called him back to apologize, but Mrs. Chan swung her sad eyes toward me and locked in.

"I don't understand," she said.

Then she asked me a lot of questions. Good ones.

How had I identified her husband's body? Was he alone when he was found? What was he wearing? Had we recovered Michael's phone? Had he suffered before he died? Did we have any idea who had killed him? Did we have any idea why?

I answered as well as I could, but none of my answers were comforting. I reached for her hand, but it was awkward, and soon she was staring out the window again.

A half hour later, Shirley Chan was sitting in a metal

chair in Interview 2, sandwiched between Conklin and me, a laptop computer open in front of us.

I said, "Let us know if you recognize anyone."

I pressed Play and the video began showing an overhead view of the Four Seasons' lobby with yesterday's date and the time, 4:10 p.m.

Ten minutes into the tape, Mrs. Chan's eyes got big as she watched her husband enter the hotel, cross the marble floors as if he was on a mission, and head toward the reception desk.

Mrs. Chan shouted, "*There he is.* That's *him*. Michael, what are you doing there?"

Conklin and I looked at each other over Mrs. Chan's head as the image of Mr. Chan went toward the elevators. I fast-forwarded the lobby footage until a blonde-haired woman with wraparound shades and a swingy leather coat entered the scene.

I hit Pause and turned to the grieving woman beside me.

"Mrs. Chan, do you recognize this woman?"

Her eyes were fixed on the blonde.

"Who is she?" Mrs. Chan asked. Her voice was cold. Resigned.

"We don't know," I said. "But she may have been the last person to see your husband alive."

CHAPTER 14

WE ALL STARED at the image of the blonde-haired woman I had stopped in midstride by pressing a key.

We didn't know her name or her occupation, if she was Chan's date-by-the-hour, manicurist, longtime lover, drug dealer, financial planner, or personal banker. We didn't know if she was dead or alive, if she had killed Michael Chan, had set up the hit, or had gotten out before he was shot and didn't know he was dead. She was unknown subject zero.

Conklin's prediction that when Mrs. Chan saw the video we would have answers seemed unlikely to come true.

I said to Mrs. Chan, "I'll show you another view of her."

I shuffled the discs, found the footage from the camera on the fourteenth floor, and booted it up. I let the footage run as the blond woman stepped out of the elevator and walked away from the camera, down the hall to Chan's room.

I hit Pause after she had knocked and Chan had opened the door. He wasn't on camera. We only saw the frozen profile of the striking blonde and the long shadow in the doorway.

Mrs. Chan asked, "Michael was in that room?"

"Yes. He was."

"Did she shoot him?"

"We don't know."

"I want to see what she looked like when she left there."

I said, "We don't have anything else. Not long after she entered the suite, the video was corrupted. All we have is two hours of static. If she left through the lobby, she was disguised. We didn't see her again."

"She couldn't just disappear," said Mrs. Chan.

"The hotel is on floors five through twenty-one of a forty-story building. She may have left through the fire exit. Here's something else. The room may have been under surveillance."

I showed Mrs. Chan morgue shots of the two young probable snoops who might have recorded Michael Chan's last moments. Mrs. Chan didn't recognize them.

"They might have been students," I said.

She shook her head, and I made a mental note to screen student ID photos from the university, all four thousand of them. I asked Mrs. Chan for names of her husband's close friends both on and off campus, and when Richie went for coffee, I asked her personal questions about her marriage.

She got angry.

"I trust Michael. He was faithful to me. Just because that woman looks like *that*, it doesn't mean they were having an *affair*."

"We're only concerned with the nature of their connection. We have to find her. For all we know, she's also a victim."

I had plenty of questions, and I laid them on Shirley Chan one at a time. *Why would Michael use a fake ID? Why did he lie about his whereabouts? Had he lied to her before? Had she ever been suspicious of his movements?*

She answered "I don't know" and "No, no, no," and then

she put her head down on the scarred gray table and cried. By the time Conklin returned with the coffee, Shirley Chan was no longer talking to us. The interview was done.

I called the desk sergeant and arranged a ride home for Mrs. Chan with a uniformed officer, and Conklin walked her out to the street. I wanted to compare notes with my partner before we both went home. So I used this brief alone time to download the surveillance video our van had shot today on Waverley Street.

I pulled it up and watched images of me and my partner going up the walk to the Chan house, Mrs. Chan answering the door. And then I watched the light traffic running between the van and the Chans' sweet old house.

At time stamp 5:24, the Chans' next-door neighbor backed a silver sedan out of his driveway, interrupting the progress of a black Mercedes that had been coming up the street. The Mercedes was forced to wait for the sedan to maneuver, and for a long moment the Mercedes was stationary and parallel with our cameras.

Even though the Mercedes' windows were tinted and it was dark outside, I almost recognized the shape of the driver's head, the angle of the chin. My heart took off at a gallop before my mind knew what was scaring me.

I watched intently as the driver of the Mercedes turned to look at the minivan. I paused the action and refined the image of the driver, who was looking directly into the camera.

My mind reeled, did cartwheels, and nearly stroked out. *My God.* It was *Joe. Joe was driving that car.*

He'd been caught on tape driving past the home of a dead man named Michael Chan, thirty miles from San Francisco.

Even though my heart and brain had left me for dead, my fingers moved and my eyes took everything in. As I stared at the image of my dear husband, my baby's daddy, my closest friend and lover, who would never go behind my back, I fought hard to find a believable explanation.

Had Joe been looking for me? Had Brady told him where I was? If so, why, when the neighbor's car took off up the street, had Joe kept going? Why hadn't he called me?

There had to be a good reason. But I couldn't come up with a thing.

CHAPTER 15

I'VE NEVER THOUGHT of myself as a coward, but I could not show this footage of my husband driving past the Chan house to my partner until I spoke to Joe.

I texted Richie, said I was going home now and that I would see him in the morning. I took the stairs down to the lobby. I left by the back door, fled along the breezeway out to Harriet Street, and found my car standing alone in the lot under the overpass.

I drove home on autopilot. The inside of my head felt like a pileup on a Minnesota highway at the height of a blizzard. I didn't know which way was up or down, or when I would get slammed again.

At just before 11 p.m., I stood outside my front door with my key in hand.

If Joe was home, I would have to confront him. If he wasn't home, that would only prolong the agony until he arrived. He had told me he was at the airport.

He told me that. And that was a lie.

I pushed the key into the lock. Martha woofed, and as I opened the door, she tore around the corner from the living room into the foyer and hurled herself at me, nailing me in the solar plexus.

I bent down, gave my doggy a pat and a kiss, and then went into the living room, expecting my lying son-of-a-bitch husband to get up from his chair.

But the chair was occupied by our sweet, gray-haired neighbor with the big heart.

I'm sure my face was rigid, but I greeted her and apologized for being so late. I asked after Julie and if Mrs. Rose could hang in for another minute so I could walk Martha.

She said, "Of course. Are you hungry, Lindsay?"

I hadn't thought of food for hours, but the idea that something warm could be waiting for me made my stomach growl. I walked Martha in a tight rectangle on Lake Street, down to Tenth, across the street, and back up to Twelfth, and after Martha did her business, we went home.

A plate of meat loaf and mashed potatoes was waiting for me on the kitchen bar, along with a glass of wine. I thanked Mrs. Rose, hugged her, and asked about the *Fringe* marathon. I didn't hear anything she said about her show. How could I? The whiteout whirled in my mind and the warm food went down without my tasting it.

I came back to the present when Mrs. Rose said she'd just changed Julie, the new box of diapers was in her room, and she'd see me in the morning.

We said good night and I went to my daughter's room.

Julie has Joe's dark hair and long lashes, and looking at her made me think of the Chan children, who wouldn't be sleeping tight for years to come. I kissed my fingers and touched them to Julie's cheek. My precious girl.

As I cleaned up the kitchen, I thought about Shirley Chan trying to make sense of her late husband's behavior, wondering what he had done and why he had done it, and what would become of her family now.

I was having some of those feelings, but my husband was *alive.* He could speak to me. And he *would.*

While the dishwasher did the dirty work, I booted up my laptop and downloaded the camera van's street view to my PC. I had to see Joe staring into the camera's eye again.

And there he was.

Big, handsome, looking into the lens like he was a movie star and this was his close-up. After he moved on, I sped through the rest of the footage and saw nothing out of the ordinary. No one slunk through the bushes. Apart from Joe's Mercedes, no one slowed down in front of the Chan house or sped past it. Not even a stray cat raced across the road.

I calmed myself, and then I called Joe. I imagined his voice nearly drowned out by the sounds of an airliner taking off behind him, and my tremendous relief that I'd been wrong.

But no. I got a digital voice saying that Joe's mailbox was full, good-bye.

I took a therapeutic shower, toweled off hard, and slipped into a nightgown. I went to Julie's room. Her diaper was dry and she was sleeping soundly, so I sat in the rocker and stared out the window onto Lake Street.

When I next saw Joe, I would just ask him, *Why were you in Palo Alto? Why did you lie to me?*

I went to bed, and when Julie's cries woke me, it was 6:15. I turned my head, absolutely sure that Joe would be sleeping next to me.

But the spot on my left was empty and cold.

I touched that empty place anyway and felt my resolve shatter and tears leap out of my eyes.

Where was Joe?

Why wasn't he home?

CHAPTER 16

MRS. ROSE ARRIVED at 7 a.m., cheerful and rosy.

While I made breakfast for Julie and fed her, Mrs. Rose scrambled some eggs for me. She talked about her grandchildren in North Carolina while I combed Julie's hair and played patty-cake with her, and once the baby was laughing, I handed her off, strapped on my gun, pulled on my Windbreaker, and said good-bye.

As I made my twenty-minute drive to work, I was in the grip of ugly feelings. My lying liar of a husband had lied. And yet, as furious as I was, I was even more terrified, because he hadn't called me and hadn't come home. Was he hurt? Was he dead?

I didn't even know the names of the people Joe worked for, that's how wrapped up I'd been in the Job over the last crazy months.

And that made me mad at myself.

Roaring mad.

By the time I parked my car, I was more of a mess than I wanted anyone to see. I entered the Hall from the rear and immediately ran into Jacobi in the lobby. My old partner, friend, and now chief of police knew the workings of my mind almost better than I knew them myself.

"What is it, Boxer? What's eating you?"

"Just deep in thought. The Four Seasons case." That was the half of the story I was willing to tell him.

Jacobi said he was assigning a couple of teams to work with me on the hotel murders.

I said thanks, gave him a weak wave, then headed up the stairs to Homicide.

Conklin was at his desk.

When he looked up, I said, "I screened the video from our van on the street."

"And?"

"I hope you're going to tell me I'm crazy."

He looked at me like he was already of that opinion. I've tried, but I just cannot hide my feelings from people I know. I sat down behind my computer and Conklin stood behind me as I downloaded the surveillance tape from Waverley Street.

I ran the footage, halting it a few seconds before the heart-stopping incident.

"Look at this," I said. "Tell me what you see."

Conklin watched intently, and when we got to the part where Joe turned to the camera, I hit Pause.

My partner said, "Is that Joe? What's he doing driving by the Chans' house?"

"That's the sixty-four-million-dollar question, and I have no answer. As far as I know, we're looking at Joe's last known whereabouts."

"No way."

"Right."

"No," he said. "I mean, that's why he looks familiar."

"I'm not following you."

Conklin said, "The guy in the hotel," he said. "The one with the bulky jacket who eluded the cameras. Look, Lindsay." He went over to his desk, moved some papers around, and came up with the screen shots we'd taken of the stealthy man crossing the hotel lobby on the day of the shootings.

"Lindsay, don't you see it?" Conklin asked me, shoving the photocopy under my nose. "The man in the lobby is *Joe.*"

CHAPTER 17

I TOLD CINDY I had to see her, and she met me on the front steps of the Hall fifteen minutes later.

"What have you got for me?" she said.

She was wearing a different T-shirt and steel-tipped work boots. The boots signified something. My guess was that she wanted to kick butt. She was in serious bulldog mode.

"We need to identify these people," I said.

I showed her the pictures on my phone of the three unknown subjects: the mystery blonde and the morgue shots of the two PI kids, slightly 'shopped so that they looked less dead.

"Send them to me," she said.

I did and she asked, "Are they wanted for questioning in the hotel murders? What can you tell me?"

"Let's just start with you putting them out under a headline, 'Do you know these people?' and see how it goes."

"OK, OK, OK," said Cindy. "You're not giving this to anyone else, right?"

"You've got a twenty-four-hour exclusive; then the FBI is going to move in and do it their way."

Cindy said, "I'll get this up on the site, front page, as soon

as I clear it with Tyler. These photos will be on the Web today and in the paper tomorrow."

"OK."

"I'm going to say 'Contact Cindy Thomas.'"

"You've got twenty-four hours."

"Gotcha."

My phone buzzed. Brady, of course.

"Boxer, got some people here from the FBI."

"I'm downstairs. I'll be up in a second."

I hung up and turned back to Cindy.

"I don't know how long your twenty-four-hour window
is going to stay open. There's a cab," I said, pointing to one
at the light. "See if you can grab it."

She thanked me and told me I wouldn't be sorry. We
hugged, and I went upstairs.

Conklin, Brady, and I all got into the elevator and rode it
up to Jacobi's office. There we met three serious men in gray
suits, and over the next two hours, we told them everything
we knew. Everything but the one thing I wasn't ready to give
up, and I knew Richie had my back.

I didn't say a word about Joe.

CHAPTER 18

WHEN CINDY CALLED me at 10:30 p.m., I was bordering on despair. I still hadn't heard from Joe, the baby was crying, and although I had done everything I knew to calm her, nothing worked. She was frantic and I didn't know why. I had thrown on a robe and was going across the hall to get Mrs. Rose when the phone rang.

Cindy didn't wait for me to say hello.

"I got a hit," she said.

"I have to call you back."

"Really?"

Julie let out a freshly minted over-the-top howl. Why?

"Really," I said, and then, "I'll call you back."

I felt the baby's forehead and checked her diaper, and both were fine. I carried her to the kitchen, patting her back while I warmed up a bottle. Was she sick? Or was she simply channeling my anxiety?

I took her back to her room, sat down in the rocker, fed her, and tried to soothe myself. Julie took the bottle, and of course she couldn't cry and suck at the same time. Mercifully.

When she fell asleep in my arms, I put her into her crib

as gently as possible. She barely stirred, but I stood over her watching until her breathing deepened and I was sure she was in a nice solid sleep.

I nuked a cup of milk for myself, stirred in some Green & Black's powdered chocolate, and set it on the end table next to the big sofa, giving myself permission to just sit quietly and calm the hell down.

I had dozed off when the phone rang.

Joe.

I found the phone where I'd dropped it on the floor near the sofa and caught it on the fifth ring.

"Christ, Lindsay," Cindy said. "What the hell is wrong with you? I said I have a *hit* on one of your suspects."

"The baby," I said. "She was having a tantrum."

"Everything OK?"

"I think so."

"OK," Cindy said, moving on. "The blond-haired woman from the hotel. Someone wrote in saying he knows her. Are you free now? Or should I just tell Richie?"

"Put me on speaker and tell us both," I said into the phone.

Richie grunted, "I'm here."

"Good. Cindy, who is the blonde? Who the hell is she?"

CHAPTER 19

CINDY'S ANONYMOUS TIP could blow open the whole case. *If* it was good. If it was *true*.

I took my laptop to the big sofa in the living room, and, leaving Julie's door open, I got to work. I typed the name *Alison Muller* into one law enforcement database after another, and when she didn't come up, I Googled her.

At 11 p.m., I called Brady.

He cleared the sleep from his throat, and after he said his name, I said, "Cindy got an anonymous tip on the mystery blonde from the hotel. We should keep it to ourselves until Conklin and I can chase it down."

Every cop knows that the FBI doesn't like to share. Once they're involved, they take over the case and cut you out of it. You're lucky to read about it in the papers.

I said so and Brady grunted without committing himself. Then he asked, "What did you find out?"

"According to Cindy's source, her name is Alison Muller. She's thirty-five, an executive at Aptec, a software company in Silicon Valley. The tipster told Cindy that he knows her, that his family and the Mullers live on the same street in Monterey."

"You've got an address?"

"I do."

I heard Yuki in the background saying, "Brady, who's calling this late?"

Brady said to her, "It's Lindsay. We'll be off soon."

I said, "I found info on Muller on Aptec's website. She's married to Khalid Khan, the composer. They have two children, five and thirteen years old. She's a graduate of Stanford with a PhD in mathematics from MIT and she's fluent in Spanish and Chinese. Speculating, but she and Chan may have met at Stanford."

There was a pause as Brady thought things over.

He said, "OK. I'll call Monterey PD and have them sit on Muller's house until morning. You and Conklin bring her in first thing."

I called my partner and filled him in. Then I tried Joe's phone again.

As before, his mailbox was full. Good-bye.

I dragged my churning mind to bed with me and closed my eyes, but sleep stayed on the other side of the room. It was just as well. An hour after I'd spoken with Brady, he called me back.

"Here's the thing, Boxer."

"I'm listening."

"This Alison Muller. She's been reported missing. Monterey PD has a BOLO out for her. Her husband hasn't seen her in a couple of days."

"No. Really?"

"Khalid Khan spoke with her late Monday afternoon. She missed her daughter's birthday party. Said she was working and would be home soon. She never showed."

"Late Monday afternoon. That's when the shootings went down," I said.

Brady said, "Right." He and I talked it over. *Where was*

Alison Muller? Had she been abducted at gunpoint? Was she dead? What, if anything, did she have to do with the death of Michael Chan, and the other victims of that purge?

I asked him, "Anything else? Did Muller's husband get a ransom call?"

"No. And Khan has been unable to reach his wife on the phone. Total blackout. Monterey PD pinged her phone. Last time it was used was Monday, six fifty-seven, from the Market Street area."

The Four Seasons Hotel was on Market.

I no longer expected to find Muller and question her. She had disappeared, and I had no idea where to look for her, no idea at all. Another thought sprang at me with bared fangs. Joe Molinari, my husband, was also missing.

What was he doing? Was he involved in all of this? I felt cold, like I was out there on that deadly, frozen highway in Minnesota again. Only this time, I was naked, alone, and without a car.

Julie whimpered. I shot a look in the direction of her room as I said to Brady, "I take back what I said before."

"Which is what?"

"We need the FBI. We need their resources."

Brady said, "See you in the morning."

We hung up, and the full weight of what I had done crashed in on me. I had withheld important, possibly critical information from Brady, and in doing so, I'd involved my partner.

I had to tell Brady about Joe.

He could fire me. And he'd be right to do it.

I hoped that by morning, I would have a theory that explained how Joe innocently fit into this case—a theory that didn't sound like total bullshit.

Maybe he'd come home so that I could ask him tonight.

I dared to hope.

CHAPTER 20

I HATED THIS.

It made me sick to have to show anyone that questionable footage of Joe in places where logic said he didn't belong. I wanted to ask him about it. He was my husband. And I trusted him. Right? But *whatever* he'd done, he'd covered it up. He'd lied. He'd put me in a jam.

I had to do the right thing. So I put on my game face and sailed through the entrance to our squad room.

The man known as Lieutenant Badass was in his glass-walled cube. Brady is brave. He's fair. And he doesn't play patty-cake.

When I had his job, I didn't like being restricted to a desk and all that that entails. Now I report to him. Once in a while, I've taken liberties with police procedures and Brady has given me hell—with a warning.

I didn't think I would get a warning today.

I cleared the obstacle course of gray metal desks and hardened homicide cops and knocked on Brady's door, and he waved me in. He was working at his laptop and didn't look at me.

"I'm busy, Boxer. Can this wait?"

When I didn't speak, Brady jerked his head up and nailed me with his double-barreled, blue-eyed stare.

"I have a meeting with Jacobi in five, so make it quick."

"Brady. Something I have to tell you. I haven't heard from Joe in thirty-six hours. Then, yesterday, while Conklin and I were in Palo Alto notifying Chan's widow, our surveillance team recorded Joe driving by the Chan house."

"I don't get you," he said tersely. "What are you saying?"

Brenda, the department assistant, came through the doorway, dropped some papers on Brady's desk, and said, "Sergeant Chi needs to speak to you, Lieu, and your ex-wife called."

Brady said to her, "Hold everything until after my meeting."

"We can talk about this later," I said to Brady, getting half out of my chair.

"Sit," he said.

I did it.

"Make me understand," he said. "Use short, clear sentences."

I swallowed hard and pushed through my own wall of resistance. I gave Brady the short sentences he'd asked for, covering the Palo Alto footage, Joe's drive-by at 5:24, and the hotel security video from the day of the shootings.

"We saw a man on the hotel tape who looked like Joe."

Brady said, "Joe was in the hotel around the time those people were taken out?"

"Looks like him—which is far from a positive ID."

Brady said, "You're saying Joe was in the hotel and also on the block where Chan lived. What's he doing?"

"I don't know, I don't know, I don't—"

"Could he be involved in the shootings?"

"Absolutely *not*," I said with conviction, but honest to God, I had no idea what Joe was capable of. Not anymore.

"Jesus, Lindsay. You shoulda told me yesterday."

Brady was furious. As I would have been in his place. I waited for him to ask for my badge and my gun and send me home.

I said, "I wanted to talk to Joe first."

I was looking at Brady's face, waiting for the shit-storm that didn't come. Maybe he was holding back because outside of the Job, Brady and Yuki are married. Joe and I hang out with them. We're friends.

"The meeting with Jacobi is an FBI briefing," Brady said. "You're going to have to tell this Joe story again. Get the video, Boxer. Meet me upstairs."

CHAPTER 21

WORLDWIDE AIRLINES FLIGHT #888 from Beijing was in its final approach to San Francisco International Airport into a foggy sun-lit morning.

At 9 a.m., Michael Chan was seated in the center row of business class on the main deck. The seats were narrow and uncomfortable and configured in blocks of two rows of four seats facing another row of four seats, so that eight passengers were sitting knee-to-knee.

Chan had been trying not to look at the untidy American couple sitting directly across from him for the last twelve hours. They were sloppy eaters. They took off their shoes. They had littered bags of chips and newspapers on the narrow space in front of their feet.

He had done his best to avoid eye contact, but they hadn't done the same. The long plane ride had been pure hell. But it was almost over.

The pilot took the plane into another series of descending turns toward the airport. The FASTEN SEAT BELT signs were on and the flight attendants had put away the serving carts and strapped in.

But Michael Chan had his eyes on the restroom at the

front of the cabin on his left. When he had washed his hands in that restroom earlier, his wedding band had loosened and dropped into the sink. He had fished it out, but just then, the plane had lurched. He'd been thrown off balance and needed both hands to catch himself, and the ring had spun away from his grasp, into a dark, germ-ridden place somewhere between the commode and the console. And that was when the "return to your seat" announcement had come on.

The flight attendant had rapped on the door, and after a brief, fruitless search for the ring, Chan had left the restroom, deciding he could retrieve his ring once the plane landed. Now, as the huge airliner made its descent, he knew he'd made a mistake.

Chan turned to the man on his left, another cramped, overtired traveler, and said he needed to get up.

The neighboring passenger reeked of sweat and bad temper. Muttering, he swung his knees toward the aisle. Chan said thanks and made the awkward climb over his neighbor's legs, bumping the knees of the woman across from him, apologizing for that.

He was steps away from the WC when the flight attendant, the red-haired one with the bright pink lipstick, unclipped her harness and blocked his path.

She said, "Mr. Chan, you have to return to your seat."

Chan said, "I'll be very quick."

He thought of the wheels touching down and the passengers from the first-class deck and all the others behind him, blocking the aisle, stampeding for the exit. He would have to wait for the aisle to clear, and for the plane to empty, and then all four hundred passengers from this flight would get ahead of him in the endless rope-lined queue to go through customs. His delay would irritate the men who would be waiting for him. It was just unacceptable.

He said, "Sorry, sorry," and pushed past the flight attendant. He had his hand on the door latch when there was an explosion directly under the plane's right wing.

Chan saw a flash and felt the simultaneous concussive boom. He was slammed off his feet, and at the same moment, a metal fragment pierced the fuselage and sheared through his left thigh. A question formed in Chan's mind, but before he could process the thought, his brain and body were separated by an inexplicable destructive force.

Two seconds passed between the catastrophic explosion and the rain of bodies and objects hitting the ground.

CHAPTER 22

I WAS COLLECTING the footage of Joe for Brady's meeting when Brady blew through the door to the squad room.

"Everyone, listen up!" he shouted.

He grabbed the remote from Brenda's desk and flicked on the TV that was suspended from the ceiling. A reporter was yelling into her microphone that Worldwide Airlines Flight 888 from Beijing had been landing at SFO when the Boeing Triple 7 had crashed somewhere west of 101.

The reporter was set up with her back to the highway. At some distance behind her was a screen of fire capped by a thick, coiling column of smoke. Her voice was nearly overwhelmed by the sirens of the emergency vehicles that were streaming out to the downed aircraft.

There were eleven of us in the squad room, and we all stared up at the images as one, cursing, gasping, stunned by what we saw.

Brady muted the sound and said, "Here's what I know. Ten minutes ago that plane crashed and likely killed everyone on board. The point of impact was the athletic fields at Mills High along Millbrae Avenue. The kids were inside, thank God, but the buildings were hit with debris and what-ever. There may be injuries. Gotta be."

As we watched the silent TV, Brady continued, saying that the airport was closed, a no-fly zone had been imposed, and the governor had declared a state of emergency. NTSB was on the scene and the National Guard was on the way.

Brady paused for breath and shook his head, and then he was talking again.

"We don't know what happened to this plane. We don't have a passenger list, and Worldwide is just stalling until they can say this was not their fault. Best guess is that there were more than four hundred people on that flight.

"This whole deal is under investigation by the NTSB, and beyond that, just about every government agency is en route. All cops are being drafted to help.

"Effective immediately, everyone here is assigned to assist wherever we're needed until y'all are relieved. I don't know when that's gonna be. Boxer, you're point man for our squad until I can get to the scene."

I was given contact info for the NTSB command post at the Millbrae Avenue exit off Route 101.

And then we were dismissed.

Conklin and I joined the flight to the stairs. Once we were in a car, I dialed up the news on my phone. The smoke-veiled visuals from SFPD's eye-in-the-sky looked like noth-ing I'd ever seen before.

A half mile of highways, airport on- and off-ramps, the Burlingame Plaza Shopping Center, a couple of blocks of small business and light industry, and oh, my God, not one, but three schools were within range of the crash site.

Conklin had thrown on the siren, and as we sped through the traffic on Bryant, he said, "Let me see, Linds."

I said, *"Richie. Watch the road."*

My fight-flight reflexes were all on high alert; my heart pounded, sweat sheeted down my body, and my thoughts sparked along multiple neural pathways before coming up against an impenetrable fact: I had no experience that could prepare me for catastrophic, wholesale human destruction.

CHAPTER 23

A WHITE RV with blue lettering and the logo of the National Transportation Safety Board was parked in the right lane of Millbrae Avenue after the Millbrae exit from 101. A line of trailers from ATF, FBI, Homeland Security, and the Sheriff's Department formed a roadblock, leaving a small break in the barricade to admit emergency vehicles.

Conklin parked our car behind the RV. We got out and stepped into the eerily silent roadway.

A man wearing an NTSB Windbreaker met us at the door to the RV. Captain Jan Vanderleest was in his midforties and had a heavily lined face and a strong handshake. We followed him into his command center, a small space with very little headroom that was banked with NTSB techs working crouched over their computers.

We stood behind them, and Vanderleest gave us the live-streaming virtual tour of the crash site and surrounding debris field. He put his big forefinger on a monitor, nailing the point of impact: the playing field at Mills High, only a hundred yards or so from the classrooms.

Vanderleest drew a circle around the inner perimeter, an area about a quarter of a mile across with the crash site at dead center. Then he circled the outer perimeter, a half mile in diameter across the bull's-eye, which included the two elementary schools.

My mind reeled as I thought about the children: Had they seen fiery plane parts falling onto the playing fields right outside their schoolrooms? Had they seen any casualties? Vanderleest said, "We can't let anyone into the school buildings. There's every kind of hazard: fire, toxic fumes, falling objects."

He ran his finger along the images of the congested roads, pausing at the car pileups, and I knew we were looking at an agonized crush of frantic parents trying to get to their kids.

"These roads have been closed, but One-Oh-One South is open and so is—maybe you know it—Mills-Peninsula. A health care facility just south of Trousdale."

Vanderleest went on, "Highway Patrol will be shuttling the kids from the schools to this medical center. It's close and it's big. This is where you can help."

Conklin asked, "Does anyone know what caused the crash?"

"All we know right now is that this flight from Beijing was coming in for a normal, on-schedule landing. The pilot was talking to the control tower, which had cleared them to land on runway Twenty-Eight L when the plane turned into a fireball at three thousand feet.

"As for what happened. I don't know how, who, or why, and that goes for all of us. Right now, no one knows shit."

CHAPTER 24

CONKLIN STARTED UP our car and we set course for the Mills-Peninsula Medical Center, a detour that would take us past ground zero, only a quarter of a mile away.

As soon as we cleared the barricade and rounded the turn onto the flat four-lane expanse of Millbrae Avenue, we could see the length and breadth of the disaster. I've driven along Millbrae Avenue any number of times, bought lunch, gassed up, cashed checks on this broad stretch of suburban highway.

It was now completely unrecognizable.

Off to our left, the dry grass on the median of Rollins Road was blazing. Ahead, looking west toward the hills, a dense roiling bank of smoke nearly blocked out the sky.

The closer we got to the crash site, the more the smoke made us cough. Visibility became limited to about three car lengths on all sides. But what we could see was horrible.

Luggage was strewn loosely across the road, spilling clothing and personal articles: books, and a pink dress, as clean as if it had just been unpacked, hanging across the median strip.

Conklin jerked the wheel, cutting the car around a chunk of charred flesh, a decapitated passenger, his clothes torn off by the blast. I put my head between my knees, but it didn't help.

"Linds. It's OK. Hang on."

He stopped the car and I opened the door and did what I never do. I barfed at a crime scene. Then we were rolling again.

Directly up ahead were red flashers, a lot of them. A half dozen fire trucks lined the street next to the Mills High School playing field. It was a sight out of a science-fiction movie crossed with a late-night horror film.

In place of kids jogging on the track and scrimmaging were several detached rows of seats with dead passengers still strapped in for landing. And in the center of this grue-some field were three misshapen sections of the airframe standing like grotesque sculptures, rising twenty feet into the murky air. NTSB agents in hazmat suits were taking pic-tures, putting down markers next to bodies and body parts.

Wind blew smoke across the field, sparking small fires and making my eyes water. Conklin crossed himself.

A team of airport cops came up to our car. We identified ourselves and reviewed the best and only route to the health care facility: straight ahead three blocks, left on Camino Real for three long blocks, then right on Trousdale.

"Mills-Peninsula. A big glass building," the cop said.

"We know the place," said Conklin.

"Drive safely."

I was never going to forget seeing this. No matter how hard I tried.

CHAPTER 25

THE MILLS-PENINSULA Medical Center parking lot was jammed to a standstill with hundreds of cars driven here by the parents of the kids at the three crash-affected schools. They had left their cars and ganged up at the police line at the barricade en masse.

It was a big parking lot and we were still out on the street, but even from a hundred yards away, I could see and hear that the parents were freaking the hell out. And who could blame them? They wanted to get their children. They were getting roadblocks instead.

As Conklin and I watched, a school bus rounded Trousdale and entered the lot from the rear. The parents reversed their direction and stampeded toward the bus, coming to a stop at the blockade of police vehicles across the Trousdale entrance.

For the first time since Brady had yelled *"Everyone, listen up!"* I became furious at the horror, at the outrageous loss of life, at the trauma everyone in San Francisco would bear for the rest of their lives.

The same type of question I asked myself every day on the job came to me now.

What had happened to WW 888? Was the crash due to pilot error or a structural flaw? Or had some person or persons deliberately brought down this jet with four hundred passengers?

Was the downing of WW 888 an act of war?

The dispatcher's voice came over the car radio.

"Boxer, Conklin, sit tight. San Mateo County Sheriff is going to escort you into the building."

I copied that, and my partner got on his phone.

He waited out a ringing phone for a few seconds, then said, "Cin? Yeah, it's me. I don't know. It's bad. Extremely, horribly bad. How are you?"

I watched the shifting mob in the parking lot and the caravan of school buses attempting to deliver young children safely to the health care facility. And I listened to my partner and my very dear friend Cindy sharing what they knew and consoling each other.

I checked my phone to see if Joe had called.

He had not.

CHAPTER 26

IT WAS RAINING softly when the taxi pulled up to the very romantic Hotel Andra in the center of the Belltown neighborhood in Seattle.

The doorman brought an umbrella out to the taxi and opened the door for the elegant woman in black who extended her stiletto-heeled shoes and stepped gracefully out onto the street. She slung the strap of her bag over her shoulder and pulled her soft knitted cap down to her eyebrows. She was on the phone as she entered the Scandinavian-style lobby.

She put away her phone when she reached the front desk, which was really a piece of art. It was a beautiful walnut-and-maple construction with glass below the granite counter and above the floor, giving it the appearance of floating.

The attractive woman loved this place.

She exchanged words with the concierge, showed him her government-issue photo ID as required, and he handed her a white #2 envelope. She thanked him, then crossed the colorful hand-knotted rugs, passed the blazing fireplace flanked with bookshelves, and stopped at the elevator.

When the lift arrived at the ground floor, a young couple got out holding hands, going out to dinner, no doubt. The guy was laughing at his own joke, the girl saying, "Funny. Yah. Good one, Brad."

The woman smiled at young love, then got into the elevator alone. She was twenty minutes late, but if a thing was worth doing—and it was—it was worth waiting for. She checked out her reflection in the mirror on the back wall and adjusted her cap, playing with the ends of her newly brown-and-gold-streaked hair. Her brown contact lenses completed the look.

She liked it. She hoped *he* would.

The elevator bumped upward for several floors, then opened into a thickly carpeted hallway with watery light. There were only twelve rooms per floor, and she walked all the way to the end.

She scratched at the door with her nails, as if she were a cat; then she tore open the envelope she'd been given by the concierge and removed the key card.

She swiped the door lock with the card; the light turned green and the handle turned easily in her hand. She lingered in the open doorway for a moment, just watching him amid this lovely setting of woodsy colors and satisfying architectural lines. Then she closed the door.

He knew she was there, but he didn't look up. He was sitting on a sofa in front of a coffee table, naked with a towel across his lap, and he was cleaning his gun.

Ali entered the room unbuttoning her swingy leather coat, dropping it on the half-moon-shaped ottoman at the foot of the bed. Then she took off everything else.

When she was wearing nothing but her heels, the man put the gun down. He stood up and took her into his arms.

He pulled her to him, swayed with her, kissed her neck, then took her by her shoulders and shook her.

"Why do you make me wait?" he said. "Why do you want me to worry?"

"I'm sorry," she said. "I'll never do it again."

PART TWO

CHAPTER 27

THAT EVENING, I parked the squad car next to my Explorer on Harriet Street under the overpass and headed out of the shadows. Claire had called, saying she had to see me right away. I was hungry, depressed, and worried sick on about six levels, but when Claire said she had to see me, I had to go.

I didn't get far.

A BMW came squealing out of the dusk and braked in front of me. I had a thought that that BMW had been on my tail since I'd left the Mills-Peninsula Medical Center, but I couldn't be sure. A man got out of the black car and walked directly toward me. He was Asian, thirties, had a wide face with a thin scar on his chin. He was wearing a black shirt and jeans.

"You police," he said to me. It wasn't a question.

"Yes. How can I help you?"

"My son inside there."

Relatives of WW 888 passengers had heard that the deceased would be brought here, but that was only partly right.

The ME's office was the first port of call. But after it had filled to capacity, bodies were distributed to hospital morgues all over the city. When the hospitals ran out of room, the deceased had been stored in refrigerated vans parked inside a hangar at SFO.

There was no way the man standing this close to me with bunched fists could know the location of his son's body.

I said, "I'm very sorry, sir. But the ME's office is off-limits now. Please call this number," I added, taking a card out of my jacket pocket and handing it to him. "Someone will let you know where to find your son and when you may claim his body."

"You lie. This number all bullshit. I need to go inside and see him now," he said.

I could see the four cops stationed along the breezeway that runs from the rear exit of the Hall of Justice past the ME's office and out to the street. Could they see me?

I told the Asian man again that I was sorry and to please call the central number I had given him, but he was radiating fury, cursing me in his own language. I thought he was going to take a swing at me.

I was prepared to throw him to the ground and cuff him if he got physical, when Inspector Monty McAllister broke from the breezeway detail and came toward me. He was big. Very fit.

"You need assistance, Sergeant?" he asked as he let me pass through the cordon.

"Thanks, McAllister."

"No problem."

Three more men got out of the BMW and came toward us.

I kept walking. Claire was waiting for me at the ambulance bay. As I reached her, I heard shouts at my back: McAllister's crew threatening to put the Asian men under arrest.

Claire reached out her arms to me and brought me inside. We held on to each other.

"I've never seen anything like this," she said. "And I never want to see anything like this again."

CHAPTER 28

IT WAS ABOUT 6 p.m. when I followed my best friend into the morgue and saw the double row of sheet-covered gurneys lining the stainless steel–clad room.

"I've got sixteen decedents here, all crash victims," Claire said. "We're officially full up, but we took on some overflow. Got six people in there," she said, lifting her chin toward the autopsy suite.

"How are you holding up?"

"OK, considering that this is the most exhausting night of my life. Most of these victims don't have ID. I've got a three-year-old with no name. Hope I can tag him tonight."

Dr. Germaniuk, the seasoned on-call pathologist and Claire's backup doc, was sliding a body into a drawer and three sweaty techs were cleaning up, setting up a body for her next autopsy.

Claire called out, "Dr. G. I'm gonna take a fifteen-minute break, OK?"

"Take twenty," he said.

I followed Claire along the hallway to her office and she shut the door behind us. She took her desk chair and I dropped down hard into the seat across from her. Claire had made this room as homey as possible, meaning only passably.

A gardenia floated in a bowl of water on her desk, a few finger paintings were under the glass desktop, and framed photos hung on the wall behind Claire: her friends in the Women's Murder Club and snapshots of her family. Her husband, Edmund. Her two grown-up sons. Her little girl, Rosie.

My eyes got stuck on the baby.

Claire's eyes were on me. "Talk to me," she said.

"Richie and I were tasked with escorting kids off school buses today," I said. "The buses came up to a side entrance to Mills-Peninsula Medical. The parents were behind police lines and crazy with fear. They couldn't do what they wanted to do, you know? They wanted to rush the buses.

"We had to get those tiny terrified, traumatized kids into the building, make sure they didn't need emergency care. We got their names. Gave them water. Then we tried to match the kids' names to the list of parents storming the barricades.

"When we had a match, Highway Patrol would call out the name over a megaphone. Rich and I would escort these five-year-olds outside into this freakin' mob scene of moms and dads screaming at the child, 'Do you know my daughter? Did you see my little boy?'

"We had all of the one-at-a-time parent-and-child reunions. Oh, my God, Claire. Each and every time a scraped-up little kid with ripped clothes broke away from me and started running toward loving arms, I thought my heart was going to blow through my chest."

I had to stop speaking. Claire reached across her desk and grabbed my hand.

I said, "I kept thinking about Julie. How can I protect my own daughter when the world is like this?"

There was a long silence as we pondered the imponderable. Then Claire asked me, "Any word from Joe?"

I shook my head.

"What the fuck has happened to him? How could he not call me? He has to have a good reason, right, Claire? I have to trust that he would call me if he could. But what if he's hurt? Or dead? No one is going to look for my missing husband in the thick of all this."

Claire murmured comforting words. "He's OK. He has a reason, sure. He'll call soon."

I looked up at my friend through the tears in my eyes. "I have to get home," I said. "You haven't said why you called."

Claire said, "Right." She opened a file drawer, took out a small sheaf of paper, and put it down on the desk facing me.

"This is the passenger manifest," she said. "I'm looking, you know, to see if I can find the name of that little boy and maybe three people I've got here who still had wallets in their pockets. And I see this name, Michael Chan. I'm thinking, there's probably a lot of people named Michael Chan."

I stared at Claire, and I really didn't understand what she was saying. Michael Chan had been chilling in this morgue since he was murdered in the Four Seasons Hotel three days ago.

But Claire was saying something different. She was tapping the passenger list where a name had been highlighted in yellow.

"Look at this, Linds," she said. "Chan. Michael. Professorville, Palo Alto. This is your victim from the hotel shooting, am I right? He *couldn't* have been on that plane. He's *here*—in a drawer with his name and number on a toe tag. I double- and triple-checked. It's him."

My mouth was open. I tried to clear the smoke from my head and absorb the highlighted name on the passenger list.

Who was *this* Michael Chan? Our dead man had been identified by his widow. Even with two shots in his face, he was a match for his DMV picture.

Claire's incredulity mirrored mine.

"Where is this Michael Chan right now?" I asked, stabbing the highlighted name.

"Metropolitan Hospital," she said. "He was sent to Metro's morgue."

CHAPTER 29

METROPOLITAN HOSPITAL IS a huge general hospital with a lab and morgue that occupies the entire basement level.

At 6:30 p.m., Metropolitan's parking lot was nearly impassable. Claire carefully maneuvered her car up and down the aisles of hastily parked vehicles. There were no open spots, not for cops or doctors or patients. Meanwhile, Metro's overextended director of pathology was waiting for us inside.

Claire said, "I'll call Dr. Marshall, let her know what's happened to us."

She took out her phone and I used the moment to call Mrs. Rose—only to find that my phone battery was dead and that I'd left my charger in the squad car.

Claire was saying, "Fine. We'll park on Valencia. Blue Chevy Tahoe."

We left the hospital lot, parked on Valencia in the no parking zone in front of an auto repair shop. We didn't have to wait long. A fantastically fit glossy-haired woman wearing a green leather coat over bloody blue scrubs knocked on Claire's window.

We got out and I was introduced to Dr. Pamela Marshall. Right after that, we had an ad hoc meeting across the hood of Claire's car.

"Busy night," Marshall said, "following the most hellacious day ever."

"I'll second that," Claire said. "Look. We just want to walk back to the morgue with you, get a quick look at Mr. Chan, and get out of your way."

"Here's the thing, Dr. Washburn," said Marshall. "We've got sixty bodies and counting. I've got Jane and John Does in double digits. You're lucky Mr. Chan had ID. I gotta be honest with you, I wish I had known and saved you the trip. I couldn't show you Chan's body right now if you offered me a million bucks and a house in Cannes."

"Wish you'd known what?" asked Claire.

"Chan was in line to be autopsied," Marshall said, "but someone moved his gurney somewhere. He's been temporarily misplaced."

I said, "Dr. Marshall. You're saying you lost Chan?"

"Misplaced. He'll turn up. Don't worry about that, and I'll call you when he does. I've got to get back," she said. "I'll call you. Good night, ladies."

"Wait," I called after her. "I need to see his ID."

Dr. Marshall kept walking.

Claire said, "If she doesn't have his body, she doesn't have his ID, either. His personal effects would be on his person."

I didn't want to believe this. Chan's body and his ID had been *misplaced?* Was this for real?

"I don't like this," I said to Claire.

"Lindsay, nothing makes sense today. Go home. Marshall will call us in the morning."

Yeah? What if she doesn't?

CHAPTER 30

ALI MULLER PARKED her rented Lexus on Waverley Street in the Professorville section of Palo Alto. It was early morning and the lights were on in the sage-green house with the name Chan on the mailbox.

Ali fluffed her bangs, reapplied her lipstick, and put her makeup kit away. She took another moment to admire the cute house, the beagle digging in the flower beds, the trike on the walkway, lacy curtains in the windows. It was the very picture of a middle-class home in a middle-class neighborhood.

The American ideal.

She looked for security cameras on the Chan house and the ones across the street. When she was sure there were no cameras, no eyes, no traffic passing by, she got out of the car and locked it up.

Instead of going to the front door, she went to the side of the house and opened the little chain-link gate between the wall and the tall boundary-line hedge. As she expected, there was a short flight of stairs leading up to a door with panes from top to midpoint.

Ali walked up the steps and peered through the glass.

Shirley Chan was unloading the dishwasher, putting dishes away. One of the children was sitting at the table in the breakfast nook eating cereal. It was the younger one, a girl.

Ali turned the doorknob and gave the door a little shove. It opened and she stepped inside.

Shirley Chan looked up, startled, trying to put it together. *Why was this woman in her house?*

"Hey," she said. "Are you a reporter? Because you have a lot of nerve. Get out of here now. Or I'll call the police."

"Shirley, don't worry, I'm not with the press. I swear."

"What is it? What do you want?"

"Calm down, please, please. I'm Ali Muller. I knew your husband, and I'm so sorry to hear about his death. We were working on a project together. Michael may have spoken of me. He told me that if anything ever happened to him, to give you this letter."

Shirley Chan told her daughter to go get dressed. The little girl complained that the dog was still outside and Shirley said, "I'll bring him in in a minute. Now, scoot."

"Have a seat," she said to the composed and well-dressed woman in her kitchen. "I only have a few minutes, but tell me how you like your coffee, and please—let me have that letter."

"Yes, of course," said Ali Muller. She put her bag on the floor and bent to open the closure.

Shirley went to the coffeemaker. "How do you like your coffee?" she asked again.

"With a splash of milk, if you don't mind."

"Don't mind at all," Shirley said.

She poured coffee into two blue earthenware mugs, filled the creamer with milk, and said to Ali Muller, "The police tell me you were the last person to see my husband alive. Is that true?"

She turned to look at the woman sitting at her table.

Ali Muller had the gun in her hand. She aimed. She fired. The bullets were silenced by the suppressor, making only two soft sounds, *pffft-pffft*, piercing Shirley Chan's forehead.

Michael Chan's widow fell dead to the kitchen floor.

CHAPTER 31

I GOT HOME as the *Late Late Show* was starting. Martha barreled toward me and Mrs. Rose swung her feet down off the sofa. While she searched for her shoes and straightened her clothes, she said, "Lindsay, the baby's fine. Joe stopped by."

"Joe was here? When?"

Mrs. Rose said, "He left an hour ago. He said that he got pulled into the crash investigation full-time and he doesn't know when he'll be home again."

Mrs. Rose took a breath, put on her shoes, then continued. "He said to tell you he's sorry he hasn't called."

"Was he okay?"

"He looked tired. I gave him a beer and he sat with Julie for maybe ten minutes. Then he changed his clothes and left. He said he had to get back. He was in a big hurry, Lindsay."

"Did he say he was going to call later?"

Mrs. Rose said, "I'm sure he will. Of course, he will."

I was still in stunned disbelief when Mrs. Rose said good night to me at the door.

I hardly slept.

My mind had writhed all night with all-too-realistic images of crash victims and other unsolved mysteries from both the job and personal fronts.

I was at my desk in the squad room at eight and ready to ambush Brady when he came through the gate an hour later. He waved me into his office and gave me the welcome news that Homicide was off airliner crash duty—the Feds were in charge—and we were back to solving homicides.

The Four Seasons murders in particular.

He said, "Yesterday morning we were talking about Joe. Have you seen him?"

"Yes. I mean, no. According to our nanny, he came home last night while I was still working. He changed his clothes, and he left me a phone message saying he'd been swept into the WW 888 investigation. That he was up to his eyebrows in it."

Brady threw me a skeptical look.

"He's an airport security consultant," I said emphatically. "Formerly with Homeland Security."

"I know that."

"Listen, Brady, he's not a fugitive. He will contact me again. And right now, we've got a new, very weird angle on the Michael Chan murder."

I had Brady's attention on Michael Chan, version 2.0.

I said, "Metropolitan's head pathologist has misplaced this Michael Chan's body. She could find him later today or sometime next week. She said she'd call when his body turns up. So I called Shirley Chan a little while ago. There was no answer at home or at her office, but I'll try again. I want to talk to her again. Find out more about her marriage. Their financial situation. Anything odd about his behavior. She was in no condition to answer—"

"Go," Brady said. "Go now."

Thirty miles and forty minutes later, Conklin and I

pulled up to the green house on Waverley. The old one-and-a-half-story house was set squarely on its lot, everything neat except for the trike on the walk and a beagle-dachshund mix lying across the front steps. When the dog heard our car doors close, he got to his feet and set up a howl.

"Dogs love me," I said. "Watch."

I walked up to the dog, saying, "Hi, buddy," and put out the flat of my hand. He wagged his tail, backed up, walked up to the door, and lifted his head toward the knob.

Conklin joined us. He pressed the doorbell. I knocked and called out, "Shirley? Anyone home?"

We were turning to go back down the walk when the lock clattered, the doorknob turned, and a little boy wearing pajama bottoms stood inside the doorway. I remembered the child's name.

"Brett? I'm Sergeant Boxer. I met you a couple of days ago. Do you remember me?"

He looked up at us and burst into tears.

I pushed the door open. The boy's PJs were wet and his footprints on the wooden floor from the kitchen to the front door were red.

His hands and feet, his chest, and the sides of his face were *red*.

Brett Chan was covered with *blood*.

CHAPTER 32

"GIVE ME YOUR hand," I said to the little boy. I remembered Shirley Chan telling me that Brett was seven. He was small for his age. Dark hair, his glasses askew, tears sheeting down his cheeks.

He held out his hand, which looked rusty with dry blood.

I grabbed his little wrist to pull him outside the house, closed the door, dropped to a crouch, and looked him over.

"Where do you hurt?" I asked him. He cried—bawled, actually—but I saw no injuries. The blood wasn't his.

"Who's inside the house?"

"My mom. And Haley."

"No one else?" I asked. "Are they hurt?"

The little boy just sobbed.

Had the perp or perps fled? Or had Shirley Chan gone mad, shot up the place, including her daughter and herself? Had Brett been sent to the door under a threat: *Don't say anything or I'll kill you?*

Conklin said, "Brett? Let's go out to our police car, OK, buddy? I'm going to call for more police. I need you to stay in the front seat and listen to the police band for us. OK?"

Brett Chan nodded.

Conklin put his hand on the boy's small back and walked him twenty feet out to our unmarked. I saw my partner talking into the mic, locking up the car, getting a couple of vests out of the trunk, then coming back up to the front steps.

"Local PD is on the way," he said. "We can't wait."

Brett Chan was covered in blood. He might be the last living member of his family, or someone inside could be bleeding out right now. No one would blame us if we waited for backup before going into a hot situation, but my partner and I would blame ourselves if someone died because we were too late.

We got our vests on and our guns in our hands, and I shouted at the doorway, *"This is the police! We're coming in."*

Then I nodded to Conklin and he kicked open the door.

The foyer and front room floors were crisscrossed with bloody footprints. Conklin took a right toward the bedrooms and I followed the tracks to the left.

As I approached the kitchen, the hair at the back of my neck lifted like I'd been brushed by cold, dead fingers. What would I find at the intersection of all those small footprints? Was I walking into a room where a shooter had his gun braced and was ready to fire again?

I hugged the doorway, and with gun extended, I peered into the kitchen.

Shirley Chan was lying faceup on the floor between the counter and the refrigerator, her blood forming a wide red halo around her head. I stooped beside her and felt for a pulse that I knew I wouldn't find. Her skin was still warm, and the smell of gunpowder lingered in the air.

I looked around. There was no brass on the floor and no sign of forced entry through the kitchen door. A bowl of milky Cheerios was on the table. A broken coffee mug and a puddle of coffee were at my feet, and a matching

blue earthenware mug was on the counter near the coffeemaker.

I saw how this had gone down. Shirley Chan had been
making coffee for another person. Maybe she'd turned to say
something when she was shot through her forehead. This
was no suicide, no accident, no holdup gone wrong. No shots
had been wasted. Mrs. Chan had been killed by a pro.

I heard Conklin saying, "You're OK now, Haley. Let's go
find Brett, OK?"

I left the kitchen and shook my head, indicating to my
partner, *Do not take her in there.* I lifted my arms and Conklin
handed Haley to me, saying, "You were in the closet, weren't
you, sweetie?"

"Haley," I said as Conklin checked out the scene in the
kitchen. "I'm a police officer. Did you see someone in the
house this morning? Someone who didn't belong here?"

I took my phone from my pocket, pulled up a photo of
Ali Muller, and showed it to the five-year-old.

"Haley? Do you know this woman? Have you seen her?"

The child tightened her hold on me and sobbed hot tears
into the crook between my neck and shoulder. Poor little
girl.

What was her life going to be like now?

CHAPTER 33

FIFTEEN MINUTES AFTER we'd parked in front of the Chan house, our car was hemmed in by cops, CSI, an ambulance, and the coroner's van.

Six CSIs were processing the scene inside the house as Conklin and I met with Lieutenant Todd Traina of the Palo Alto Police Department.

Of course, Conklin and I wanted to work this crime. Not only had we been first on the scene, but we were also involved with Shirley, her murdered husband, and the mysterious wrinkle of a *second* dead Michael Chan, killed in the crash of WW 888.

Bottom line, we were thoroughly briefed and highly motivated.

But this hideous crime had happened in Palo Alto, not our turf. The best we could hope for was a free exchange of information between our department and the Palo Alto PD.

Conklin, Lieutenant Traina, and I stood under a tree on the parched grass between the sidewalk and the street, and we told the lieutenant how we'd happened upon a fresh murder scene in Professorville.

I said to the young lieutenant, "We wanted more time

with Mrs. Chan. We hoped she might have remembered something that would help us with her husband's murder. We knocked. Brett Chan answered the door."

After describing the little boy's heartbreaking appearance, I gave Lieutenant Traina my take on the crime scene.

"Looks to me like Mrs. Chan knew the shooter," I said. "There was no forced entry and she was making coffee for two when she was shot in the forehead at close range. I saw no sign of a robbery—just a well-executed hit."

Traina took notes and said, "Uh-huh. Please go on."

Conklin said, "Haley, she's five. She was eating her breakfast when a lady with 'striped' hair came in through the outside kitchen door. According to Haley, Mommy told her to get dressed for school. When she went back toward the kitchen, she heard 'big bangs,' so she ran to her room and hid."

Traina asked, "Striped hair? What's that mean to you?"

I said, "Like brown hair with blond streaks."

"Hunh. Did she know this lady?"

"Never saw her before," Conklin said.

"And the little boy? Brett?"

"He was in the shower when this went down," I said.

I told Lieutenant Traina we would share information and he said he'd do the same, "Sure thing."

We exchanged cards and were getting into our car as Child Protective Services arrived.

Why had Michael and Shirley Chan—two college professors—been targeted hits? And what, if anything, could this tell us about the dead man with Michael Chan's name and address who'd been on WW 888 from Beijing?

Was there a connection?

Someone had to know.

CHAPTER 34

THE BEAUTIFUL AND expansive Stanford University campus is accessed by broad palm tree–lined avenues and dotted with hundreds of other varieties of trees. The handsome buildings are predominantly Mediterranean- and Spanish-style sandstone with red-tile roofs. Just lovely.

We had an appointment with the history department chair, Michael Chan's former boss, Eugene Levy. Levy was short, bearded, wearing thick eyeglasses. He got up from behind his desk, shook our hands, asked us to have seats, and closed his door.

Levy said, "What a tragedy. I only knew Michael professionally, but for more than eight years. I liked him. He was reliable. Conscientious. Knew his stuff cold. Although, in light of how he died, maybe I didn't know him at all."

Levy had prepared a list of several of Chan's colleagues and students, in alphabetical order with phone numbers. He'd starred the names of a few people he thought had personal relationships with Chan.

"I'm just sick about this. The whole school is rocked. You'll let me know if I can help further?"

I told Levy we would do that. After leaving his office,

Conklin and I interviewed two dozen people over the rest of the morning, ending late in the afternoon.

We asked the standard questions: *How well did you know Michael Chan? Had he been acting strangely? Did he have any enemies? Can you think of a reason why someone might have killed him last week in a five-star San Francisco hotel?*

Not one person offered a shadow of a clue.

By five in the afternoon, we were no closer to cracking open a door into Michael Chan's death than we had been four days ago. We were heading for the car when a breathless voice called out, *"Officers."*

A brawny twenty-something young man in shorts and a school T-shirt was jogging up the walkway behind us. When he caught up, he stopped and introduced himself as Stiles Paul Titherington, assistant football coach. According to Levy's list, he was a friend of Michael Chan.

He said, "Got your message. Yeah, Michael and I were tight."

The man was bouncing on his feet, seemed hot to tell us what he knew.

"OK, I don't know who the hell killed him, but I can tell you this: he was having an affair, like made-in-Hollywood in-love. Michael was not, like, an emotional guy and suddenly, he meets this woman, and she's the meaning of life."

Titherington went on to say that Michael hadn't been planning to leave Shirley and that apparently Alison was also married with children.

The name Alison hooked me.

"He had plans to meet her a couple days ago," said Titherington. "He was going to let me know how it went. Next thing, I heard that Michael was dead."

I said, "Did Michael tell you Alison's last name?"

"I've told you what he said. She's gorgeous, smart, funny, a total package."

After leaving Titherington, Conklin and I talked nonstop on the drive back to the city. We had some leads to go on, but we couldn't tie them into a bow. Alison Muller had gone to Michael Chan's room at the Four Seasons. He was in love with her. Both were married; it was an assignation.

Many questions remained. Why hadn't Muller called the police when her lover was shot? Had she been abducted? Was she dead? Or had she killed Chan and had gone into hiding?

I was calling Brady to tell him about our day at Stanford when Conklin's phone rang.

He said, "OK, sure. Thanks, Cin. We'll meet you there."

"What was that?" I asked him. "We'll meet Cindy where?"

CHAPTER 35

THE GRAND PACIFIC Hotel was just south of the airport on Old Bayshore Highway. Folding doors between three adjoining conference rooms on the mezzanine level had been opened to create a hall big enough to accommodate the hordes who had come to hear NTSB's update on the investigation into the crash of WW 888.

The cream-and-maroon room was packed, standing room only, no chairs at all. I stood off to the right of the room with Conklin and Cindy, in view of the rear exit.

At six o'clock on the dot, a blond-haired woman in a charcoal-gray suit with an NTSB patch over her breast pocket walked smartly along a hastily built stage at the front of the room. She took her place behind a podium, tapped the microphone, and, without waiting for the room to quiet down, she began to speak.

"My name is Angela Susan Anton and I'm chairman of the National Transportation Safety Board. I know you've been waiting since our initial announcement, but we have been working hard to gather meaningful information in the face of the near-total destruction of the aircraft and the tragic deaths of the passengers and crew."

Waves of weeping swept the room as friends and family of dead passengers heard once more and with official certainty that they would never see their loved ones again.

Chairman Anton resumed her presentation.

"I've been working closely with our chief investigator, Mr. Jan Vanderleest, who heads our team of twenty-five investigators. The work so far includes interviews with those who knew the four pilots and relief pilots."

Anton described the pilots' seventy-two-hour preflight work-rest history, concluding that the flight crew had been rested and in good physical and mental health, all of which was borne out by the progress of the flight from Beijing up to the moment of the incident.

The chairman pushed through the shouted questions, saying that the air traffic controllers who were in SFO's control tower when the tragedy occurred had reported that the pilot had checked in on San Francisco tower frequency for landing on runway 28 Left at 8:56 Thursday morning. That landing clearance was issued to WW 888 about a mile and a half from the threshold.

She said, "This is what the air traffic looked like just prior to the incident."

Anton flicked on her PowerPoint and a large screen to her right depicted a simulation of WW 888's approach toward the runway, including the explosion and a graphic interpretation of the breakup of the falling aircraft.

She said, "There have been reports of a flash in the sky just seconds before the aircraft failed. Because of the direction and altitude of the plane in its last moments, we don't have a clear angle on the right wing, which was the point of impact. And when the fuel inside the wing exploded, the wing failed upward, which can look from the ground like the contrail of a missile.

"That said, the possibility of a missile strike exists...."

The chairman was interrupted by a tsunami of questions and screams and shoving as photographers jostled for a view of the projected visuals. Anton shouted into her mic, "Chief Vanderleest has additional details. Thank you."

Anton was barely offstage when Vanderleest took the lectern. He stood like a block of stone until the room was silent again.

Then he spoke. "As the chairman said, the possibility exists that WW 888 was brought down by a missile, but until the flight recorders are found and the remains of the 777 are assembled and analyzed—the reason for the crash of WW 888 is still undetermined. Information on the location of those of the deceased who have been identified is on our website and with Worldwide Airlines, who will give daily briefings.

"Thank you for your attention."

Conklin called out to me and Cindy over the tidal raging of the crowd, "Stay with me."

We were in the hallway outside the ad hoc auditorium when an Asian man in jeans and a black jacket body-slammed me. I staggered back into a group of people, somehow getting my balance before I fell. I looked around wildly to see who had assaulted me and for a half second, I got a clear look at his face: wide forehead, thin, white scar across his chin.

Just then, the doors opened at the back of the room and hundreds of people stampeded toward the exit, carrying us along with them.

CHAPTER 36

I WAS OUT of gas when I came through the doorway that night. Martha charged me and I held her back by her shoulders and called out, "Honey," forgetting that I hadn't seen Joe in days, or maybe just hoping he would answer.

Mrs. Rose sang out a sweet hello and appeared in the foyer, wiping her hands on a dish towel.

"Joe isn't here, but Julie is fine. Are you OK?"

I nodded and tried to block the images of Shirley Chan's body and the complete devastation of her children's lives.

Where was Joe?

I wanted my husband. I wanted him to be all right. To be innocent of what felt like betrayal. To spend the night holding me and being held and talking and making love.

"Lindsay, I wasn't sure when you'd be home."

"I'm so sorry," I said to Mrs. Rose. "The day got away from me."

"Not a problem. I made a roast—"

"I love you," I blurted.

"I love you, too," she said. She opened her arms and hugged me and she told me to go see my daughter. "She's really chatting up a storm."

She brought a glass of wine into the baby's room and I rocked Julie and stared out the window and told myself that I was fine, I just needed to sleep.

By nine, Julie and I were alone. She said, "Story," and it was a demand, not a request. Joe had taught her that word. I took her and Martha into bed with me and told Julie the story of finding Martha at a border collie rescue league.

"We fell in love at first sight, didn't we, Boo?"

Martha barked and Julie laughed, and I had a few laughs myself. First time in a few days, that's for sure.

I intended to return Julie to her crib in just a few moments, but she woke me around three with the little distressed cry that usually precedes a meltdown.

"Sweetie, sweetie, Mommy's here."

Where was Daddy? Where was Joe?

CHAPTER 37

CLAIRE WAS RACING as she left Metropolitan Hospital.

It was definite. Dr. Marshall had lost Michael Chan's body. Her earlier statement, "I'll call you," had been amended to "Damned if I know what happened to him," and a moment later escalated to "I'm starting to wonder if we actually had Mr. Chan, or if we just had his wallet in a plastic bag."

"So where's his wallet?" Claire had asked.

"Damned if I know. Look, I haven't slept in three days."

It was Saturday morning and Lindsay wasn't answering her phone, and Claire didn't want to wake her.

Still.

Claire got into her car and called again, and this time Lindsay picked up.

"What time is it?" Lindsay asked with a scratchy voice.

"Quarter to eleven," Claire said. "You're asleep. I'll make it quick. Michael Chan's body is still missing and Metropolitan has stopped looking for him. This isn't over until I have his body in my morgue."

"Never mind," Lindsay said to her. "They tried."

"They *tried?* What's wrong with you, Lindsay?" Claire said.

"Nothing. Everything's fine," Lindsay told her.

"Joe? He's come home?"

"Nope. He'll turn up."

Claire said, "OK," hung up, and started her car. It was time to do something about this weird and unhealthy state of affairs. She called Cindy and Yuki, and by the time she arrived at Lindsay's address, both of them were waiting for her in Cindy's car.

Claire knocked on the window.

"Ready?"

"You betcha," said Cindy. "It's a good day for an intervention."

The three of them, carrying shopping bags, went to the doorway of Lake Street and Twelfth, and Claire pressed the buzzer. When Lindsay answered the intercom to say, "No one's home," Claire shouted, "It's me, lazybones. Open up."

The buzzer sounded and Claire, Cindy, and Yuki entered the old residential building and climbed the wide stairs to the third floor, and Claire rang the bell.

Barking preceded the clacking of locks and the opening of the door.

"Claire, what? Can't I sleep in once in a while?" Then Lindsay saw the rest of the gang and threw the door open. Claire saw that Lindsay was wearing maternity pajamas and gave her a questioning look.

"No, I'm not expecting," she said. "This is all I have that's clean."

Martha danced, the baby cried from somewhere inside, and Lindsay said, "Just so you know, I'm not leaving this apartment until Monday. I might not leave then."

"Agreed," said Claire. "Time for us to all have a good visit."

"We got sandwiches and cookies. Also coffee," said Yuki.

Cindy said, "Linds, just so you know. Anything anyone says here is off the record. Even if you know who really shot Kennedy. Even if you know the location of the Holy Grail."

Lindsay laughed and Yuki got the baby out of her crib and handed her to her mom.

"Lindsay, sit your ass down," said Claire. "Let the feast begin."

When the four best friends had gathered around the finger food on the coffee table, Claire announced, "Now that we're all settled in, Lindsay, let's have it. When was the last time you saw Joe?"

CHAPTER 38

IF CLAIRE HAD called first, I would have said, "Thanks, but no way. I'm going to sleep in, all day long."

But she didn't ask, and without warning or my permission, my well-earned deep funk was shattered by Yuki's infectious laughter, Claire's bossy mothering, and Cindy's genuine joie de vivre.

Plus food.

Julie loved a crowd and was super-glad of the company. I put her in her bouncy chair about five feet from the action and Martha curled up at my feet, so it was all girls and all good. Correction, it was great.

Claire said, "Time to work, Linds. When did you last see Joe? When did you last hear from him?"

"And what do you think is going on?" Cindy added. "No matter how bad this is, you know we're not going to judge."

"We just want to clear up the mystery," said Yuki. "We need to know what we're dealing with, am I right?"

Yuki, her legal mind at work, asked for a calendar of events. So I started from the beginning and proceeded in chronological order.

I started with the remarkable fact that Joe hadn't come

home Monday night but had been snoring beside me on Tuesday morning. I told them he'd been perfectly fine—in fact, romantic. He'd made breakfast for me and Julie Anne, and I'd left him home with her as I ran out to work.

I said, "Monday was the day of the shootings at the Four Seasons. Rich and I were consumed with it. We got an ID on Michael Chan the next day and went out to see his widow."

My friends were nodding, saying "Uh-huh, uh-huh" and encouraging me to keep talking.

I said, "I spoke to Joe on Tuesday while Rich and I were driving Shirley Chan back to the Hall. Late that night, I reviewed the surveillance video from our van we had sitting on the Chan house from across the street. He was on that tape.

"Wait, I'll show you."

I woke up my laptop, and as the girls stood around me, I showed them the clip of Joe stopping his car on Waverley and staring directly into the SFPD's dedicated spy cam. And I told them about Richie picking out a guy in the hotel's lobby footage who looked like Joe.

"Joe's face on that tape—that's the last I've seen of him."

A lot of questions came at me from my clever, mystery-solving friends, but they were questions I couldn't answer.

"Here's what I think," said Cindy. "He's involved in this, Lindsay. I don't mean in a bad way, but his drive-by in Palo Alto can't be a coincidence."

"I don't know, Cindy," I said. "I agree it means something, but we may not know all the angles."

"Meaning?"

"He's a consultant. He knows everything about port security. He could be working some kind of hush-hush job. He might be prohibited from contacting me. Maybe phones are being hacked."

"Did you call the people he works for?"

"I would if I knew who they were."

Cindy was undeterred.

"So keep going with your ticktock," she said.

"OK, OK."

I told the girls about the mysterious blond woman who'd been seen entering Chan's room at the Four Seasons. Cindy jumped in, saying, "I posted her picture on our site and got a tip."

"The next day," I said, throwing my hands into the air, "before we could follow up—"

Claire finished my sentence: "The crash of WW 888."

I said, "That night when I got home, Mrs. Rose said I had just missed Joe. He'd been home to change his clothes. He left me a message saying he'd been pulled into the plane crash nightmare, and, like, don't wait up."

"So he's definitely *alive*," said Yuki. "He's not *hurt*. He's *working*."

"That's what he said."

I believed what I was saying, but damn it, it was weird that Joe couldn't get in touch at all. Actually, it was inexplicable. When our lunch was over and the last of my friends were gone, I bathed Julie, gave her some applesauce, and called Joe.

"I'm sorry," said the mechanical voice, "but the subscriber's mailbox is full. Good-bye."

Honestly? This was killing me.

CHAPTER 39

I SPENT THE rest of the day doing laundry, and by dinnertime I was hungry and bored. I took Julie across the hall to Mrs. Rose, saying, "I'll be right back," and headed out to our local Asian grocery store.

It was dark when I got down to the street. I was considering what kind of veg I wanted to go with last night's pot roast when something happened—a shock or a blow.

All I knew for sure was that my face was on the pavement so fast that I never got my hands down to break my fall. Had I tripped? Had I had a stroke?

My head throbbed and my vision was distorted, but I made out the shapes around me as *shoes*.

Lights flashed, headlights zooming past. Nothing made sense. I wanted to throw up. I had struggled up to my hands and knees when I took a blow to my side and was down again. I rolled into a ball and covered my eyes, and heard two voices, maybe more, speaking to me in heavily accented English.

I looked through my fingers and saw four blurry Asian faces looking down at me. I thought I recognized the one who had confronted me in front of the ME's office. Same guy who slammed into me after the NTSB press conference.

He was wearing black, and he had a wide face, and he was shouting at me, something like "You know Chan?"

Was I making that up?

"Back off," I said. "I'm a cop."

I reached for my gun at my hip, but it wasn't there. There was another shout—"Who you work for?"

"What? Get away from me."

I took another blow to the back of my head, and when I woke up, I was in an ambulance moving at high speed. The EMT at my side was saying, "Welcome back. What's your name?"

I called Conklin from the ambulance and, shouting painfully over the sirens, I asked him to call Mrs. Rose.

Right after that, I was wheeled into the ER. My clothes were removed and stuffed into a plastic bag. A nurse took my blood pressure and temperature and layered on two blankets. Eventually a Dr. DiDonato appeared.

He checked me out.

"On a scale of one to ten, with ten being excruciating, how do you feel?"

"I feel like someone beat me up."

"You remember that?"

"Vividly."

"Have you ever had a CT scan before?"

"No."

"Well, get ready for a new experience. I'll let you know how your head looks, and then we're going to keep you here overnight for observation."

"I left my one-year-old with a neighbor. Someone needs to look for witnesses."

"I'm on duty until eleven," DiDonato said. "Dr. Santos will take over after that. Maybe he'll release you in the morning."

Conklin arrived while I was waiting for my CT scan. He looked both scared and mad.

"What happened? You were mugged? You?"

"I was beaten up by four Asian guys, but I'm alive. I wasn't robbed," I said, waggling the ring finger of my left hand with its sparkling array of diamonds.

"So why were you beaten? What did they want?"

"Something about Chan, I think. I can't swear, Richie. It happened too fast. Why me? I've got no idea," I said.

CHAPTER 40

AT AROUND EIGHT the next morning, Rich wheeled me out of the hospital, helped me into his Bronco, and strapped me in.

Then he let me have it.

"You're overtired. You could have been killed. You have nothing on the guys who beat you—nothing. No names, vague descriptions, and you didn't get a lick in. You know what that tells me, Linds? That you're off your game. It's Sunday. Day of rest and you should take it. Go to bed and stay there. I can handle this by myself."

I wasn't having it.

"What am I going to do at home, Rich? Watch the plane crash over and over again on TV?"

"That. And sleep."

"Look. I admit I was stupid, OK? I should have had my piece with me. I should have had my head on straight. But I repeat. I was just going to the store for a minute. And, by the way, I outrank you. You don't get to bench me."

"You want Brady to put you on medical? Because I have him on speed dial," said my partner, my brother, my backup, my comrade, my friend. When I didn't answer immediately, he said, "You need to listen to me. Stay home."

"No way."

I held on to his arm as he helped me into my apartment building's creaky elevator. Mrs. Rose opened the front door and told us to hush. "Julie is sleeping."

"Can you stay? I have to go to work," I said.

Rich gave me a scalding look, but Mrs. Rose didn't catch it. She stepped up once again, saying, "Of course, Lindsay. At this rate I'll be able to retire to the South of France pretty soon."

"Before you retire, I'm promoting you to captain of the Emergency Baby Care Squad."

"Fine. I'd like a salute," she said. "No one's ever saluted me before."

I did it and she laughed so hard that I laughed, too.

Which really hurt.

While she made coffee, I hit the rain box. I examined myself as I stood under the spray. I was bruised from armpit to knee, from midriff to halfway around my back. But I had no internal injuries and my brain was OK, too. Thank God. I concluded that the four Asian hoods hadn't tried to kill me. If it was a warning, they might work me over again.

I dressed, hiding the scrape along my jaw and cheek with makeup, and strapped on my gun. Locked and loaded, I went back out to the living room. Julie was awake, wearing a sunflower-yellow onesie and bobbing up and down in her bouncy chair.

She looked adorable and like she'd grown an inch or two since yesterday. My little girl. She stretched out her arms to me and howled. My heart just lurched.

What if I had been killed last night?

What then?

I picked her up and hugged her, cooing a little bit, before handing her off to Mrs. Rose.

I had work to do, and at the same time, I was leaving my heart, my precious little girl, with the nice lady from across the hall.

"You coming or not?" Rich said.

I followed him out the front door.

CHAPTER 41

MY PARTNER OPENED the passenger-side door and helped me into the Bronco with the care one might give to a baby chick.

I buckled up, plugged in my phone charger, and knocked back a couple of Advil, already thinking about Alison Muller.

We were days late to be following up on our only suspect in the Four Seasons killings. But the airplane crash had bumped all other cases, even this quadruple homicide, to the back of the line.

Because of the crash that was immobilizing a section of the city and nearly every member of law enforcement, a wide range of criminals, from shoplifters to psychopathic serial killers, had been given a cop-free holiday. And that might include Alison Muller—wherever she was.

As we headed out, Conklin told me he had worked last night scanning social media and websites of companies where Muller had worked during her corporate career. He had downloaded an assortment of her photos onto his phone, and while he drove, I checked out versions of "Ali" with her hair in different lengths, styles, and colors. Even the "striped" look was represented.

"Rich, you're one of a kind, you know?"

"That's two of us," he laughed. "I'm not sure that's a good thing."

We took 101 South, passing through that stretch of road bounded on the right by scorched grass and littered with airplane parts and on the left by San Francisco Bay before we hit the straightaway that hugs our famous coastline.

We turned off the radio and used this time to examine the ragged edges of our case, starting with Michael Chan and the three other victims at the hotel. We wondered if the crash of the airliner and the missing body of the second Michael Chan were in any way connected to the death of Michael Chan, the First. We discussed Joe's video appearances and his uncharacteristic disappearance and how the Asian men who had knocked me around last night fit into this mess of mismatched parts.

All we knew for sure was that Alison Muller was a central figure. And without her, we didn't have a clue in the world.

We were still sixty miles out from Monterey, just south of San Jose, when I wadded up my jacket, tucked it between my face and the window, and napped for about an hour. I woke to nauseating stop-and-go traffic, and then Conklin was asking, "You going to file a report on your beatdown?"

"I'm thinking about it."

The car stopped. I looked out at a sunny street lined with beautiful homes.

"Now that I've thought about it," I said, "I don't think it would be a good idea. Do you?"

He shrugged. "There are pros and cons. Like I said, Brady will sideline you, pronto."

"I'm fine, Rich. I'm perfectly fine."

He turned to face me, looking at me with heartbreaking kindness and concern. "You tell me if you don't feel perfectly fine, Lindsay. I don't want anything bad to happen to you."

"I know."

My partner turned off the engine.

"We're here," he said.

CHAPTER 42

ALI MULLER'S 1920s Mediterranean-style home on Ocean View Boulevard was stunning. The many-windowed white stucco house was roofed in terra-cotta tiles and punctuated by a six-sided tower at the right-angle juncture between two wings.

I looked up through the windows of the squad car at the spiky native plantings on a rising slope up to the carved oak front door and I felt—warned off. The place was beautiful, and as welcoming as a fortress.

Conklin said, "You OK, Linds?"

"Why do you ask?"

"Fine. Let's go."

The man who opened the front door was handsome, just over six feet, in his midforties, wearing a cashmere pullover, dark trousers, slippers, and a gold wedding band. He looked well put together and not happy to see us.

He said, "Yes? What can I do for you?"

Conklin introduced us, showed his badge, and said we were looking into Alison Muller's disappearance because she might have been a witness to a homicide.

"I am Khalid Khan," said the man in the doorway. "Alison is my wife. Come in."

We followed Khan past a spiral staircase inside the entrance and into a blond and airy great room ripped from the cover of *California Living*. It had a high ceiling, and the tall windows I'd admired from the street offered a ten-million-dollar view of the bay.

Khan offered us seats on the pale leather sofas, and he took a matching armchair. Soft music surrounded us, a string composition I didn't recognize. There were no paintings or photographs or anything personal in the room. Again, I felt that forbidding air about the house.

I said, "We're investigating four killings that took place early in the week in the Four Seasons Hotel."

I showed Khan my phone with the still shot of Muller from the hotel security footage. Khan scrutinized the image.

He said, "I could see how someone might think that's Ali, but this woman's hair covers her face except for her nose. I don't believe this is my wife."

"Do you recognize her coat, Mr. Khan? Could it be Alison's?"

He shrugged, just as two girls came down the stairs and entered the great room. They were beautiful children with thick, glossy hair, one about thirteen, the other about five. Khan said, "Caroline and Mitzi, these are police inspectors from San Francisco. They are looking for Mama."

The younger child, Mitzi, said sternly, "I hope you are looking very hard."

I said we were, and after the children ran off toward the kitchen, Conklin continued questioning Khan.

He said, "When was the last time you spoke with your wife?"

"She phoned me on Monday, saying she'd be home that

night. She didn't come home, but this is not unusual for Alison. She has a very busy life."

Conklin asked, "You're not afraid something has happened to her?"

Khan answered no to all of Conklin's questions without apparent emotion or curiosity. No to ransom demands, unusual behavior, strangers in the neighborhood, hang-up phone calls, and whether he knew the name Michael Chan.

Why was Khan so unperturbed when his wife had been missing for almost a week?

So I asked him. "You don't seem concerned, Mr. Khan. Why is that?"

Said Khan, "This isn't the first time Ali has taken off for a few days without leaving word. They're walkabouts. What she calls focus downs. She just checks out to think by herself."

Really? Without saying a word?

"I trust my wife," he said.

I asked Khan if anyone might have wanted to hurt her: a coworker, a competitor, a stalker, or a jealous friend.

"Ali is successful, yes. And there are always jealous people, but she is a wonderful woman. She'll be home when she's ready. I'll have her call you the minute she comes home," he said without a shred of sincerity.

Khan was sure Alison was alive. Or he didn't give a damn about her.

I said, "We have video of the woman we believe is Alison. If you can identify her, we can at least establish her whereabouts last Monday afternoon."

"Naturally, I'll look at the film."

I asked if I might use the bathroom and he said, "You mean you'd like to snoop around my house? By all means, have at it," and he turned his back to me.

By all means, I would.

CHAPTER 43

WITH KHAN'S PERMISSION, I gave the second floor a thorough visual inspection, concentrating on the marital bedroom. Like the great room, the bedroom looked like a photo in a lifestyle magazine: expensively furnished and entirely untouched.

The bed was precisely made. There were no clothes on the floor, no clutter on the dressers, no sign of pets, handcuffs, dust bunnies, or bloodstains.

We had one possible witness to the Four Seasons bloodbath: Alison Muller. She was also our only suspect. In the absence of the flesh-and-blood woman, and without a warrant, this was my only chance to frisk her clothes.

I walked past the tower view of the bay to the far wall, slid open the closet doors, and turned on the lights.

Alison's closet looked like a designer showroom: twenty-five feet long by ten feet deep, with built-in drawers and treed shoes under the eighty linear feet of clothing racks.

Her executive wardrobe filled one section with silk blouses, expensive suits, boots made in Italy, and six-hundred-dollar red-soled high-heeled pumps. Next to her office apparel was a frankly dazzling evening wear collection—casual, formal, all with European designer labels. Above and below the racks were shelves of wraps, bags, and boxes of strappy heels.

I saw no A-line, knee-length black leather coat.

While the presence of that coat might confirm Alison Muller as the blond-haired woman at the Four Seasons, the absence of the coat proved nothing. She might still be wearing it. Or she might have been buried in it.

As I was wrapping up my tour of Ali's wardrobe, I saw an anomaly: a nearly hidden seam between two sections of built-in drawers.

I pressed on one side of the seam and a door sprang open—revealing a stash of racy, lacy, extremely fine lingerie.

I was examining a boned bustier when Khan came through the closet doorway.

"Find anything, Sergeant? A murder weapon, perhaps? Or a pile of bloody clothes?"

He stopped short when he saw the display of sexy underthings.

"What is this?" he asked.

"You haven't seen it before?"

"That's not Ali's style at all."

"And still, here it is, in a secret closet. Have any thoughts on this, Mr. Khan?"

He blinked at the lingerie, then returned to the bedroom door and stood there until I made my exit. He followed me down the staircase, and when Conklin and I were standing at the open front door, I thanked Mr. Khan and gave him my card, saying, "Call me if you hear from Alison."

"Absolutely," Khan said stiffly. "The very first thing."

CHAPTER 44

EVEN MEN WHO'D killed their wives had demonstrated more concern for their missing spouse than Khalid Khan, the man in the fortress overlooking the bay.

"Nice guy," I said to my partner once we were inside the car. "What's your take?"

"You first."

"OK," I said. "Once again, I'm wondering if Alison is the doer, or if she's moldering in a dump somewhere. And does her husband give a crap either way?"

"Cultural affect, maybe. What is he?"

"Arrogant. For starters. Here's a thought."

Conklin had taken out his phone and was checking his messages. I kept going.

"Say Khan found out about Alison's thing with Chan and paid a pro to make her disappear? Maybe Chan was part of the contract, too. Looks like Khan could afford the very best. The snoops and the housekeeper were collateral damage."

"Brady called."

"OK. Give me another minute, here."

I was telling Conklin about Khan's reaction to Muller's

lingerie collection when a sharp rapping sound on the wind-shield made me jump. What the hell?

I twisted my head around to see Caroline, the older of Khan and Muller's daughters, knocking on the glass.

Conklin buzzed down the window.

"Quick," Caroline said. "I don't want him to see me."

Conklin unlocked the back door, and Caroline got in, slipped down below window level, and asked Conklin to drive. He took the car one block down Ocean View, pulled around the corner, and braked on another residential street.

Caroline said, "Listen. My father is an idiot. I've told him, but he's brain-dead when it comes to her. My mother is a psycho. She has no feelings and she *lies* all the time."

Conklin said, "That must be pretty rough, Caroline. Does she lie to *you?*"

"All the time."

"Give me an example."

"There's like four million examples."

Conklin smiled and said, "Pick one."

By now, the girl was pressing her face to the grille between the front and backseat. She was talking fast. She wanted to have her say and get out of the car.

She said, "Like, she'll say she's working late. And I'll call her and there's no answer. And she'll come home just before we have to get up for school, and she'll put on a robe and pretend she's been home all night. And when I look at her speedometer, she's driven like five hundred miles.

"So I'm thinking, OK, she has a boyfriend somewhere. A couple of times I heard her talking all flirty on the phone. I go and hit Redial and an international area code jumps up. Her job is *here.* Who could she know in Berlin?"

I said, "Caroline, your mom hasn't called or texted?"

She shook her head, her long hair slapping her cheeks. Tears wet her face and she wiped them away, fast and hard, with the flat of her hand.

"Please don't ask me if I love her."

I didn't have to ask. Obviously, she did.

I said, "Show her the picture, Rich."

He swiped at his phone, pulling up the photo of the striking blond-haired woman in the lobby of the Four Seasons Hotel.

"Is that your mom?" I asked.

"A hundred percent. Those glasses are her Guccis. That's her Zak Posen coat. And check out her hand on the phone. What did I tell you? She's not wearing her wedding ring."

Conklin showed Caroline the DMV photo of Michael Chan. He asked, "Have you ever seen this man?"

"Yeah."

"Where?"

"Duh. It's all over the Internet. I can *read*. You think my mom had something to do with him?"

"We're asking everyone if they know him," Conklin said.

My partner thanked the girl, gave her his card, and told her to call anytime. Then she got out of the car. I got out, too, and watched her walk up the block with her chin tucked down. When she turned up the walk to her house, I got back into the passenger seat.

My partner said, "Here's what I think. Alison Muller is a cheat, a narcissist, and a terrible mother. Going out on a limb, here, she's also a pathological liar. You know where that leaves us?"

He touched his thumb and forefinger together, held up the zero for me to see.

"Exactly," I said.

I called Brady to check in.

He said, "Monterey PD forwarded the Muller file to me an hour ago. They're treating her as a missing person. Detectives talked with neighbors, friends, business associates. They've got nothing."

That made all of us.

CHAPTER 45

I HAD TOLD Conklin that I was just fine after my beating last night, that I was cleared by the hospital and fit for duty. But even the pressure of buckling my seat belt caused a starburst of pain to radiate out from my ribs, wrap around my back, and shoot up to the top of my head.

I did my best not to wince. Or scream.

We were heading north on Ocean View Boulevard, Conklin saying we should stop off somewhere and grab something to eat.

I said, "Fine," but I was preoccupied.

I was looking into the side-view mirror, seeing a black BMW crossover holding steady a few car lengths behind us. I thought I'd seen that car parked across the street from the Muller-Khan house through the bedroom windows. And now I was thinking I'd glimpsed it peripherally when I was watching Caroline Khan return to her home.

"Rich, the BMW behind us. The Asian guys who got into my face outside Claire's office the other night. They were driving a vehicle like that."

Conklin flicked his eyes to the mirror and said, "OK, we'll

keep our eyes on it," adding that there might be a few thousand identical cars in this town.

I tried to relax.

Monterey Bay was on our left, with gorgeous houses along the right, as we headed in the direction of downtown Monterey. The view was a fine backdrop for my roiling mind. I was thinking about Ali Muller, wondering where the hell my husband was and what made Joe any different from Ali Muller. I didn't like where my thoughts were going, so I glanced into the side-view mirror again.

The BMW had dropped back behind a panel van, but it was still keeping up with us when we passed Lovers Point Park and veered right onto the arterial.

"It's still on our tail," I said to my partner when we stopped at a light in downtown Pacific Grove. We took a right down a street lined with shops and restaurants, most of them closed on a Sunday, and yes, there it was. The black BMW was two cars behind our taillights.

The Pacific Grove post office was ahead on our right.

"Rich. Pull up over there."

Conklin braked at the curb, and while the SUV had time and distance enough to slow and cruise past, the driver freaked. He jerked the wheel hard, then hit the gas and shot through the stop sign at the corner.

"Go," I said to my partner.

As we tore up the asphalt, I radioed dispatch, saying to notify Monterey PD that we were in pursuit of a suspicious vehicle. I gave them the make, the model, and the two numbers I'd been able to grab off the plate.

Conklin switched on the lights and siren and I gripped the armrest. We flew along Lighthouse Avenue, following the BMW onto a residential block called Ridge Road. Ridge T'd into another block of homey houses with front yards, and as Conklin took a two-wheeled turn, I prayed that no dogs, cars, or children would get between us and the SUV.

I switched the mic to bullhorn mode, leaned out the window, and shouted, "This is the police! Pull over. *Now.*"

The BMW kept on going.

CHAPTER 46

THE DRIVER OF the BMW had the bit in his teeth, and also a solid lead. He sped past the gate in the residents' lane and switched around on the winding roads, taking us out to 17 Mile Drive, the scenic route that goes around the peninsula and through Carmel.

I was beat up again from the chase, slammed from side to side against the straps, feeling like I'd been thrown into a commercial-grade clothes dryer.

But as soon as we hit the divided two-lane drive, our speed was cut in half. Traffic filled in between the treed divider on our left and the vegetation and backyard fencing on our right.

Our lights and sirens flashed and screamed, and as cars scrambled to get out of our way, we passed Rip Van Winkle Open Space at a jerky forty miles per hour. Conklin was doing a fine job under the circumstances, weaving around the balky cars and the ones that were hugging the edge of the golf course on our right.

It was clear to me that the guy we were chasing knew his way around this town when he pulled hard to the right, cut across scrub terrain, and skirted the Pacific shoreline before clipping a pickup truck at a stop sign and making a breath-taking and hazardous left onto Ocean Road.

Horns blew. Brakes squealed and pileups ensued. I radioed dispatch again, reporting that we were still in pursuit and needed assistance. Forthwith.

The driver of the black BMW took Bird Rock Road, a narrow and winding road that passed through a forested stretch of yet another golf course, and he did it at seventy. Then he broke from the road and cut across the links.

We followed into chaos and panic as golf carts tipped and golfers scattered. Flags were mown down and sand sprayed out from under tires before the BMW got back onto Bird Rock Road, taking a wide loop toward 17 Mile Drive again.

We lost ground on the links.

Our well-used Ford was a repurposed drug dealer's ride that had been ridden hard for three hundred thousand miles. It was no match for the spanking-new four-wheel-drive crossover. By the time we got out to the drive, there were dozens of cars between us, but I spotted our BMW stuck in the same traffic up ahead.

My partner focused on the road and the BMW buried inside a pack of other vehicles a hundred fifty feet in front of us. We passed Pebble Beach at a crawl, then merged onto Highway 1 heading north.

And now the traffic was so thick that our bleating sirens couldn't budge it.

Where were the patrol cars we needed to assist us?

Where was the roadblock? The choppers?

Was the driver of the BMW a deadbeat dad or a dope dealer? Or was he one of the men who had attacked me? My gut said he was one of my attackers—and not to let him get away.

I counted three black SUVs in the near distance, any of

which could have been the BMW we were chasing, but I couldn't make out the plates.

We stopped and started and gained ground where we could, but after we passed the Highway 68 exit toward Salinas, I recognized the long gash in the passenger-side door of a BMW crossover cruising at high speed down the off-ramp.

"Ah, shit, Richie, we lost him."

"Christ," Conklin said. "Sorry about that, Linds."

Just then, a couple of cherry-lit Highway Patrol cruisers came up from behind. They weren't after the BMW. They were signaling us to pull over.

My partner said, "What now?" and cursed as he braked the car on the verge.

We buzzed down our windows, put our hands where they could be clearly seen, and waited for the cops. Gravel crunched under hard-soled boots. A pair of uniformed Sheriff's Department officers approached our windows.

"We're on the job," I said to the one who appeared two yards off my right shoulder. "I'm opening my jacket to show you my badge."

PART THREE

CHAPTER 47

MONDAY MORNING, I cracked my eyes open around 3 a.m.

Joe's side of the bed was stone cold and I heard Julie crying from her room next door. I rolled gingerly out of bed, trying not to press hard on my full-body bruises, and within a couple of minutes, I was cuddling with my daughter in our favorite rocker. I even sang her back to sleep with one of my mother's Irish lullabies.

Mission accomplished, Martha and I grabbed another couple of hours in the big bed before our nanny rang the bell.

I left Mrs. Godsend in charge of the baby and the border collie, and at 8 a.m., I was having breakfast with Conklin.

The crummy break room looks its best on Monday mornings. It wasn't Muller-Khan clean, but at least it didn't look like potbellied pigs had had a party in there.

I made a fresh pot of French Vanilla roast to go with the bag of churros my partner had brought with him. We were soaking up the relative calm while waiting for Brady to get out of a meeting with the brass and the NTSB on the WW 888 disaster.

Conklin had the morning paper and opened it to Cindy's column on page eight. She'd run the pictures again of the young snoops in room 1418, asking for anyone who recognized either of them to please come forward.

"They're from out of state," I said. "Or out of the country. Could be tourists, right? Any other time, we'd have an ID, but…" I didn't have to say the obvious. The city's agonized attention was focused on the crash and the ongoing search for answers. Of which there were none.

Richie closed the paper, straightened out the sections, and said, "I'm just going to float something. Blue sky. Don't jump all over me."

I said, "Go ahead."

"It's about Joe."

"OK."

"He's an airport security consultant, right? He's working on something related to the crash. That's what he said in the message he left you."

"Right."

"So we see him on the hotel security tape. We see him outside the Chan house. Why? What if Joe had high-level intel that a Michael Chan was involved in terrorism? He finds out that there's a Michael Chan in Palo Alto. He goes out there and follows Chan back here to the hotel, OK?"

"OK, OK, I'm with you."

"So Joe's waiting in the lobby for Chan to leave, say, but instead, we arrive with CSI and Claire, et cetera, heading up to the fourteenth floor. Joe can't get involved in that, but he drives out to the house in Palo Alto the next day—"

"Why does he do that?"

"He doesn't know Chan is dead. He's waiting for him to come home."

"OK."

"And he sees our car in front of the house and peels off. Hell, maybe when he looks into the van's lens, he knows full well that it's doing surveillance on Chan."

"So you think Joe's on assignment to bird-dog Michael Chan?"

"Yeah. Then, two days later, the plane goes down. And now Joe's got the same passenger manifest Claire's got. And Michael Chan is on the plane. And he can't call *you*," said my partner. "There's some blackout protocol, whoever he's working for. They don't want to be hacked by terrorists."

"That's good, Rich. I like it."

And I did. It was the first meaningful and still innocent explanation for where Joe was and what he was doing.

It made sense.

So why wasn't I buying it?

Brady appeared in the doorway of the break room.

He gripped both sides of the doorjamb for a couple of seconds, just long enough to say, "We've got Alison Muller's lease car. Brown Lexus. Left in a parking lot at Seattle-Tacoma International. It's white-glove clean, like it was detailed inside and out. No prints, no trash, no body in the trunk. No nothing. And Muller's name isn't on any airline passenger list.

"Thought you'd like to know."

CHAPTER 48

I CALLED OUT to Brady as he broke from the doorway.

"Lieu, I need a minute."

He turned, saying, "A minute's all I've got. They're waiting for me upstairs."

He shut the door and joined Conklin and me at the table, moving the paper and the sugar canister aside to make room for his massive arms. Then he looked at me as if to say *Well, what is it?*

I thought about what Conklin had said, that if I told Brady about the beatdown, he was going to take me out of the game. But now I had to tell him everything. I took a breath and got started.

"There are some Asian guys dogging me," I said, "four of them, and I've never gotten a good look at any of them. Night before last, I was roughed up on the street—"

Brady got up, opened the door, and shouted across the room to our steady and uncomplaining squad assistant, Brenda, "Tell Jacobi I'm running late."

When he came back, he was glaring at me. He looked conflicted—furious and worried. He was checking out the scrape on the side of my jaw, which I'd somewhat covered with makeup, and my blackening eyes.

"How bad?"

"I'm good. I went to the ER. I'm bruised, but no broken bones, no internal injuries, no concussion. They kept me overnight and released me in the morning."

Now he let me have it.

"You got beaten by four guys and you didn't tell me? What's wrong with you, Boxer? Don't you think knowing that would impact decisions I have to make? Do not ever, *ever* keep intel away from me again. And watch your ass. Do not work alone. Understand?"

"Yes. I'm sorry. Really."

"What did these guys want?"

"I cannot figure it out. One of them shouted at me. Heavy accent. It sounded like 'Do you know Chan?' And maybe 'Who you work for?' I can't swear to that, Brady. But they didn't kill me and they could have. I never got in a punch."

Conklin was crossing and recrossing his legs, sighing, his body language conveying frustration and maybe suffering along with me.

Brady said, "Tell me all of it."

I had to do it. I told him there might have been as many as four incidents: the confrontation at the ME's office, the body slam at the NTSB meeting, then the beatdown outside my apartment building, and yesterday's cross-country steeple-chase in and around Monterey—which might or might not have anything to do with the other three incidents.

"We never got a look at the driver," Conklin said. "But the point is, Lindsay, you have been harassed and assaulted."

"Could you ID these guys?" Brady asked.

"Maybe I could identify the man who confronted me out-side Claire's office, but otherwise, their faces are a blur."

"Tell me what happened outside the ME's office."

"That guy wanted to see his son. I took it to mean that his son had been on the plane. Brady, he couldn't have known if his son was with Claire or at Metro or still on the highway.

"I gave him a phone number. He didn't like that. Maybe everything that followed was payback for that. That's speculation. What do you think?"

Brady said, "I want you to go home. No argument. Keep your gun with you. You want to speak to someone? A shrink?"

I shook my head. I could feel the marbles inside my skull rolling from ear to ear.

"Call me if you see these guys again. Even if you *think* you do."

I nodded and Brady left the room.

I got my jacket, and after Conklin walked me down to the car, he told me, "For God's sake stay home, lock your doors, and get some sleep." It was touching how much my friend and partner worried about me. How much he cared.

We hugged. Then, without agreeing to anything, I drove home.

CHAPTER 49

I PARKED MY car at Eleventh and Lake, a block from the apartment. It was humiliating to have to admit to being beaten by dirt bags who'd gotten clean away with it, dirt bags I couldn't identify.

But I was glad Brady had sent me home.

Underneath my horrible mood was a sense that I was burying something really big and really deep. As if I'd had a profound dream of losing something. And now that I was awake, I had to figure out what I'd lost.

I locked up the Explorer, stuck my hands in my pockets, and walked home, still limping from the pain cloaking my entire body. I looked up to see Mrs. Rose at the front door. She must have just brought Julie and Martha back from the park.

Wow, that Gloria Rose was cute.

She was wearing a watermelon-pink wool coat and a knitted cloche-type hat with flowers in the front. My baby girl kicked in her stroller and waved her hands and shrieked when she saw me. And Martha barked in little riffs that made me grin.

I took back my baby and dog. Then I gave Mrs. Rose a

hug and told her I'd been made to take a sick day and I'd call her later.

Upstairs, I fixed fresh banana smoothies for baby and me. We ate in front of the TV and I made up a story of a big banana that wanted to be a smoothie. Julie seemed to think I was an awesome storyteller, and when she fell asleep on my lap, I put her in her playpen with her sock monkey.

I switched on the TV to Bloody Airplane News, which was pretty much on all channels. Worldwide Airlines was giving a press conference and all the networks were present.

At the podium, in front of a dark curtain, was a red-haired man, Colonel Jeff Bernard. The title under Bernard's image said he was an aviation safety expert and former air force colonel working for NTSB.

I amped up the sound in time to hear him say that the black boxes had been recovered and analyzed. He said the recordings told the story of a perfectly normal approach to SFO with pilots in control, no prep for an emergency landing.

Colonel Bernard looked down at his notes, then raised his eyes again and continued.

"We believe it's likely that a SAM, that is to say, a portable surface-to-air heat-seeking missile, was launched within three miles of the aircraft, probably from Junipero Serra County Park. Once launched, the missile followed the heat trail to the engine on the right side of the airliner, and when it exploded, the fuel that is stored in the airliner's wing ignited. Uh, it is my opinion that the passengers never knew what happened. Mercifully, the entire incident lasted approximately two seconds."

There was shouting and shoving and the camera was knocked aside. My heart was pounding as I switched channels again. Cut to a reporter out front of the WWA building who began summarizing the news, namely that the crash of WW 888 had been an act of terrorism—and that while several terrorist groups had taken credit, none of the boasts had checked out.

I clicked on channels up and down the line, and at some point, sleep grabbed me by the shoulders and hurled me onto the sofa. When I woke up, an hour had passed and I had an idea.

I'm pretty sure I would have had the idea sooner if I hadn't been in denial. But the interview with Alison Muller's husband had been nagging at me.

If Khan was to be believed, he trusted his wife. She takes off and doesn't call and he tells me, "She'll be home when she's ready."

Meanwhile, there are secrets in Ali's closet, hard evidence of something that should have told Khan he didn't know everything about Ali.

As for me, I was pretty sure that Ali Muller was either a killer or a targeted victim, definitely not a casual bystander.

So what was the difference between Khalid Khan and me? Both of us trusted our spouses, and maybe both of us had been willfully blind to the fact that our mates were leading double lives.

I wasn't buying into blind trust anymore.

I was going to find Joe, no matter what it took.

CHAPTER 50

"JULIE-JULIE-JULIEEEE," I sang.

I picked her up, loudly kissed her stomach, and brought her with me into the master bedroom. After spreading the fluffy duvet on top of the rug, I put the kiddo down with her sock monkey and her favorite dog.

Martha is the perfect baby minder, and the two of them were having a perfectly sensible conversation as I opened Joe's closet door.

Joe's wardrobe was not as organized as the contents of Ali Muller's closet. And it was smaller, too, your standard six-by-six closet, with upper and lower rods: jackets on the top rod, pants on the lower.

I gathered armloads of clothing, making several trips from the closet to the bed, and when the racks were empty, I cleaned off the top shelves. I opened shoe boxes and Joe's gun safe. His gun was gone.

I looked in his hamper to see what clothes he'd shucked when he'd come home for clean ones a few days ago. I found only regular laundry: underwear, shirt, jeans, socks. No trace of paint, gunpowder, or lipstick was visible to my naked and angry eye. I smelled the dirty clothes. They smelled like Joe.

I ran my hands over every inch of the closet walls. I was feeling for anomalies, for secret doors or traps. I tapped on the walls with the butt of my flashlight. The walls were solid. I lifted the carpet for good measure and found only a mess of dog hair in the corners.

Next I went through all of Joe's pockets and checked the linings. I shook out his boots and put my fingers deep into his shoes. Nada.

I tossed Joe's clothes onto the closet floor and shut the door. Then I went to his dresser, where I did a similarly thorough frisking of his shirts and underwear. I not only emptied the drawers but also checked for false bottoms and examined the undersides.

After I'd looked between the mattress and box spring and under the nightstands, I remembered that I was dealing with a man who'd been trained by the FBI. If Joe didn't want something found, it wouldn't be found.

But still, I couldn't stop.

I picked up Julie and her sock monkey, whistled to Martha, and went into the back bedroom, which Joe used as an office. It was small, about nine by twelve. He had a desk under the one window facing Twelfth Avenue, a swivel chair, and a stand-alone bookshelf.

The desk was locked, so I got the key from where it was taped under the bathroom sink. Not that I'm so smart. He'd showed me where he kept it.

I returned to the back bedroom, opened the desk, and looked immediately for his laptop—and of course, it was gone. So were his iPad and his computer bag, and since the days of datebooks are long gone, I found nothing telling.

There were no cryptic notes on the pad next to the phone and no numbers in or on his desk.

But I remembered a couple of names from Joe's recent past.

I called Brooks Findlay, Joe's former employer. Findlay is a real shit who had hired Joe to draft security procedures for the Port of LA. Then, without cause or reason, he fired him. We figured Findlay had canned Joe because by doing a great job, Joe was making Findlay look bad.

Joe had given Findlay an elegant FU the last time he spoke with him, and Findlay had no reason to help me—but it was a place to start.

Findlay didn't answer his own phone, but the woman who took a message said he'd be back in the office after lunch. I used the time to empty the bookshelves, flap open every book, and run my hand over the shelves.

And I made other calls. I spoke with three federal agents I'd worked with on cases where the SFPD and federal law enforcement crossed paths. I didn't expect much, and that's what I got. No one had heard from Joe or knew what he was working on or where he was.

Then Findlay's name lit up the caller ID.

I told Findlay I hadn't heard from Joe in a few days. That the last I'd heard, he was doing a freelance job for San Francisco International Airport having to do with the crash. Did Findlay have any information on that?

"I haven't heard from Joe and I haven't heard *about* him, either. I don't think you know who you're married to, Lindsay."

I suddenly understood the expression "My blood ran cold."

I told Findlay thanks and good-bye—I think. I became aware of the beeping busy signal as I held the phone next to my side.

I disconnected the line, used the bathroom, washed my

face, gulped some Advil, and tried to think. There was one name and phone number I hated to call, but it was time.

Her number was stored on my phone from nine months ago when she'd come to SF to drop off a gift for our new baby. Her name was June Freundorfer and she was Joe's old girlfriend, still with the FBI, DC Office.

I called June.

She answered on the first ring.

CHAPTER 51

I WAS DRESSED and caffeinated when my sister, Catherine, arrived from Half Moon Bay with her two little girls and an air mattress. I was glad to see them, very darned happy to turn my household over to Julie's aunt and cousins.

I had cleared two days off with Brady, and my cab was waiting. I kissed everyone hello and good-bye at my door, grabbed my bag, and ran down the stairs.

The driver kept the radio on throughout the drive to the airport. I knew the news cold, but I listened again as reporters talked about San Franciscans in a panic. It had been bad enough when the news of the crash of WW 888 had centered on the body count and the tragic stories. Since then, the story had evolved and expanded and was now being billed as the worst terror attack on US soil since 9/11. And so far, no person, no group, no country had been identified as the terrorists.

I boarded the 10:15 a.m. Virgin America flight to Dulles International on the theory that terrorists wouldn't strike two airliners in one week, a theory that held no water at all. All the passengers were putting on brave faces, and when the nice man to my right offered me a sleep aid, I took it.

Seven hours after leaving San Francisco, I was in the darkly lit bar at the tony Hotel George, waiting for June Freundorfer to appear. I had a small table, a bowl of nuts, a watery wine spritzer, and a ton of trepidation.

I remembered a time not so long ago when a picture of June, dark-haired and glamorous in a full-length gown, and Joe, completely dashing in a tux, had turned up in the online Style section of the *Washington Post*. Joe was still commuting to DC at the time, and when I showed him the photo, he insisted that he and June were just friends and that he had escorted her to a benefit. That was all.

I'd taken it badly.

June was gorgeous. Furthermore, she had once been Joe's partner in the FBI. She was promoted to the FBI's Washington field office about the same time Joe was hired as deputy director of Homeland Security, also in DC.

Both single, they'd dated for a while back in the day, but I hadn't asked Joe for details. Not long after Julie was born, June had come to visit, unannounced, and had brought a baby gift in a robin's-egg-blue box tied with a white ribbon.

I'd thanked her, and as soon as she was out of sight, I'd dumped the unopened gift into the trash. I didn't want to see her, know her, or give the Tiffany's rattle or whatever it was to Julie.

Now I was going to have to see June again. And this time, I was going begging. She said she had information for me but wouldn't speak further on the phone. And that was how I came to be waiting for her at a hotel bar three thousand miles from home.

I was about to order another drink when I saw her coming through the room. She was in a shimmering gray suit, diamonds at her throat, perfect wavy hair—the kind of look I admired but couldn't easily pull off.

There was just too much street cop in me.

Joe's former partner and ex-girlfriend, high up in the FBI pecking order and currently whatever she was to Joe, came over to me. She said, "Lindsay, it's good to see you." I stood up and she gave me a fragrant air kiss.

I thanked her for making time for me.

"You sounded worried," she said. "I would be worried, too."

Holy crap. What did that mean?

The waiter pulled out her chair, and when we were both seated, June ordered a glass of club soda and a Jack Daniel's on the rocks. Jack Daniel's was Joe's drink.

When she turned back to me, she said, "I only have fragments of information for you, but it may be worth something."

The waiter put the drinks down in front of June and she pushed the whiskey over to my side of the table.

"This is for you," she said.

CHAPTER 52

I SIPPED AT the two iced fingers of Jack to be polite, but not only did I want to hear from June, I also wanted to be able to assess whether she was being straight with me or jerking me around. She put her phone on the table.

"I'm waiting for a call," she said.

Then she leaned in.

"Joe was involved in some heavy stuff, Lindsay."

Was?

"When you met him he was with Homeland Security, right?"

I nodded. A group of six people came into the bar and the maître d' led them to a table about ten feet away. The group settled in noisily, laughing, their chairs scraping the floor.

I said, "He'd just been appointed deputy director."

June said, "Well, as you know, he had been with the FBI before that, DC Bureau, but it isn't commonly known that right out of college and for the following ten years, Joe was CIA."

"What? He…never told me." Was that true?

"Nor me. But it's come to my attention recently. Do you

know the name Alison Muller? Sometimes she goes by Alison Khan. Sometimes by Sonja Dietrich."

Yes, indeed. I pictured Ali Muller with her Gucci shades and slow-motion blond hair. Then Joe flashed onto the flat-screen in my mind.

I said, "Ali Muller showed up on security footage around the time of a quadruple homicide last week."

June said, "I thought so. She was seen by our people, but not positively identified. I have to ask you to keep this between us, Lindsay. I could get in very deep trouble, but look. Joe is missing and I know you must be in hell."

I nodded dumbly as June said, "Joe and Muller worked together in the CIA."

"They *did?* Worked together how?"

"This is what I know," said June Freundorfer, tugging on her diamond necklace. "Muller sets what's called, in the trade, honey traps. She uses her, um, appeal, to entice her subject, get close, and once she's learned what she needs, she's gone.

"Joe was her superior, I think. At any rate, they were an effective team. Muller had connections to foreign ministers, foreign intelligence operatives, military leaders—you wouldn't believe the names. She's not only brought in actionable information, she's turned enemies into defectors to our side. She's kind of a legend in the CIA."

I must have been blinking like a bat under a bright light. I was trying to process information that just didn't compute. Joe. Managing a Mata Hari for the CIA? No. No way. June could be making this up, but why would she? I thought she was being sincere. Maybe she really could help me. I had to ask.

"June. Is she working with Joe now?"

"I don't know, Lindsay. But you should know that it's not impossible. Alison and Joe were close."

There was a lot of static in my head. "Close." Meaning sexually. Romantically. Joe and that blond flytrap. I could actually picture that.

"I'm just guessing," June said, "but maybe his relationship with Alison Muller got out of hand. Maybe that's why he moved over from the CIA to the FBI. This is speculation built on rumor—but then, that's my stock in trade."

I took a swig of the whiskey and coughed most of it up. June handed me a cocktail napkin, and as I dabbed at my face and the table, she said, "Mind if I ask you a few questions?"

"No. But I'm almost completely in the dark."

Not just dark, pitch freaking black. I remembered what the horrible Brooks Findlay had said to me: "I don't think you know who you're married to, Lindsay."

Wasn't *that* the truth?

June said, "To your knowledge, when was the last time anyone saw Alison Muller?"

I told June that the video featuring Alison Muller was shot Monday a week ago.

"And the last time you saw Joe?"

"I saw him on surveillance video that was shot the next day."

June sighed and sat back hard.

I managed to ask, "Is Joe alive?"

"I don't know," June said. "He hasn't answered my calls. Look. I have a name for you. John Carroll. He used to go by the tag Number Six, because that was his number on our CO's speed dial."

June laughed.

"Funny guy. He was my mentor at the time, and he knew both Joe and Alison before he retired. He may still be in touch with Alison or know someone who is. You can trust him."

She wrote a name and number down on the cocktail napkin, then answered her phone. When she clicked off, she said, "I've got to go. Good luck, Lindsay. Call me if you need to talk."

CHAPTER 53

THAT MORNING'S THREE a.m. wake-up call had nothing to do with Julie. It was utterly silent in my big hotel room, but my mind was far away and it was very busy.

I ran my memories of Joe in fast forward, picturing him when I'd first met him. How he looked. How impressed I was with the way he worked our case. How smart and funny and solid he was. I tried to skip over the first time we made love, but the pictures took up a whole room in my mind.

My apartment. Our second date. Even now, as scared and as angry as I was, I could still feel the chemistry.

After that, Joe flew across the country to see me, time upon time. And then he left DC and his job and moved to San Francisco so that we could get off the roller coaster of bicoastal relating. That was meaningful. Job vs. Lindsay. He chose me. And I couldn't have loved my big handsome lover more.

When my apartment on Potrero Hill burned to the ground, Joe said, "Move in with me."

I did it.

I thought about the fights we'd had, and how he'd walk us back down. I liked that he was older than me, and I saw a good husband and father in his values and his manner and his actions.

When he proposed marriage, I had no hesitation, and since then, no regrets.

Until now.

Now it seemed that he had lied to me. Not "No, you don't look fat." This was enormous, a huge honking omission the size of a city. He'd not only left out a telling chunk of his life story, but he'd also skipped right over a relationship with a woman who'd been very important to him, a woman who might be a killer.

I couldn't fool myself any longer.

Joe's disappearance alone was a betrayal. And if he had been "involved" with Alison Muller once, he could damned well be involved with her now. It could not be a coincidence that Joe and Alison Muller had been in the same place and had disappeared at the same time.

A closetful of lacy lingerie flashed into my mind.

I couldn't stand my thoughts.

I could not bear to be alone in this hotel with no moves at all. It was too late to call Claire or my sister. And I could not call June.

I thought of the last time Joe and I had made love. How warm and silly and wonderful that romp had been. I'd held him and kissed him and loved him up and then we'd had breakfast with our baby girl in a shaft of morning sunshine.

And now?

Was he in bed with another woman?

Or was he lying dead somewhere with a bullet through the back of his skull? Had Alison Muller killed him?

Had that bitch killed my husband?

CHAPTER 54

I DRESSED FOR my appointment to meet John Carroll at seven-thirty that morning. I put on yesterday's trousers, a clean blouse, and my best blazer.

The National Mall, a long tree-lined park with iconic views of the Lincoln Memorial and the Capitol, was only three blocks from the hotel. I crossed Constitution and walked along the center path, and I have to say, the grandeur of the place was just wasted on me.

All I wanted to do was meet Mr. Carroll and listen to him say my fears were ridiculous. That he knew for a fact that Joe was working on a job that was vital to national security. And that Joe was safe and had nothing to do with Alison Muller.

I saw a man sitting by himself on a bench, staring across a wide grass median to the Reflecting Pool. He was white, rangy, about fifty years old, with thinning brown hair. He wore blue pants, a black Windbreaker, and running shoes. As I got closer, I saw that he was gripping an aluminum cane in his right hand.

I said, "Mr. Carroll?"

He looked up and nodded, and I told him my name.

He indicated that I should sit down, which I did. And he

said, "June said you wanted to know about Ali Muller, but she didn't say why."

"I'm with the San Francisco Police Department, Homicide. We think Alison may have witnessed a violent crime."

"Oh. I'm sure it wouldn't be the first time. So you're looking for her as a material witness?"

"Exactly. Can you help me?"

"The short answer is no. I haven't seen Alison in years. Thank God."

He wrapped his fingers around the handle of his cane and dug the tip into the ground, preparing to stand.

I said, "Wait. Mr. Carroll, I'm also trying to locate my husband, Joe Molinari. June thinks they may be working together." I heard myself saying these awful words out loud. "So if you can give me any kind of lead to their whereabouts…"

"Joe Molinari? Hah. That's a blast from the past." John Carroll settled back on the bench. He actually smiled.

"I don't doubt that Muller knows where Molinari is. Do you have any idea what you're poking into?"

"I think I do," I said stiffly. He didn't notice.

"I worked with Joe in the early nineties," Carroll was saying. "Bright man. With a future. I was surprised when he switched agencies. But who knows why anyone does anything?

"She was another one. Sonja Dietrich. Alison Muller. Bright as a star. Men fell in love with her, to their long-term detriment. They would do anything for her. Tell her everything. I was in love with her myself."

I didn't speak or even clear my throat. I had to hear this story. And Number Six was ready and willing to tell it.

"I was married when I knew Muller. Had a lovely wife. Sadie. Two terrific kids. She made me forget all about them.

When I was in so deep with her that I couldn't see over the edge of my own grave, she went to Central Command and said I couldn't be trusted.

"Well. In a sense that was true. I'd told her things, and she had recorded our conversations. I couldn't believe she did that to me. To *me.*"

The retired CIA operative gazed at the still waters of the Reflecting Pool, lost, no doubt, in memories of Alison Muller. He'd already told me he was a dead end, but I gave it another shot.

"Mr. Carroll. If you were me, where would you look for Muller? Any kind of a lead would help me and the SFPD."

"The last time I heard from Alison Muller was the night before she ruined my career and my marriage and my belief in myself. All I've got for you is the benefit of my experience.

"I believe she actually loved Joe when I knew them. I thought he must be the luckiest man in our galaxy. But here's the thing. If she's got her hooks into Joe again, I advise you to call your lawyer and get ready to dissolve your marriage.

"Or hope for the best. See how that works out for you."

"Thanks. For your time," I said. If I'd had my gun with me, I might have shot him through the heart.

Just like he'd done to me.

CHAPTER 55

I HAD MY carry-on bag slung over my shoulder and was outside the hotel with a loosely connected group of people who, like me, were waiting for the shuttle bus to the airport.

I was thinking, *There's the evil you know, and then there's this place.*

I couldn't wait to get home.

A limo pulled up to the bus stop and the window buzzed down. A voice called out to me. A beautifully manicured hand waved through the open window.

"June?"

I walked over to the limo.

"Lindsay, I called and the desk said you'd just checked out. I'm glad I caught you."

June Freundorfer opened the door, said, "Get in," and slid along the backseat, making room for me.

"I have to catch the bus," I said. "My flight…"

"We'll give you a lift. Virgin America?"

How'd she know?

I got into the car and closed the heavy door behind me. June pressed the com button and gave the driver instructions. Then she leaned back.

"What's going on?" I asked her.

"Lindsay, completely off the record, maybe we can help each other. I hope you don't mind, but I did a little poking around on your Four Seasons Hotel case."

"Really? Why?"

"We were tracking Michael Chan."

My blood was beating against my eardrums. I was still in shock from my meeting an hour ago with John Carroll, that prick. And I wished more than anything that I could turn back time to—when was it? A week ago, when I'd had lunch with the girls and I was so high on my life. Now I was in a long black car with June Freundorfer, who wanted to be my friend. Crap. I was starting to like her.

"The reason we were keeping tabs on Michael Chan," June said, "was because we were interested in his wife."

June definitely had my attention.

"Shirley Chan has been on the CIA watch list for years. Ours, too. She was working for MSS, China's intelligence agency. The Ministry of State Security. MSS recruits heavily from the academic sector. This is a big talent pool for industrial and military spies, and they also plug into the universities to keep informed about our trends and advances."

I remembered Shirley Chan crying in the backseat of our squad car after learning that her husband was dead. She had been an emotional wreck. She was a Chinese spy? Now I pictured the woman with the "striped hair," taking her out with three well-placed shots from across the kitchen table.

June was saying, "We were thinking that maybe Michael Chan was also MSS. That could explain Muller's interest in him. Or maybe Chan was just a way to get information about his wife. You met her, didn't you?"

I gathered my scattered wits. I had no top secret information on Shirley Chan. Her murder was on the record in

Palo Alto and, to a lesser extent, my very minor report for our files. We'd informed her that her husband was dead. We'd hoped she could tell us why Michael Chan had been killed. That was all.

I said to June, "My partner and I interviewed her after her husband was murdered. We went back out to her house again three days later."

I told June that I'd found Shirley Chan dead and that her daughter's description was vague. It seemed possible that it had been Alison Muller who had pulled the trigger.

"Three shots," I told June. "No misses. Very professional. The shooter left no prints and no trace."

June said, "Yeah, well, that's Alison's style all the way."

When the limo stopped at Virgin's curbside check-in, June reached over and hugged me. Out of reflex, I hugged her back. It felt OK. I got out of the car and moved through the airport like a zombie on Xanax.

Once on the plane, I collapsed into my window seat and buckled in. The flight didn't scare me at all.

This was the fastest way home.

CHAPTER 56

I HIT THE ground running and was home within an hour. I was spending some cuddle time with my daughter and gab time with my little sister and darling Brigid and Meredith when Cindy called, saying, "We're meeting at the clubhouse in thirty minutes. Your excellent presence is requested."

I checked it out with Cat, who said, "Go. Please go ahead. We'll be fine."

Twenty minutes later, with my stomach growling and my bruises throbbing, I breezed through the entrance to a little joint on Jackson Street called Susie's Café.

The four of us thought of this place as our clubhouse and tried to meet within these ocher-colored, sponge-painted walls every week.

With the catchy beat of steel drums coming from the front room and the aroma of Caribbean-style cuisine fanning out from the kitchen, we had shared years of laughter in "our" booth at the back of the house. And we'd solved a few knotty crimes while we were at it.

I sighed happily once I was inside.

I nodded to the old acquaintances at the bamboo bar and to Susie, who was penning the specials on the whiteboard.

I passed through the narrow channel that skirts the pickup window and empties into the smaller back room.

As usual, Claire and Yuki had arrived first and had taken one side of the booth. Also as usual, Yuki had ordered a margarita. After all my years of knowing Yuki, she still didn't care that tequila put her under the table. In fact, giddiness suited Yuki. Her ringing laughter was one of life's pleasures.

Claire's seat was on the aisle, so she stood up and hugged me, saying, "You OK, darlin'?"

"Never better."

"Right," said Claire, calling me on my bullshit with just her inflection.

I swung myself down to the seat across from my friends and ordered a beer, and that was when Cindy entered the back room with Richie in her wake.

True, Richie is not in the club, but we all love him dearly, and sometimes testosterone can move our thinking in a different direction.

Cindy sat next to me, and Richie pulled up a chair at the end of the table. Lorraine took our orders for the specials du jour and more beer. Then everyone turned to look at me.

The volume in this place was so high that unless there was a microphone buried in the jerked pork, this was as discreet a venue as possible for a conversation about Joe Molinari, Chinese spies, and a blond government operative who set honey traps.

I spilled the beans to a rapt audience.

"I have it on good authority that Alison Muller—that's one of her names—is a CIA spy."

I waited out the "What?" and "Who said so?" from Cindy and Claire, who were both familiar with the names of the victims. And then I said, "The same good authority told me that Shirley Chan was also a spy—for China."

There were more gasps and OMGs and Richie said, "So what about Michael Chan? Was he a spy, too?"

I shrugged. "Maybe. Or maybe he got caught in the cross-fire. But the same source, and this has been independently validated, dropped a bomb. Joe was in the CIA long before I met him. That makes me think maybe he's working for the CIA now."

"That would explain why he hasn't been in touch," said Rich. Discussion of Joe as a CIA operative rounded the table a few times; then the conversation turned back to Ali Muller.

Cindy was curious about what kind of woman slept with men in order to betray them. Claire added, "Sex for secrets. And she kills people, right?"

"Psychopath," said Yuki. "Or patriot. Maybe she's both."

I tried to keep my head in the conversation, to feel the love and the safety in this coziest of places.

But my mind kept veering toward what I hadn't said. That Ali Muller had worked for Joe. That they had been close. I hadn't told my best friends in the world the fear that I was harboring, that Ali and Joe were back together again.

Music came from the front room. People were clapping and shouting "Lim-bo. Lim-bo." I drank my beer. I didn't even have to form questions in my mind anymore. I ached for my missing husband. I ached for him all over.

CHAPTER 57

CAT AND I had a good long talk that night, and we fell asleep in the big bed. Early the next morning, with promises both ways to stay closer in touch, I kissed my sister and nieces good-bye at the curb.

I took Martha for a good long run to the park and back. Panting and blowing, we returned to the apartment, where I showered, while Mrs. Rose made oatmeal and coffee. Breakfast time for Julie, Martha, Gloria Rose, and me was becoming almost normal, except for the empty sunlit chair where Joe had been sitting with his pancakes more than a week ago.

I drove my car through morning rush out to the airport, this time to meet Conklin for an update on the worst tragedy visited on the city of San Francisco since the great earthquake of 1906. We boarded a little red bus full of cops and journalists, and after zipping across the tarmac, we were deposited at the yawning mouth of the SuperBay at the northeastern turn end of the airport.

The SuperBay was huge, large enough to hold four jumbo jets. But under the lights, laid out on the football-field-sized concrete floor, was a giant, unsolved jigsaw puzzle made up of the blasted wreckage of the Boeing 777.

Vanderleest gave nothing away with his expression, but he was thorough. He walked the large group around the perimeter of the loosely assembled airplane carcass, showing where the tail section had broken from the fuselage; pointing out the fuselage itself, with its many rows of seating; indicating the ignition site, including the fragments of the wing; and showing us the nose of the plane with the intact cockpit, one of the few parts that bore any resemblance to its original form.

Vanderleest capped off his lecture by saying, "Anything that needed analysis was sent to our lab in DC. Investigations like this one typically take a year, sometimes a year and a half, to close. I'm always available to give updates, as needed."

I asked Vanderleest if there was any news of parties who had fired the missile and he told me, "There are still no credible claims to this—this horror."

It was a wrenching experience, seeing that total destruction, imagining the people who'd been only moments from a safe landing and reunions with friends and family. The explosion had killed hundreds for no reason anyone could explain, and to date, no one had been charged with any of it.

When we'd seen and heard it all, Conklin and I took the bus back to the domestic parking garage, where we'd left our cars. While in transit, my partner said to me, "Brady and I went to the Chan funerals while you were out."

"In Palo Alto?"

"Yeah. Small church, but it was packed," he said. "Lotta crying. I saw some of the people we met out at Stanford. That runner friend of Chan's. And the department head, Levy, gave one of the eulogies. A lot of people only spoke in Chinese."

"You didn't see Alison Muller, by chance?"

"That woulda made it worth the trip. But I think I saw the guy who slammed into you at the NTSB briefing."

"You think?"

"His face was sort of triangular. Wide forehead. Eyes sort of wide apart. A narrow white scar across his chin."

"That's *him*," I said. "That's the *guy*."

"He saw me looking at him and just dissolved into the crowd. What's he got to do with Chan?"

"Maybe he wanted to confirm that Michael Chan is dead," I said. "Maybe he doesn't know which Chan is the real one and which is the doppelganger. Fifty bucks says he's with Chinese intelligence."

"You know what I think?" Conklin said. "Flight WW 888. That plane flew outta *Beijing*. Michael and Shirley Chan and the Chinese thugs who've been dogging you. They're all part of the same thing."

"I buy it, Richie. Now we only need to figure out what this 'thing' is."

CHAPTER 58

AS SOON AS I got to my desk that day, I called Claire and asked, "Any news from Dr. Marshall regarding the whereabouts of Michael Chan, version two?"

Claire said, "This is what she said, and I quote. 'I am still sorting out body parts. I'll call you when or if I locate Mr. Chan or parts thereof. Any more questions?' She's made herself clear. Still, whatever she says, she's responsible."

I had just rung off with Claire when Brenda paged me. I picked up line two and turned to look at Brenda at the same time.

Standing at her desk was a tall, dark, and immaculately dressed man. Brenda's voice came to me in stereo.

"Mr. Khan is here to see you."

"Send him back," I said.

Khalid Khan pushed at the gate and came through our gray and depressing squad room. He sat down in the chair next to my desk and blew his nose into a handkerchief. I could swear he'd been crying.

He said, "It's hard to admit this, but when you left the house the other day, I knew I'd been an ass. I apologize for the way I spoke to you. No, you don't have to say anything. Thanks for what you did. I've been deluding myself for years, and now that I'm willing to look at the truth, I don't know where to find it."

"Tell me what you do know," I said.

Khan told me his daughter was sure that the woman in the Four Seasons security footage was Alison. Caroline had listed some of the lies Alison had told him, and he was shaken to his soles by her mendacity. Khan told me now of several times when Ali had gone on her "focus downs," coming back a week later without telling him anything about where she'd been and what she'd done.

"We have always said that what was good for each of us was good for the marriage," he said now. "That made sense. Ali was never cut out to be a traditional wife, and I loved that about her. And now I'm paying the price for my incredible gullibility. Please tell me what to do."

I told Khan we were looking for his wife in San Francisco, that Monterey police were looking for her also, and that the FBI was involved because of the four people who were killed in the hotel.

I said, "The crash has sucked up the time of every law enforcement officer in the state, Mr. Khan. But no one has forgotten that Alison is missing. She hasn't called you or your daughters?"

"No."

"Before the hotel shootings, had you ever heard of Michael Chan?"

"Never."

"What about Joe Molinari? Is that name familiar to you?"

"I don't think so," said Mr. Khan. "Who is he?"

"A person of interest, that's all."

I'm pretty sure my face colored, but Khan didn't notice.

"I don't know if I want her back," he told me with a broken voice, "but I have to talk to her. It just can't end like this. I need to see her."

"We want to find her, too, Mr. Khan."

I was thinking, *If I was any good at finding lost spouses, I would find mine.* It came together then. *Sure. Why the hell not?* I would find them both.

CHAPTER 59

I WAS BATHING Julie when the phone rang.

I grabbed it, stabbed the button, and growled, "Boxer." It was a juggling act, pinning the phone under my chin while keeping my slippery baby in hand.

A voice said, "Mrs. Molinari, this is Agent Michael Dixon from the CIA."

"Yes?"

My thoughts were as slippery as my daughter. CIA? What the hell was this? Good news or bad? Had they found Joe?

"We'd like to have a few words with you."

"OK. When?"

"We're downstairs."

"Here? Now?"

"Yes, ma'am."

"Well, give me a second. Make that five minutes and then buzz me."

I rinsed Julie off, wrapped her up in a towel, and from there dressed her in PJs. She was not tired and she was not going to bed, so I put her in the playpen. I left Martha loose, but I got my gun out of the cabinet and tucked it into the waistband of my jeans.

When the intercom buzzed, I told Dixon and his partner to put their badges up to the camera. They did it. And still, I checked them out through the peephole in my door. Satisfied, I undid the chain lock and let the two men inside.

They introduced themselves as Agents Michael Dixon and Chris Knightly from Langley. They were both in their thirties, both in business attire, jackets and ties and well-shined shoes. They weren't a twin set. Dixon was average height, dark hair, button nose. Knightly was large and blond with an American flag lapel pin.

Dixon was the man in charge.

When they were seated on the wide leather sofa, Dixon said, "I understand from John Carroll that you're interested in locating Alison Muller."

"She's a possible witness," I said. "She may have been the last to see a victim of a recent homicide."

"Yes, we understand that she may well have been with Michael Chan." Dixon went on. "We want to level with you, Mrs. Molinari. Call it interagency cooperation. But in exchange, we need you to back off your inquiries into Alison Muller."

Really? They didn't have the authority to take me off my case. If that was what they wanted, they shouldn't have come to me here. What was up?

I said, "That's not my call. Not yours, either. Muller is a person of interest in a quadruple homicide. Our case. SFPD."

"I want to assure you that Muller didn't kill Michael Chan," said Dixon. "Muller wanted him alive. We all do."

"So what happened?" I said, not promising anything.

Knightly looked around the apartment from his seat on the sofa. He got up. Went to the large windows facing Lake Street and looked out. Keeping watch, I thought.

Dixon said, "We've been in contact with Muller. She was working Chan, trying to establish if he, like his wife, was in Chinese intelligence."

"And was he?"

"Muller didn't know. She had already left the hotel and was walking northeast on Market at the time of the incident. This is documented. She doesn't know anything about the other victims."

"I'd like to talk with her myself," I said. "Officially. Once I've cleared her, I'll be happy to move on."

Julie started to fuss. I made an educated guess that she needed changing and that she was about to make this need extremely well known.

"That's not possible," Dixon said. "She's undercover on a job. When her current assignment wraps up, we'll put her in touch with you."

Pretty much what Khalid Khan had said to me a few days ago. I pressed on.

"What can you tell me about a passenger named Michael Chan who was on WW 888?"

"Nothing. What do you mean?"

He was lying. But maybe he'd tell me the truth when I asked the question that was most important to me.

"Joe Molinari," I said. "Do you know where I can find him?"

Knightly returned to the sofa and said, "I know of Molinari, but he's ancient history. We have no current information about him, I'm afraid."

"I just want to know if he's alive. Can you tell me that?"

"Believe me, I would tell you if I knew," said Agent Knightly of the CIA. "He's not one of ours."

Julie let out a wail. The two men put their cards on the kitchen island and let themselves out of the apartment.

What the hell had just happened?

Alison Muller's colleagues had said she was alive.

And for all I knew, Joe Molinari, my husband, the father of my crying little girl, *that* man was dead.

CHAPTER 60

AS SOON AS Julie was asleep in her crib, I filled the tub with the hottest water I could bear and got in. But even lavender-scented bubbles couldn't relax my mind.

Those men from the CIA had lied to me. Maybe they had been in contact with Alison Muller, maybe not. My gut was telling me they just wanted me to stop looking for her, calling attention to her, speaking to the FBI about her. As for what they'd said about Joe, I couldn't read them. Not for sure.

I imagined Joe, working out of his home office, that small room that he could almost wear like a sweater. Those months when he was home all day with the baby—had he been working for the CIA? Had he been working with *her?*

The day of the killings in the Four Seasons, had Joe been there because he had been teamed up with Muller? Maybe while she was on the fourteenth floor killing Chan, he had been waiting to get her out of the hotel unseen.

Far-fetched? Maybe. But it was too damned much of a coincidence that the two of them had disappeared at approximately the same time.

I went to bed, but I couldn't sleep. In the light of the

streetlamp coming in through the window, I stared up at the juncture between the walls and the ceiling and wondered now if Joe had been alone in his car when he looked into our camera outside the Chan house.

Had Muller been sitting beside him in the passenger seat? Had the two of them come to the Chan house—not to do their own surveillance, but to take out Shirley Chan? Had our squad car in the driveway delayed Shirley Chan's murder?

I cannot explain why an idea suddenly jumped into my mind, but it did. I sat up straight in bed.

Joe had taken all of his electronic devices with him before he disappeared—hadn't he? I'd gone through our bedroom and also Joe's office. But I hadn't gone through Julie's room.

I got out of bed and went to the nursery next door. Martha trotted behind me. I whispered to her to sit, and then I turned on the *Finding Nemo* lamp on the white-painted dresser. The light from the lamp was pale and yellow, but I could see the whole room. I peeked in on Julie and she was breathing softly. So I began opening her drawers.

I took out folded onesies from the top drawer, baby blankets from the second, diapers from the bottom, and when I didn't find anything of interest, I put it all back and stepped over to her closet.

I pulled the chain on the closet lightbulb and took stock. Julie had very few clothes needing hangers, but Joe and I both had stored excess clothes here. I grabbed up armloads of coats and ski outfits we never wore, putting them on the floor. Then I took boxes of shoes off the shelf.

Once I had the boxes on the floor, I flipped the lids on the dress shoes, both mine and Joe's. And then my heart froze solid. On top of the shoes Joe had worn when we got married was a tablet. I'd never seen it before. The charger was in the box with the shoes.

CHAPTER 61

MARTHA LICKED MY face as I plugged in the charger and turned on the tablet. I pushed her away and stared at the box that was requesting a password.

I had no idea what Joe's password would be. And then the image of a number jumped into my mind. It was the haziest kind of memory because I hadn't thought about it when I saw it. Now I wasn't sure if I'd seen it at all. I bolted to Joe's office and opened the center drawer. I had put all of the contents back after I had tossed it, failing to find clues or evidence of Joe's whereabouts.

Now I pulled the drawer all the way out. I dumped the take-out menus and pens and paper clips onto the rug, then took the drawer over to the desk lamp and looked at where the bottom met the sides of the drawer.

Something was written in pencil close to the seam, a long line of numbers and letters that added up to nothing.

Like the best kind of password.

I brought the empty drawer to the tablet on the floor of Julie's room and typed the alphanumeric into the password box on Joe's page. I got blocked several times. There were eighteen characters in this chain, and I blew it a few times.

The third time, I was slow and deliberate, and I was sure I'd typed in the eighteen characters perfectly.

And still the password was rejected.

I typed in a few obvious combinations of birthdays and names, but no luck. *Joe was a spy.* Triple *threat.* CIA, FBI, Homeland Security. He wasn't using a password he'd written in his pencil drawer. He wasn't going to use *password1234,* either. He wouldn't use his daughter's name to guard his secrets. Right?

Just for laughs, I typed in *JulieAnne,* and bam. I was in. Imagine that. Folders populated the little desktop.

It was immediately clear to me that this storage account was for Joe's personal stuff. The Brooks Findlay file wasn't there, for instance, nor any of Joe's freelance clients. I found a file for football scores, and clips from blogs he followed. I found nothing marked *top secret.* And his contact list didn't include Alison Muller's info.

Before giving up, I clicked on the calendar icon, and when it opened, I flashed over the entries for the many empty days and months when Joe had worked from home.

The notes were brief and straightforward, but there were a couple of cryptic entries at the end of March. Joe had taken a trip back east to see his mother, who'd just had surgery to put in a pacemaker. He'd made notes of his flight reservations on this, his personal calendar.

But what I was reading showed me that Joe hadn't made a round trip from SFO to New York's JFK. He had booked connecting flights from SFO through JFK to Brandenburg, an airport in Berlin. And he'd noted the confirmation numbers for two seat assignments.

One for J. A. Molinari. And the second for a fellow traveler, Sonja Dietrich.

Joe had gone to Berlin with Alison Muller.

Who was he? I didn't know my husband at all.

CHAPTER 62

JOAN RONAN MACLEAN was an attractive twenty-five-year-old bartender from Palo Alto who'd come to San Francisco on her own dime to see Conklin and me. She made herself comfortable in the visitor's chair next to our desks, flipped her sandy-colored hair out of her eyes, and said Michael Chan frequented the Howling Wolf and had been at the bar a couple of nights before he was killed.

According to MacLean, "Chan was drinking alone, and he had more than his usual two beers."

"How did he seem to you?" Conklin asked.

"Pensive. The bar was kinda empty and he wanted to talk. I speak a little Chinese because I had a Chinese nanny, so we're kinda friends. But I was completely unprepared for this."

"Please go on," Conklin said.

"Yeah, yeah. He told me he was in love with a woman, not his wife, and that they were going to run away to Canada together."

"Did he mention the woman's name?"

"He called her Renata one time, and the other times he called her 'my love.' I asked him if he was serious about running away, because he has a wife and kids, you know? And he said she was married, too. And he said this lady carried a gun. So I said, 'She's a cop?'

"And he said, all dreamy-like, 'I don't really know.'"

I asked MacLean, "As you see it, does this affair have anything to do with Chan getting killed?"

"Well. It made me wonder if his wife killed him. Or if his girlfriend did."

More questions in a case that was nothing *but* questions. I thanked MacLean for the tip and walked her out to the gate. When I got back to my desk, Conklin was hanging up the phone. He said, "Chi has a lead on the Chinese guys who've been dogging you."

Chi was Sergeant Paul Chi of our homicide squad. He was born here but speaks some Chinese and has cultivated a stable of CIs in and around Chinatown.

I said to Conklin, "What's he got?"

Conklin tapped on his keyboard and said, "Here you go."

I was looking at a low-res photo of a broad-shouldered Chinese man, maybe in his twenties, wearing a black T-shirt, sports jacket, and jeans. He'd been snapped getting out of a partially obstructed vehicle that might be a BMW SUV.

"When was that taken?" I asked.

"Yesterday, half past noon, near a noodle shop in Chinatown."

"What noodle shop? Where, exactly?"

Conklin turned his head and looked up at me. "What do I look like? Google Maps?"

I laughed, went around to my desk, and threw myself down into the chair. I pawed my mouse and opened my browser.

"Name of noodle shop? Or is that too much to ask?"

"Mei Ling Happy Noodles."

I put the name in, clicked a few times, and got a picture of a noodle shop on Stockton, a major artery through Chinatown. I swiveled my monitor so my partner could see the shop and then the wide view of the street. At midday, the stores and markets on Stockton and the neighboring intersecting streets of Washington and Jackson were fairly seething with traffic and pedestrians.

"So, this was taken noonish," Conklin said. "Maybe this guy was stopping for lunch."

"Uh-huh. Noodles to go."

"I could go for some yat gaw mein," Richie said.

I was ready to punch out and go home to my child before nightfall for once.

"You mean now?" I said. "How about tomorrow, first thing?"

"That works for me," he said.

I thought, *Little Julie. Here I come.*

CHAPTER 63

IT WAS JUST before six p.m. when I headed out to the parking lot on Harriet Street. Rain had been threatening most of the day and was now bordering on torrential. I ran with my head down and my keys in hand. After disabling the alarm, I swung up into the Explorer's high driver's seat, which, after ten years of daily use, fits me like my Calvins.

I turned on my lights and got the wipers going, then pulled out to my left, heading along the narrow one-lane street, which was banked by chain-link fences and parking lots. I could see my turn onto Harrison a block away when a car came barreling straight at me through the gloom, hitting its brights when it was only a few car lengths in front of me.

I had no time to think.

I swerved my wheel hard to the right and jammed on my brakes, and at the same time, the oncoming vehicle screeched to a full stop, smashing my left fender and shattering the headlight.

Freaking idiot. Was he *insane?*

I had my hand on the door handle and was about to get in that driver's face when another vehicle pulled up on my left, stopping right *there.* A chain-link fence was on my right, effectively blocking my exit from the passenger-side door. Then brights in my rearview mirror brought it all into sharp focus.

I was completely boxed in. I was *trapped.*

I whipped my head around to face the driver on my left and was hardly surprised to see the Asian man with the scar on his chin, the one who'd body-blocked me as I was leaving the NTSB meeting.

I yelled, *"What do you think you're doing?"*

He grinned, lifted a handgun, and took aim at my face.

I ducked a fraction of a second before a succession of bullets shattered my window. I kept my head down at the level of the dashboard, pulled my gun from my shoulder holster, and fired back. I got off a couple of shots, but the man with the scar ducked, and I didn't wait to see if I'd hit him.

I jerked the gearshift into reverse and stepped on the gas. I backed up hard and fast into the car behind me. Metal shrieked as the rear of my vehicle and the front of his crumpled from the impact.

At the same time, bullets from the car to my left and the one in front of me came through my windshield, spiderwebbing the glass, which fell onto my dash.

I hunched down and shifted into drive, and the Explorer lunged forward. I had to avoid hitting the car that had caved in my left headlight and was still partially blocking the road. I veered to my right, scraped along twenty feet of chain-link fencing, and floored it.

My car filled with light.

I peered over the steering wheel for a split second and saw that the shooter in front of me, taking up his lane and half of mine, had opened his car door and was using it as a shield. His head was haloed in the streetlights behind him, and I could see him very well as he rested his gun on his door frame and took aim.

I stayed bent over the wheel, pedal to the floor. There were a loud crunch and a scream as I hit the shooter's door with him wedged behind it.

I kept going, flying toward Harrison with driving rain coming through my empty windows. Bullets pinged into my car's chassis and took out my rear window. One after the other, my rear tires blew out. The gas tank would be next.

My car shimmied and hydroplaned as I came to the end of Harriet, and when I took a hard, jackknifing left turn onto Harrison, I nearly lost control.

Horns blared from all sides and panicky drivers jumped lanes to get out of my way. I couldn't see much through the rain in my eyes, but the Hall of Justice loomed on my left. I sped to Eighth, taking turns onto one-way streets until I cruised to a creaking stop, halting my battered ride beside two cruisers that were parallel-parked in front of the Hall.

A couple of uniformed cops were standing on the sidewalk staring out at the mess I'd made of Bryant Street traffic.

I yelled out to them, "I need some help here."

My badge was hanging from a ball chain around my neck. I held it up to the window frame.

The cops came over and took a look at me. One said, "Mother of God." And the other leaned in and asked, "How bad are you hurt?"

My face prickled like I'd been stung by a hundred bees, and I could feel blood trickling down my collar. I was soaked and freezing, but I hadn't been shot.

"I'm OK," I said. "There's been a shooting around the corner on Harriet, couple blocks down. There are multiple heavily armed suspects still on the scene. Call all cars and be very careful. And get an ambulance. Someone got hurt."

CHAPTER 64

I PHONED CONKLIN from the street, and what I said scared him enough that he and Brady met me before I could reach the front steps of the Hall.

Conklin said, "I'll take you to the hospital."

"Thanks, but no way. I wasn't hit."

He insisted and I shut him down.

"I'm cold and wet and, yeah, shaken up, but not *shot*."

We repaired to Brady's office forthwith. I gave him my gun and he got on the phone and ordered the armorer to get me a new one. Then he called Jacobi.

Conklin found a blanket in the break room and draped it around my shoulders and was pulling splinters of glass out of my cheeks and hair when Claire knocked on the glass. Who called her? Brady?

Claire took one long look and said, "My God, Lindsay. I just heard. Come with me."

"What for?" I said. "I'm *fine*."

"Come with me, sweetie. Come on."

I grumbled but followed my doctor friend to the ladies' room, where she said, "You only get out of going to the hospital if I say so."

I submitted. I took off my clothes.

Claire gave me a full 360-degree inspection, saying "Oh, my God" at the sight of my bruises. She turned me gently around, lifted my arms, and ran her fingers over my scalp.

Finally, she said, "If you feel good enough to go home, you get a pass."

"I should be dead," I said, my chattering teeth biting my words into syllables. "Those shits knew my movements. They waited for me and were determined to kill me. Why? And now I killed one of *them*."

"Come home with me tonight," Claire said.

"I can't. I'll be OK, Claire. Brady will keep eyes on me, put cars in front of my place. I'll be fine."

Brady was still on the phone when I returned to his office. I sat with Conklin, and as Brady talked to whomever, I sifted through the events of the last half hour. The best outcome would be if the man I crushed behind his car door was alive so that I could get him to talk. God knew, I wanted answers.

Brady took another call. He listened, said, "Thanks," then hung up.

He said, "The guy you hit with your car, Boxer—"

"Yes?"

"He walked away. Or his friends scraped him up and threw him into the trunk. There was no corpse on Harriet."

I had a moment of relief, and then the next thought rolled over me like a tidal wave.

We had no suspects or witnesses, no IDs, no plate numbers. The men who'd attacked me could be heading for LA or Mexico or points east, or hell, they could be idling their engines on Bryant, waiting to take another crack at me.

"Here's your new gun," Brady said, handing over a Glock identical to my old one. "The chief's on the way down."

Damn it. Now I was going to have to tell this story to Jacobi.

CHAPTER 65

CHIEF OF POLICE Warren Jacobi is big and gray-haired and he walks with a limp because of two bullets he took to the hip on a bad night in the Tenderloin. I was also shot that night, but unlike Jacobi, I remained conscious and called for help. That night Jacobi and I bonded for life.

Over the last dozen years, Jacobi has been my partner, my subordinate, and now my boss. I stood up when he entered Brady's small office. He reached out and folded me into a gentle hug.

My eyes welled up and I dried them on his jacket.

"I'm OK. I'm really OK."

He released me and shook his head.

"Boxer, I want you to listen to me. You're a target. I don't know why, and from what I hear, you don't know, either. And I know you weren't careless or stupid. Regardless, you've been beat up and chased and shot at, and next time these guys get you in their sights—I don't need to spell it out, do I? So don't fight me. Don't make me pull rank. Just do what I say. Take some time off. Leave town until we nail these guys."

As I listened to Jacobi's litany, something inside me heated up and boiled the hell over. I went off. I just blew.

"With all due respect, Jacobi, that's a load of bull. It was bad, but I handled it. That's what the job is. I hardly have a scratch on me. So stop treating me like a victim. I'm fully functional and absolutely sane. This is my case and I'm on it. OK? OK?"

I went to my desk and typed up a report. I handed it to Brady, then went down to the street and emptied my glove box and got my bag out of the front footwell before my fatally crippled Explorer was loaded onto a flatbed truck and taken out to the forensics lab.

Conklin drove me home. I didn't talk during the ride, but I grabbed his hand and squeezed it before I got out of his car. And then he came around and opened the passenger door. I gave him a look that should have stopped him.

"Shut up," he said. "I'm going in with you."

Once inside my apartment, I greeted our nanny and said good night and good-bye to my partner. I showered, then ate something with tomato sauce, I don't remember what.

I played blocks with my daughter and put her to bed. After that, I rechecked the locks and the security system and looked out at the patrol cars parked down on the street. I put my gun on the night table, and then I got into bed with Martha and fell asleep. I didn't think and I didn't dream.

When I woke up in the morning I was madder than I'd ever been before in my life. I understood now that I was being treated like an orphaned kitten not just because I had been repeatedly attacked and almost killed. It was also because Joe had left me without a word.

The men who'd tried to kill me would answer for what they'd done if it was the last thing I did in my life.

And that went for my husband, too.

CHAPTER 66

OFFICER EVELYN FINLEY drove me slowly and carefully to the Hall that morning, as if she were transporting vintage glass Christmas ornaments. She also walked me through the lobby and waited with me until the elevator came.

"Following orders," she said.

Damn it.

"Thanks, Finley," I said. "I can take it from here."

I rounded Brenda's desk at the entrance to the bullpen and saw that Conklin, Chi, McNeil, and Brady were in some kind of huddle near Chi's desk. Apparently, a meeting was in progress. Maybe I hadn't been purposefully excluded. Maybe it just felt that way.

Conklin waved me over and both he and Brady scrambled to get me a chair. I almost laughed. Instead, I muttered, "Thanks. I've got it. I've *got* it."

Cappy McNeil is almost fifty, carrying too much weight around his middle, but he's a steady old hand and a very good cop.

His partner, Sergeant Paul Chi, is ten years younger and one of the sharpest cops in the city. The two of them were getting their first look at my face of a million cuts, but they'd already heard about the turkey shoot last night.

Cappy said, "Ahh, sheet, Boxer. This is just wrong."

He patted my arm and passed me one of his two untouched donuts.

Once I was settled in, Chi resumed his briefing.

"Lindsay, to bring you up to speed, I have a CI who lives over a grocery store on the corner of Jackson and Stockton. He called me last night to say he's seen about four Asian businessmen, well dressed, driving deluxe vehicles, coming and going at odd hours. They're apparently based in a crappy apartment building right here."

Chi pulled up a map on his computer, street view. He stabbed a location on Stockton, middle of the block, east side.

"This is it," said Chi. "Ten Thirty-Five Stockton. Low-rent joint with a dry cleaner downstairs. Now, the tenant of the presumed crappy apartment is Henry Yee. Two small-time drug busts. He works in the noodle shop over here. Corner of Jackson. He's subletting his place to these guys, sleeps at the restaurant.

"Now, rumor has it that these men are here on some kind of government business. They're not into drugs or—"

I stopped him. "Wait. What government?"

"Chinese, I'm guessing, but no one knows," Chi said. "My CI called last night because last week, he sees these men unloading long, heavy boxes from a black or blue SUV. He didn't think much of it until last night.

"According to my snitch, around eight p.m. last night, one of those slick Chinese guys parks his SUV on Stockton near the corner of Jackson. The car's got two busted headlights. And now my snitch is thinking back on those heavy loads that were taken out of the SUV last week and wonders if that stuff wasn't artillery. My guy's a junkie, but he's not stupid. I tend to believe him."

I said, "Some kind of dark vehicle smashed my front end last night. And then I backed hard into the vehicle behind me. This SUV you're telling us about had to be one of those cars."

Brady called Jacobi, who came downstairs and joined us. An hour later, we had a plan.

CHAPTER 67

BY FOUR-THIRTY that afternoon, three teams from Homicide and our SWAT unit were deployed discreetly around Stockton and Jackson, a neighborhood known for its traditional Chinese shops and also for its drug, gambling, and gang activity.

I took it all in from where Conklin and I waited in our parked car on Stockton.

Our focus was on a three-story beige stucco apartment building across the street from us in the middle of the block. Next to the dry cleaner Chi had referred to was a gray-painted door that led to the apartments upstairs.

SWAT SUVs bracketed the apartment building and covered the open stores, their bins of merchandise spilling out to the sidewalks teeming with shoppers and passersby. Traffic stopped and started at the intersections, delivery trucks double-parked, a school bus dropped off children, and laughing tourists came out of a restaurant.

I kept scanning the street.

I could see Lemke and Samuels of our squad, parked at the corner of Washington. Michaels and Wang, also in Homicide, were in their car at the Jackson end of Stockton, watching the noodle shop where the waiter worked.

Brady was across the street from us, leaning against the wall of a ginseng company, reading a paper.

Chi and McNeil were in plain clothes, examining the produce in the corner market across from us, when a blue BMW SUV with a long gash on one side double-parked fifty yards up the block from the apartment house with the gray-painted door.

Brady flicked his eyes toward us.

Conklin and I got out of our car and crossed the street through traffic as Chi and McNeil walked up behind the two Asian men who were heading toward the apartment building.

I was too far from Chi to hear his voice, but I knew he was introducing himself, saying he had a few questions and he'd like to see identification.

The taller of the two men smoothly pulled a gun from his waistband and got off three shots while the other man opened the door to the building. Chi grabbed at his neck and went down.

McNeil dropped behind two cars at the curb and fired on both men, who disappeared through the doorway. SWAT swarmed out of their vehicles in full tactical gear—helmets, shields, armor, and M-16s. That was when automatic gunfire sprayed down on the street from the apartments above.

In the space of a few seconds, an everyday street market scene had turned upside down into panic and utter chaos. Pedestrians shrieked and ran for cover as Brady and McNeil dragged Chi out of harm's way.

Conklin and I kept moving, throwing open the gray door,

running toward the stairs. A trail of blood drops spattered the treads leading up.

I called Wang and told him to pick up Henry Yee, the waiter who lived in the top-floor apartment. Seconds later, SWAT entered the building. The ten of us thundered up the stairs.

CHAPTER 68

CONKLIN AND I were wearing Kevlar under our jackets and had our Glocks in hand. This wasn't much protection, but I was so pumped on adrenaline, I didn't care.

When the top-floor hallway was packed with the SWAT force, the commander gave me a nod. Conklin and I took positions on either side of the apartment door.

I knocked and announced, screaming, "*Police!* Drop your weapons and come out."

There was no answer, no sound but the pounding of my heart. We stepped aside and SWAT battered the door open and tossed two stun grenades into the room before closing the door again.

A deafening concussion knocked plaster off the ceiling, and a dozen heartbeats later, SWAT stormed the premises. I heard shouts. Automatic rifles chattered in long bursts, and then there was the sound of heavy boots as our team walked the rooms, opened doors, shouted "Clear."

When the commander said we could do so, Conklin and I entered the small apartment.

The bodies of four armed and very dangerous men were sprawled around the front room. The tac team had done the job they were trained to do. They'd done it by the book.

Bullet holes pocked the walls, and blood had spattered and sprayed and was pooling on the floor.

A half dozen automatic rifles lay on the floor under the windows, along with many open boxes of ammo. And something unusual was on the kitchen table. It was like a metal tube about five feet long, with a scope, a muzzle, a handgrip, and a butt end that was meant to brace against a shoulder.

I'd never seen one before, but I knew a portable missile launcher when I saw it. I was pretty sure it had a range of three miles and was used to take down aircraft.

Two thoughts slammed together in my mind. These men who had been after me since the day of the crash were *arms dealers*.

Were they involved in what had happened to WW 888?

Counting casualties on the ground, 430 people had been *killed* in that crash. Had these men taken part in that unspeakable horror?

I turned back to the array of dead men lying shot to pieces in this shabby room. I walked from one to the other, getting an angle on their faces, looking for the one who had made me his personal target, the one who'd leveled his gun at my head last night.

And then I saw him at the far end of the room near the bedroom doorway. After he'd been shot, he'd slid down the wall into a sitting position on the floor and had left a long, wide smear of blood behind him. His head and shirt were entirely bloodied, and his arm and shoulder had taken bullets in several places.

I moved closer. By God, I wanted to be sure.

The man's closed eyes were widely spaced and there was a thin scar across his chin.

This was the son of a bitch who'd tried to kill me.

I wanted him dead. But I wanted to talk to him even more. I leaned down and grabbed his shot-up arm, hoping he would scream, hoping he was faking it. I got nothing. No scream, no taunts, no answered questions.

But I swear, the way his lips were set in death, he was still smirking.

I released his shoulder and he toppled, dead weight falling sideways onto the floor.

I was still staring at his body when Conklin called my name. He was on the phone. He said to me, "Wang's on the line. They've got that waiter guy, Henry Yee. He's in custody."

CHAPTER 69

TWENTY-FOUR HOURS after the takedown on Stockton Street, we were still cleaning up the mess and trying to get answers.

Chi was recovering from surgery and in stable condition. Two pedestrians had been hurt, a woman and her young daughter who had been hit by the spray of gunfire when the men in the apartment opened up on the street.

The press was all over us. It didn't matter that the shots that had injured the passersby had been fired by criminals. The fallout was all on the SFPD.

Under pressure, Jacobi gave a press conference, saying that military-grade automatic weapons had been seized from apartment 3F at 1035 Stockton, but he didn't mention the missile launcher and he didn't take questions, saying only, "I can't discuss an ongoing investigation."

No documents or identification had been found on the dead men in 3F. There were also no fingerprint matches, and no one had come forward to claim the bodies. We had too many questions without answers, but we did have the sorry patsy, young Henry Yee.

Conklin and I were with Yee and his lawyer in our small, gray interview room. A camera rolled tape from a corner of the ceiling, and the observation room behind the glass was packed with high-level cops, including Brady, Jacobi, and our DA, Leonard Parisi.

Henry Yee was five feet tall, nearsighted, and pretty much lost. His lawyer, Ernest Ling, was a mild-mannered man who went by the street name of Daddy. Mr. Ling negotiated for Yee, and given Yee's importance as a material witness, Parisi himself had agreed to drop the gun charge as long as we were satisfied with what Yee told us.

So far, we had established that Yee was twenty years old with two years of high school. He had two small-time drug arrests and no parents.

The lease for apartment 3F had passed to Yee when his mother died. And then, about a month ago, Yee had sublet the apartment to four men from China who paid him eight hundred dollars over the rent for him to sleep elsewhere. Yee worked as a waiter and dishwasher for Mei Ling Happy Noodles and had been sleeping in the storeroom. His subtenants hired him to bring them take-out and do occasional odd jobs. He also stopped by the apartment to change clothes.

Sometimes the four men joked around with him, and he also overheard some of their conversations. So he said.

Yee had been carrying a gun under his apron when Wang and Michaels snatched him up. He had no license to carry, and certainly no need for a gun in his job. The Colt .45 was a gift from his subtenants, and apparently, to Yee, it was a prize.

That gun had been lucky for us, too.

Yee was an adult with a sheet. He was looking at prison time for the illegal possession, and if he could be implicated in the crash of WW 888, he would be eligible for the death penalty.

Daddy Ling had made the best and only deal for his client. Now we needed Henry Yee to tell us everything he knew.

CHAPTER 70

HENRY YEE WAS sipping from a can of Coke, looking at morgue photos of the deceased.

Said Yee, "This one. He's called Dog Head or Dog. I don't know his real name. This one is called Jake. This one speaks no English. He's called Weisei. But this one," he said, pointing to the picture of the man with the scar, "he goes by Mr. Soo. He is not a gangster. He says he works for the government."

Conklin asked, "What were the weapons for, Henry?"

"I don't know," said Yee. "Mr. Jake told me it was private business."

I said, "Did these men ever discuss the airplane that went down at SFO?"

"That airplane from Beijing? No, I didn't hear that."

I said, "We think they *did* have something to do with that airplane, Henry. Think hard. Did you hear anything at all?"

Ling said to his client, "Henry. You don't have to worry. None of those men can hurt you."

"They didn't tell me anything," said Henry Yee.

I said to the lawyer, "Mr. Ling, this isn't working. Your client has given us his name, rank, and serial number. That's not the deal we made."

Daddy Ling said, "He's afraid it's going to come back on him. That's not crazy, Sergeant."

Ling had a whispered talk with his client, who looked up at me through the thick lenses of his glasses. He nodded and heaved a long sigh.

Then he said, "This is the only thing I know about the airplane. I don't think it means anything, and please don't get mad at me."

I felt a chill, as if we were on the edge of a breakthrough, but I was afraid to trust the feeling. This mutt had been a total disappointment.

"Night before last," said Yee, "me and Mr. Soo both got home at the same time and I notice that Mr. Soo's car is all banged up. I say, 'What happened, Mr. Soo? You all right?'"

"He's very mad. He got into a car fight with a police lady he calls Dirty Mary."

Did he mean *me*?

"Why Dirty Mary? Like Clint Eastwood?"

The kid nodded and went on.

"Anyway, Mr. Soo had already told me after the crash that he needed proof for his boss that some man was on that plane. He said Dirty Mary stopped him from doing his job. That made him look bad. But I think he did find the body," said Yee.

"What makes you think that?" I asked.

"Like a week and a half ago, I helped him unload his car and I saw a body in the back wrapped in a sheet. I just saw a foot that was all burned. Mr. Soo shut the trunk before I could see more."

Pictures were coming up in my mind and tumbling end over end. The first time I saw Mr. Soo outside the ME's office, he'd said he wanted to see his son. I'd turned him away and a bunch of cops had backed me up.

"Was he looking for his son?" I asked Henry Yee.

"No, it wasn't his son," said Yee. "It was someone else."

I thought of the missing victim of WW 888. The body had gotten mysteriously lost at Metropolitan Hospital. I remembered the chaos that night, the exhausted, traumatized people, more corpses than any one morgue could handle.

I could imagine someone disguised in hospital scrubs, looking at rows of bodies on gurneys, reading toe tags. I could imagine someone wheeling a corpse out of the hospital emergency room.

No one would have stopped a person in scrubs. Not that night.

I was breathless, almost faint. I stood up and, placing the flats of my hands on the table, I leaned toward our only material witness.

"Think, Henry. Did Mr. Soo mention the name Michael Chan? Was he looking for the body of Michael Chan?"

"He never said the name," Yee said.

The kid looked terrified. Of me? Or of retaliation?

Ling said his client had cooperated fully. The interview was over. Yee was released.

I still had questions. Plenty of them.

PART FOUR

CHAPTER 71

CINDY CALLED TO say, "*Lindsay*. I've got breaking news. Big-time. Can you meet me downstairs in five minutes? I'll drive you home after."

"Give me a hint," I said, shutting down my computer and locking my desk drawer.

She was speed-talking. *Warp* speed.

"A tip came in twenty minutes ago. From a guy who saw the photos I'm running of the Four Seasons' Jane and John Doe, and he says he's got *video of them*. In the *hotel*. On a hidden *camera*. He's going to show me the video. Is that enough *hint* for you?"

It certainly was.

"I'm on my way."

Conklin had already left for the day. I asked Brenda to call off my ride while I phoned Mrs. Rose to say I'd be late. Then I zipped up my jacket and ran down the stairs.

Cindy had my attention for sure. Was the tipster solid? Would there really be a video of the kids in that room? And if so, would the video reveal their killer? Had Cindy cracked the case on four homicides? I was hoping. I guess I'm still an optimist after all these years.

Cindy was waiting for me in front of the Hall as traffic rushed and dusk fell. I got into her '09 Honda Civic just two steps ahead of Traffic Control, who was about to shoo her away.

"Start talking," I said as I buckled up. "Where are we going? You've got my undivided attention."

The car lurched as Cindy put it in gear. "His code name is Jad," she said. We were heading northeast on Bryant, Cindy turning her head every few words to pin me with her big blue eyes.

"'Jad' was doing surveillance for somebody. I took it to be a government agency, but he wouldn't say who. He was, however, *emphatic* that what he caught on tape could get him *killed*. I could feel him sweating over the phone."

"And so why did he contact you?"

"Because in my copy I begged anyone with information as to the identities of John and Jane to get in touch with me, confidentially. He also said that what he knew was eating him up inside. His voice was cracking up, Linds. He was *freaked* out."

"Did you tell him you were bringing me?"

"Well, what I said was that I wasn't going to meet a stranger alone. That I was bringing my associate. Like Woodward and Bernstein. You know?"

"Oh, man."

I was shaking my head. This wouldn't be the first or even the fifth time Cindy had waded into a highly flammable situation because she was onto a big story.

"Linds, he said it was OK to bring you. And there's more," said my crime reporter friend. "Along with the video of those two kids, Jad also has footage of what could be *Chan and Muller*. Yeah, Lindsay. Really. Asian guy. Blond woman. I'm thinking, *Oh, my God*. It's now or never. Jad could take off. This time tomorrow he could be on another *continent*."

"We should be going in with a tac team, Cindy."

"I agreed to keep this confidential. And I *believe* him. He's going to show us the video. He *wants* to. He called *me*. Look, we're meeting him in the *parking lot* at Washington and the Embarcadero. It's *wide open*. We'll be perfectly safe."

I told her, "We'll be sitting ducks."

"Wait a minute. Didn't you just outwit three armed desperados with nothing more than a quick draw on your stick shift?"

I laughed. "You have a way with words."

"And that's why they pay me the OK bucks."

Cindy grinned at me and threaded her car through a narrow opening in traffic. She maintained maximum possible acceleration from Bryant to the Embarcadero, where she smoothly entered the lot right across from the Ferry Building. She took one of the empty spots facing the street and left the motor running.

She fished her phone out of her bag and made a call. "Jad? It's Cindy. I'm here."

There was a pause.

"The blue Civic. Front row. OK."

Cindy clicked off.

"Our date with destiny," said my friend. "He's on the way."

CHAPTER 72

AN OLD BLACK Lincoln with a noisy muffler took the looping turn off the Embarcadero, crossed the wide roadway, and nosed into the parking lot where Cindy and I sat waiting.

The Lincoln's driver braked at the back of the asphalt, plates up against the chain-link fencing and partially hidden from our view by a staggered row of parked vehicles.

I watched over my shoulder as he got out of his Town Car and headed toward us. The tipster was overweight. He wore a thin, gray knee-length coat and carried a nylon computer bag in his right hand. He came up behind us and knocked on Cindy's window, which she buzzed down.

Cindy said hello and introduced me as "Lindsay, my partner on the crime desk."

Jad took off his gloves, put them in his pocket, and said to me, "Pleased to meet you. Let's sit in the back."

Cindy and I disembarked from the front seat and arranged ourselves in back so that the big man was sitting between us. When I got a closer look at him, I saw that he was young, early to midtwenties, with pale hands and brown eyes that couldn't quite meet mine.

I quashed a nervous impulse to laugh. Sitting in the shadows next to this stranger who was passing secret information made me feel like I was inside an old comedic spy movie. Was this improbable spy the real deal? Had he caught a professional killer on video and in the act?

I tuned back into the moment as Jad was saying, "I told my bosses that the equipment didn't work. You know, shit happens. So, this is video, here. I've seen it and you're going to see it, and then I'm gonna destroy it. This footage is never coming to a theater near you."

Cindy said, "How am I going to report this if I don't have the footage to back me up?"

Jad opened a very thin laptop and it lit up the backseat. He said, "Cindy, that's your problem. I agreed to meet with you conditionally. After you see the video, you're either going to get independent corroboration or you're not. This is as far as I go."

Jad tapped at his keyboard and said, "On your mark, get set." And then he pressed Play.

I instantly recognized the image on the screen as room 1420 of the Four Seasons Hotel. Michael Chan was sitting at the end of the bed, flipping channels on the television. A doorbell sounded and Chan turned off the TV and walked toward the door, out of camera range. A moment later, I heard Chan saying, "You're late." And the door closed hard.

Chan and Muller entered the frame. Muller's legs were clasped around Chan's waist and he was holding her tightly as he walked her toward the bed. Her glasses were gone and I could almost see her eyes beneath the curtain of bangs.

They laughed and kissed deeply, and then Chan laid Muller down on the bed facing him. He removed her boots and tossed them aside, all of his movements confident as though he'd been through this ritual before.

I caught bits of their game play. Chan said that he was the Prince of Gorgonzola. She said her name was Renata and that he had paid her for sex once before in Rome.

The teasing continued as Chan unbuttoned and peeled off Muller's clothes, then stripped off his own. She moved under his hands, and if she didn't just love the hell out of how he was turning and touching her, she could have won the golden statue for best actress.

The two were nearly naked on the bed, their heavy breathing sucking in all the air in the room, when the computer screen went black. Dead black.

Cindy said, "*Hey*. What happened?"

Jad said, "Yeah, that's a bitch, right? I thought it was my equipment that lost the connection. Well, that wasn't it. The Wi-Fi in and around the hotel was blocked.

"Stay tuned," said Jad. "There's more."

CHAPTER 73

JAD WAS CUEING up another video.

He clicked the arrow and the video rolled.

I recognized 1418, the room next to Chan's. There were two single beds, a sofa, a desk, and a coffee table, and the two young people, a black male in cords and a sweater, and a white female in jeans and a pastel plaid shirt. They were sitting at their ad hoc computer stations, looking at their screens.

Jad said, "Nothing happens in here for a couple of hours." He fast-forwarded the video and the time stamp sped from 4:30 to 6:20.

As Jad had said, there wasn't much happening in 1418.

The boy sat at the desk, the girl hunched over the coffee table, both gravely watching their computer screens, which were turned away from the camera. I couldn't see what they were watching, but presumably, it was Chan and Muller in the room next door.

They ate sandwiches, chugged from their water bottles, and wheeled the room service cart outside the room, all without incident. At the 6:20 marker, Jad slowed the film and said, "Don't look away. Don't even blink."

The young man in the video poked a key on his laptop and spoke to someone on his screen.

"Hey, Joe. You on the way up?"

A voice came over the computer's speakers.

"Bud, where's Chrissy?"

I felt a shocking chill and a sensation of falling. I gripped the armrest and tried not to move or speak or cry out. That was Joe's voice. I couldn't be mistaken. *My* Joe.

"I'm here, Chief," said the girl at the coffee table. She got up from her chair, leaned over her colleague's shoulder, and waved her hand at his computer screen.

"OK. Good. I'm still in the lobby," said the voice of the man I'd loved for years, the man who'd promised to love me through sickness and health, the father of my baby. He said, "What's going on?"

"They're both in there. We've got action," said Bud.

"Any talk about that plane from Beijing?" Joe asked.

The girl said, "Nothing yet. They're all about each other, Chief."

"OK. I'm coming up."

"Copy," said Bud.

And then, at 6:23 on the nose, Jad's picture dissolved into static.

I was falling again, but my mind stayed in gear.

Sometime between the time the Internet feed went down and when Liam Dugan, the head of hotel security, showed us the dead housekeeper in the closet, a total of four people had been murdered.

Jad was saying to Cindy, "The two dead kids. Bud and Chrissy could be their real nicknames. If you run their pictures again with those names, maybe someone will come forward. You heard 'Joe' ask about an airplane from Beijing?

"Three days later, an airplane from China was blown to

hell over Route 101. Maybe Bud and Chrissy were killed because they knew about the plane. I wish I didn't, but I know it, too. And now so do you," Jad said.

He said to Cindy, "Someone should put it out there that there was foreknowledge of that plane crash, don't you think? But it can't be me.

"And now say good-bye to the video."

"Wait," Cindy said. "Play the last minute again."

Jad sighed, then reversed the footage and ran it forward. I heard Joe ask about an airplane from Beijing. Joe knew about that plane. *Joe knew.*

Jad closed down the video and dragged the file to an icon labeled DESTROY. Software flames consumed the files.

The videos might be permanently destroyed, but they were part of me now.

I couldn't forget them if I tried.

CHAPTER 74

THE WIND HAD picked up during our fifteen-minute meeting in the parking lot, whipping the young trees standing in their concrete planters on the sidewalk as traffic illuminated the six-lane Embarcadero.

It looked like any normal summer evening in San Francisco, but nothing would ever be normal for me again.

Joe had prior knowledge of a plane crash that was shaping up to be one of the worst air disasters on record.

Cindy and I got out of the backseat of her car. Jad told Cindy that his phone number was now a nonworking number, and that no offense, he would stand there and watch us leave so that we couldn't follow him.

We all shook hands, and Cindy wished Jad good luck. I wondered if Jad's superiors actually believed his recording equipment had failed. Or if they were following him even now, watching Cindy and me as we climbed back into her car.

Cindy was practically bug-eyed as she drove us away from the parking lot.

"Check me on this," she said to me. "The dead kids were taping Chan and Muller. They were told to hit the kill switch, and they did. During the blackout, someone came in and shot them and maybe killed Chan, too, right? That guy talking to them…?"

"That was Joe."

"I *know* his name was Joe," Cindy said. "Wait. Lindsay." She turned to look at me. "You don't mean that was *your* Joe?"

"Off the record. That was him."

"Oh, no. Please don't tell me that."

"*Cindy.* Watch the *road.* Yes. That was Joe Molinari."

"But what does Joe have to do with those people, Lindsay? I don't get this at all."

"I'm thinking," I said.

My thoughts were scrambling for cover, but they couldn't hide.

What role *had* he played in the lives and deaths of Bud, Chrissy, Chan, and Maria Silva? Had he killed them? Were he and Muller working this operation together? And I had to know—what had Joe known about flight WW 888? And what, if anything, had he done with that information?

I couldn't share these thoughts with Cindy, not yet.

"Lindsay, are you thinking Joe is the *killer*?" Cindy was staring at me again, her eyes as big as headlights.

I said, "No—look, no. Joe's a freelancer. It's more like he was hired to monitor the action in Chan's room. So what if, as Joe was going up to supervise those kids, someone heard him say he was going upstairs and sent a 'go' signal to the killer?"

I was winging it, but I was imagining it, too. I kept talking. "And so the kids were expecting Joe, but the killer knocked on the door and they let him in."

Cindy said, "Yeah. Yeah. I'm following you. The killer

shoots them, shoots Chan—and Joe got there *after* the shootings?"

"It's a good theory," I said, while wondering, *Is it?*

"What happened to Joe? And what happened to Ali Muller?"

"I wish I knew," I said sincerely.

"According to my calculations," Cindy said, "the plane went down about sixty-two hours later. Right?"

I nodded, remembering the run-up to that crash vividly.

I'd worked the hotel crime scene with Conklin, Clapper, and Claire, and that night, Joe had come home very early on Tuesday morning, two days before the crash. We'd made love and had breakfast together and I'd told him about the hits at the hotel. *We talked about it.*

Then I'd gone to work.

That day, we got an ID on Michael Chan. Conklin and I had driven out to Palo Alto and notified Shirley Chan that her husband was dead.

And except for the recording of Joe watching us at the Chan house, I hadn't seen him again. As Cindy had said, two and a half days after the shootings in the hotel, WW 888 had blown apart.

Cindy was doing her best to drive and process everything we had just seen on Jad's fifteen-inch laptop.

She said to me, "Look, I have a problem writing this story. Joe is *pivotal*. He talked about the plane from Beijing. That information, if it had been used properly, might have saved a few hundred lives. So how do I write about that? I have no fricking *evidence*. I can't print this as a *rumor*."

"Can you sit on this for a day?" I said.

"Why?"

"Because I have to get some answers."

"From whom?"

"I'll tell you as soon as I can tell you."

"Lindsay."

"You don't have to say it, Cindy. I promise. You get the exclusive. If I find out anything at all."

CHAPTER 75

WHEN I WALKED through the front door to the apartment I once shared with my husband, the wonderful Mrs. Rose said to me, "Lindsay, I have to go. My son is waiting for me at Tommy's and I have to dress. You'll find some pasta salad in the fridge. Oh, Martha has to go for a walk and the baby hasn't eaten or had her bath. She just wouldn't play ball with me. Sorry, dear."

I told Mrs. Rose thanks for everything and have a good time and stood at the open door until she was gone. Then I closed the door and leaned against it, exhausted by the meeting with Cindy and Jad, thinking, *No more. Please, I can't take any more.*

I was a mess.

I was the primary investigator on a quadruple homicide without witnesses or forensic evidence, and it was further compounded by a tangle of international players, a terrorist attack, and intelligence agencies working on the sly.

My husband was party to some or all of this, and he'd sucker-punched me, kneecapped me, and left me alone in a blind alley.

I was grateful to Cindy for including me in her meeting

with Jad, and also thankful that she had agreed to sit on the story until I had answers.

But she wouldn't sit on it forever.

I'd fed her the only theory of the murders I could think of, which presumed that Joe was not guilty of murder.

But he might well have had foreknowledge, if not his actual hand on a trigger. And for all I knew, he was a killer, many times over.

I became aware of Martha, who was whining and pushing at my legs. I said, "OK, OK, I hear you."

We went to Julie's room. I woke my daughter up very gently, and of course, she started to cry. I talked nonsense while dressing her in fleece and a hat. Then I awkwardly opened her stroller and strapped her in.

Martha was ebullient, and I hated to disappoint, but this was going to be a short, short walk.

I wheeled Julie into the elevator, keeping Martha on a tight leash, and somehow, Martha's business was quickly done. She was desperate to go for a run. She pulled and barked at me when I turned to go back into the building.

"You don't always get what you want," I said to Jules and Martha. "And that goes for me, too."

I then proceeded to do what single mothers all over the world do—that is, everything at once.

I fed the baby and I fed Martha, and after drinking the dregs of the opened bottle of Chardonnay in the fridge, I dished up some pasta salad and wolfed it down.

On the way to the dishwasher, I grabbed a basket that I keep on the counter near the microwave. It's eight inches square, four inches high, a catch-all for receipts and the odd paper clip, marking pen, and business card.

Two men from the CIA had paid me a call last week, the point of which was to tell me to stop looking for Alison

Muller. They had left their business cards on the counter. I couldn't remember seeing those cards again.

I hoped Mrs. Rose had put them in the receipt basket.

I upended the basket and pawed through the contents, and *yes,* I found the cards. Michael J. Dixon. Christopher Knightly. Case officers, Central Intelligence Agency. Phone numbers were in the lower left corner.

I remembered that Dixon, the dark-haired one, had seemed to be the one in charge.

It was nearly 8 p.m. Would he answer his phone?

I had to try.

I dialed the number and he answered on the third ring.

"Agent Dixon, this is Lindsay Boxer. You visited me a couple of days ago to talk about Alison Muller."

"I remember, Mrs. Molinari. How can I help you?"

"I need to see you. I have information that concerns national security. It also concerns my husband, and I think you'll want to hear all about it."

Dixon gave me an address and told me to come in the next morning at nine. I didn't know what I was going to say when I met with him, but I had all night to figure it out.

The whole minute-by-minute sleepless night.

CHAPTER 76

I GOT OUT of bed before my baby girl woke up. I showered to get my blood running, and while Mrs. Rose buttoned down the corners of my household, I called in sick, asked Brenda to tell Conklin that I would talk to him after lunch, and then ordered a taxi to drive me to the CIA office on Montgomery Street.

I dressed to impress, meaning I put on my best blue gabardine pantsuit, just cleaned, a good-looking tailored shirt, and my smart Freda Salvador shoes, which I'd last worn to meet in DC with FBI honcho June Freundorfer.

Mrs. Rose topped up my coffee mug while I Googled the address Dixon had given me and found that it was the location of a CIA division called the National Resources Program, or NR.

I read and clicked and read some more.

And what I learned was that the NR was to the CIA at Langley, Virginia, what schoolyard pickup hoops were to the NBA.

The NR recruited largely untrained people with access to information: foreign nationals living in the United States who were willing to gather intel for cash and probably a feeling of self-importance. The NR also hired on Americans with overseas access to government workers, aircraft manufacturing plants, newspapers, and the like.

These part-time operatives came with a variety of backgrounds. Some were college students, some were corporate executives, entertainers, and young techies—like Jad. And like Bud and Chrissy, who had been secretly filming Michael Chan and Alison Muller.

And while these geeks had been spying on spies, Joe Molinari had been right in the thick of it.

My taxi driver buzzed the intercom.

I told Mrs. Rose I would call her in a few hours and hugged everyone at the door.

My driver asked, "Alexander Building, right?"

I said, "Right," as the cab lunged from the curb and out into traffic.

Twenty-five minutes later, I was on the street in front of an early-1900s neo-Gothic, tan brick office building. I entered the lobby, stopped at the desk, and showed my credentials to the security guard.

He called upstairs to Agent Dixon's office, then wrote my name on a peel-and-stick tag, handed it to me, and said, "Fourth floor. You can go on up."

I followed his pointing finger to the elevator bank.

CHAPTER 77

I WAS ALONE in the elevator that whisked me smoothly to the fourth floor. The doors slid open and I stepped out onto a granite floor leading to a pair of glass doors etched with the eagle-centric, round blue logo of the Central Intelligence Agency.

The reception area was thickly carpeted in blue, and a cluster of upholstered chairs gathered around a circular glass coffee table. A gallery of gold-framed portraits lined the long wall behind the reception desk: all former heads of the CIA, including President G. H. W. Bush and our current CIA chief.

I gave my name to the woman behind the desk, signed a log, and took a seat. There were no magazines on the table, but I didn't have to wait long.

Agent Michael Dixon entered the room through a door to the left of the receptionist, greeted me as Mrs. Molinari, and asked me to follow him. We walked past many open cubicles with young staffers inside and other offices with closed doors.

At the end of the hallway, Dixon opened the door to a wood-paneled conference room and showed me in. Christopher Knightly, the second of the two agents I'd met in my apartment, was standing at the windows, looking out over the city with his back to the door.

He turned and said, "Morning, Sergeant Boxer. Please have a seat." And to the man I had assumed was his senior partner, "Thanks, Dixon. I'll take it from here."

I sat in one of the eight swivel chairs around the smallish mahogany conference table. I refused an offer of coffee or bottled water, although my mouth was dry. I was wondering if I'd made a monumental mistake in coming here.

Knightly pulled out a chair across from me and lowered his football player heft down into it.

He said, "You told Dixon you have information that may be of importance. That you know something about Worldwide Flight 888. What do you want to tell us?"

The inference was plain and almost laughable. This was the CIA, an arm of a huge intelligence-gathering agency with fingers in pies I couldn't even imagine.

I was a cop. Just a cop. But if I'd had Christopher Knightly in the box, I could have fired questions at him for hours. So I assumed that attitude.

I said, "I'm working a quadruple homicide, and I'm fairly certain that this isn't news to you. I want to know why Michael Chan was murdered and by whom. I want to know who killed the housekeeper and the two CIA computer techs in the room next to Chan's at around the same time. I want to know why I was followed and beaten by four Asian men who had a Stinger missile launcher in an apartment they were renting in Chinatown. And I want to know what my husband, Joe Molinari, had to do with all or any of that.

"If you can't give me answers and compelling reasons why I should keep what I know to myself, I'm going to let the press know that the CIA knew about WW 888 before it went down and may even have had something to do with that disaster."

I was suddenly afraid that I'd said too much; that like a little terrier on the street going after a pit bull, I'd taken a bigger bite than I could chew.

If I was seen as a danger to national security, I might be taken into government custody. Or worse. I thought of the sweaty young man with the clandestine videos on his laptop, afraid for his life. I thought of Bud and Chrissy dead on a hotel room floor.

Knight gave me a patronizing smile and said, "We're not going to hurt you, Sergeant. I'm not the bad guy."

I exploded.

"So who *is* the bad guy? That's what I want to know. Who's the bad guy in all this?"

The door opened behind me. I swiveled my chair and saw a man who looked a lot like my husband come into the room.

My God. It was really *him.*

"I guess I'm the bad guy," Joe said, dragging a chair out from the table and dropping down into it.

My mouth had fallen open, but the rest of me was *paralyzed.* Joe looked terrible. He had a beard, there were bags under his eyes, and his clothes were filthy.

What the hell had happened to him?

Why didn't he look glad to see me?

I managed to croak, "Joe?"

He looked at me with an expression I can only call sadness.

"What do you want to know, Lindsay? I'll try to tell you what you want to know."

CHAPTER 78

I'D BEEN SHOCKED into silence.

This was my husband. My *husband*.

I looked across the table at Knightly and back at Joe. Joe said, "Chris, give us a moment. And kill the cameras."

"Got it," Knightly said. When he'd left and the door was closed, Joe moved over to the chair next to mine and reached for my hands.

I pulled away.

It was pure instinct. This man resembled the man I had loved and married, but I no longer knew who he was.

He said, "Lindsay, I know you're upset. I would be, too."

"Upset?"

"Wrong word. I know you're furious at me and I...and that I deserve it. I know I've hurt you, and I can't tell you how sad that makes me. I know what I'm saying isn't working, but please, if you can, trust me."

Trust him? How? Why?

"Where have you been?"

"I can't say. Not yet."

I shouted, "I've been thinking you're *dead*!"

"I know."

"And sometimes I *wished* you *were*."

That was a lie, but I said it with vehemence. And Joe didn't take his eyes away from me.

I kept going. "You didn't call me or leave a message or send me a lousy text to say you were OK."

He sighed and looked down at his hands. Was he remorseful? Was he thinking what to say to me? I didn't care.

"You walked out on me and on Julie. In the last ten days, I've been viciously attacked. I've been beaten, shot at, outnumbered, and outgunned. And what have you been doing? Playing I Spy games with Alison Muller?"

He was looking me with sad eyes and I was doing second-by-second gut checks. Was he lying? Was he in trouble? What or who was Joe Molinari?

"Oh, God, Lindsay. I didn't know you were attacked. Were you hurt? Are you OK?"

"Talk to me, Joe. Tell me everything and I'll let you know if I'm OK after I've heard you out."

He tried to take my hands again, and again I pulled away. This was pure reflex. I didn't know if I still loved Joe, or if he had ever actually loved *me*.

CHAPTER 79

"BE RIGHT BACK," Joe said.

He got up and left the room. I watched his empty chair spin lazily in his absence. I wondered what he could possibly say to me that would make me trust him—or if he would even try.

A few long minutes later, Joe came back into the room with two bottles of water, put one down in front of me, and uncapped the other. He drank half of it down.

Then he said, "Ali Muller used to work for me, I don't know, eighteen years ago. We were both pretty young, idealistic, and she had a gift for intelligence gathering."

"What kind of gift?" I asked.

"More than one, actually. Her IQ was off the charts. She was beautiful. People trusted her. She spoke a couple of languages. And she was pretty fearless."

I had heard enough about Ali Muller from June Freundorfer, her CIA friend John Carroll, and her husband, Khalid Khan, and now Joe was singing her praises.

I didn't want to know more. But I wasn't letting myself off easily. Alison Muller was central to this sickening amalgam of secrets. And I was pretty sure she'd killed Shirley Chan.

Joe was saying, "She volunteered to set honey traps. You know?"

"She seduced men, slept with them, beguiled them into giving her information."

"Right. That's right."

"And she slept with you, isn't that also right, Joe?"

"We were in our twenties. It was kid stuff and it's long over, Lindsay. What is relevant is that she was successful, well regarded in the Company, but eventually, she hated that kind of work. By then I was with the FBI and had lost touch with her."

"Joe, come on. You've seen her recently."

"I'm getting to that. When I was with Homeland Security, we knew Michael Chan was a spy for the Chinese, but we thought it was better to leave him in place. And I learned that Ali Muller, who was still with the CIA, had asked to get involved.

"Not long after, I moved here to be with you. Ali lived down the coast, had a good high-level day job that enabled her to travel without scrutiny. She was married with kids. It was a perfect setup for her real job. And as I came to find out recently, Chan fell for Muller. Very hard."

"I was in the Four Seasons the day Chan was taken out."

"I know that."

Joe arched his eyebrows.

"I have you on tape. I also have you on tape out at Chan's house the next day."

Joe nodded, and sighed deeply. "That surveillance van."

I searched his face, looking for tells or twitches. But Joe was a trained liar, government grade. Triple threat.

"It was getting very complicated then," Joe said. "We'd lost track of Muller. Chan and those two tech kids had been gunned down right under our noses. And we were aware that a big operation was in the wings."

"Like the takedown of a passenger jet?"

"Yes, yes. We were aware of a possible threat. We didn't know details. We thought Chan might know. That's why Muller was with him. We didn't know who his contacts were or if our information was any good at all. We didn't have dates or times."

Joe looked—heartbroken. Because the plane had gone down? Because the techies had been killed? Because Muller was missing?

I kept my hands in my lap and said, "What are your plans?"

"I have to locate Muller."

"Were you planning to come home?"

I didn't mean to say that. It just jumped out of my mouth and into the room.

Joe looked into my eyes and reached for me again, and this time, I let him wrap his big mitts around my hands. I wanted to believe in him. I wanted life to go back to the way it had been only a couple of weeks ago.

Was that possible?

He said, "I can't make a plan, Lindsay. Country first. This is what I do. It's what I've always done. I'm sorry."

CHAPTER 80

I WAS SIMMERING. But I didn't want to boil over, not here, not now. I said to Joe, "I can find my way out."

He said, "Let me walk with you."

We walked silently down the carpeted hallway to the reception room. Joe held the glass door for me and waited with me at the elevator. I didn't look at him, and when the elevator came, I got in without saying good-bye.

I called Cindy as soon as I got to the street. I told her I had learned absolutely nothing, but—off the record—I had seen Joe.

She shrieked into my earpiece. She wanted to know what Joe had said, where he was now, when she could talk to him.

"Cindy, he's in an ongoing operation with the CIA. That's all I can tell you, and don't blow his cover. Please. But if you want to run Bud and Chrissy's pictures with their names and a request for information, you should do it."

She said, "Consider it done. Talk to you later."

I called a cab, and as my mind churned, I waited on the corner of Bush and Montgomery Streets.

I was thinking I owed it to Conklin to tell him everything I knew. I envisioned a very serious meeting in Jacobi's office:

me and Conklin and Brady and, by special permission, Cindy. I had a duty to report criminal activities. I had professional ethics that required me to get clean with my partners. I also wanted their advice and, with it, relief from the pressure that was like none I'd ever experienced.

But as soon as I imagined that collegial scene, new thoughts powered through. Where did my true loyalties lie?

With my husband, who until ten days ago, I had loved entirely?

Or with my coworkers and friends, who had trusted me with their lives as I had trusted them?

The taxi arrived. I had to give the driver a destination, and I heard myself say, "Take me to Lake and Twelfth."

The driver got on the phone with his girlfriend, and I put my head back and closed my eyes. I woke up when the driver said, "Lady. Here you are."

Ten minutes later, I was in my jeans and a T-shirt in Joe's office, going through his things again. I talked to Julie as she bounced in her jumper seat.

"I don't know what I'm looking for, Jules," I cooed. "I don't know what I could possibly find that would trump what Daddy told me an hour ago. He's a spy on active duty. Yes. Active duty."

Julie let loose with a peal of laughter.

I got up from Joe's desk and went over and kissed her.

I said, "I want to make sure I haven't missed something, little girl. I just want to know what he was doing all those months when he was here with you playing Mr. Mom."

There was a box of Joe's stationery in the top drawer, right-hand side. I'd opened it before, frisked it with my fingertips, but this time, I took out the note cards and envelopes and found a stubby little key Scotch-taped to the bottom.

The key had a number.

It could be to a safe-deposit box.

For all I knew, it could be to a safe-deposit box belonging to *us*, a fireproof lock box with life insurance policies and the deed to our condo.

Or it could be a secret trove of love letters and boarding passes and locks of Muller's hair.

I put the key in my pocket and lifted Julie out of her chair. I took her into the bedroom, pulled the curtains closed, and got into bed with my baby. Martha curled up on the rug beside us.

It was completely still. We were alone. Maybe we'd always been alone. I had had to accept the depth of Joe's deceit. That I'd been betrayed by my husband, my best friend.

"Country first," he'd told me. "This is what I do."

That son of a bitch.

CHAPTER 81

I SET UP a conference call with Rich and Cindy, and after some back-and-forth, we reached agreement on my plan.

I called Brady, saying, "I need to see you out of the office. It's important."

He said, "You sound—terrible."

Brady had called me out. It was as if barbed wire were coiled around my chest and forehead. My breathing was shallow, and pressure was building behind my eyes.

He said, "Are you home? I can stop by after work."

"Great. Buzz me and I'll come down."

Maybe I'm paranoid, but last week two spooks had dropped by my apartment to warn me off my search for Alison Muller. It was possible, even probable, that a mic or two had been planted in my apartment.

At 7:20 Brady texted me to say he was on the way, and twenty minutes later, he buzzed up from the intercom. I grabbed the baby and ran down the stairs.

I found Brady leaning against his Buick with his arms crossed over his chest and his hair blowing across his face. He opened the car door and I got in with Julie in my arms.

"How sick are you?" he asked. "Or was this a mental health day? You *should* take a couple days—"

"Thanks, Brady, but I'm not sick and I'm not falling apart. I have news on the hotel murders, and my place could be bugged."

I held Julie against my shoulder as I caught Brady up on Cindy's tipster, who'd gone by the name of Jad. I told him what Jad's video had revealed: that our murdered Jane and John Doe had been working for the CIA and that now, thanks to Cindy, we had their nicknames: Chrissy and Bud.

"Cindy's running their pictures today with those names."

Brady said, "Good. A positive ID could come out of that."

I nodded, cleared my throat, and kept going.

"Brady. I heard something while I was watching Jad's tapes. It was Joe's voice. He was talking to those kids over the computer. He asked them if they'd picked up anything on a plane from Beijing. They said they hadn't. But still, the CIA knew something about a plane, maybe WW 888, before the crash."

Brady voiced some colorful curses that I was pretty sure Julie wouldn't understand, and after the stream of disbelief and fury subsided, I continued.

"So this morning, I went to the CIA office on Montgomery. Joe was there," I said. "I saw him."

Brady is a pretty good listener, and although he said, "You shittin' me?" he let me speak without further interruption. I described my visit to the NR office, saying that while Joe hadn't told me much, he had confirmed that Michael Chan was a spy for the Chinese. And that Alison Muller was a CIA operative, now missing in action.

"The CIA will deny knowing anything about that plane, right, Brady? But they can't stop us from working our case.

And I think, but cannot prove, that Alison Muller either did the shooting or saw it go down."

Brady raked his hair back, stared out the window for a long minute, and said, "What do you want to do?"

I told him.

He said, "Boxer. Do you really want to take on the CIA?"

"I don't see any other way to close this case."

"OK," he said. "I'm on board."

CHAPTER 82

BRADY PUT OUT a BOLO for the driver of a black Lincoln Town Car with a dragging muffler before I got out of his car, and by three the next afternoon, a young man named Jeffrey Alan Downey, aka Jad, was in our interrogation room.

According to his driver's license and the answers he gave to the uniformed officers who brought him in, Downey was twenty-two years old, a recent graduate of a computer sciences program at Berkeley. He worked as a freelance computer tech and lived with his grandmother in Oakland.

He did not volunteer who he worked for, but from the sketchy knowledge I'd gathered, he perfectly fit the profile for a low-level recruit for our local branch of the CIA.

Brady and I watched through the glass as Conklin went into the interrogation room with Jad. The young, sweaty owner of a beat-up Lincoln in violation of the city's noise ordinance told my partner that he'd pay the fine, but there was no way, no reason to hold him. He knew his rights.

Conklin asked mildly, "Where were you last night, Mr. Downey?"

The young man who called himself Jad said, "Really? I don't have to tell you that." He looked mad and scared enough to pull his I'm-under-the-protection-of-the-CIA card. But he hadn't played it yet.

Brady said to me, "If he says the L-word, let him go."

"No problem, boss."

Downey looked up when I entered the box.

"*You*. You're the *reporter* from the *Chronicle*. What *is* this?"

I asked Conklin if I could have a private word with Mr. Downey. After Conklin left the room, I took a chair, introduced myself, and said, "Sorry we had to pull you in, Mr. Downey. But if you answer my questions truthfully, you'll be free within the hour. No one will ever know you spoke with the police."

"Am I under arrest? Because either way, I'm not telling you *anything*," he sputtered. "You played me, lady. I think you violated some code or something."

I got up from the chair, opened the door, and shouted, "Everyone, take a walk. And no cameras. I mean it."

I winked at Conklin; then I slammed the door. I went back to my seat across from Downey and leaned over the table so that we were nose to nose.

"Mr. Downey, please pay close attention. You have held back information about the WW 888 disaster that cost over four hundred people their lives. You will either tell me what you know and when you knew it, or I will turn you over to Homeland Security. I don't care who you think has your back, you are a coconspirator in a hellacious act of terrorism. Do you *want* to spend the rest of your life in a federal prison?"

Downey's face turned red and tears flew out of his eyes.

He said, "Wait a minute, wait a minute. You think I know something about that airplane? I *don't*. I called Cindy Thomas because I was sick about those dead people in the hotel room. But I had nothing to do with them, or that airplane—which hadn't gone down when I made those surveillance videos. You don't know if that guy, Joe, was talking about that particular plane. How could I know? I'm a geek. I signed on to do surveillance, period. I'm not even cleared for this stuff."

He put his hands over his eyes and sobbed noisily.

I slapped the table and snapped, "Look at me."

He jerked his head up.

"Mr. Downey, the CIA is going to walk away from you. They didn't see the video. But I did. And Ms. Thomas did. And if you don't convince me otherwise, I'm going to turn you in and we're going to testify against you."

He snuffled, used the tissues I handed him to mop his face, then sputtered weakly, "You're giving me too much credit. I'm just a *kid*. And I *don't* work for the CIA."

Oh. Now I got it. June Freundorfer had said the FBI was interested in Chan. I guess they were interested in Muller, too.

"Who, then? The FBI?"

Downey nodded and his chest heaved. It was apparent that he was verging on another meltdown. I reached across the table and patted his hands.

"OK, Jeffrey. Tell me what you know. Don't leave anything out. If I believe you, you can walk out of here today."

Downey honked into the wad of tissues. He was still agitated and frightened, but he had moved in my direction.

He said, "All I know about the plane was that guy Joe asking the kids if they'd heard anything about a plane from Beijing. They hadn't. I wasn't even sent to learn about that. My peeps are all about crushing a Chinese spy ring."

"What do you mean, 'spy ring'?"

"I was paid to watch and listen, that's *all*. If Chan was a spy, you know more than I do. Same for Muller. Is 'the

Prince of Gorgonzola' a secret code? I don't know. I just record what happens, and what happened is that those two got it on."

"What do you know about Alison Muller?"

"For God's sake. That's what you want? I've got tape on her. Give me my laptop, I'll show you what I've got."

CHAPTER 83

DOWNEY HAD VIDEO of *Alison Muller*. He had *video*.

The barbed wire restraints around my chest dissolved and my heart did a happy dance, but I wasn't about to let Jad know it. I asked him if he'd like something to drink while I got his computer, and shaking his head like a wet dog, he said no.

I left Interview 2, closed the door behind me, and asked Conklin, "What did you think?"

"He's a foot soldier. I think he's telling the truth."

Conklin disappeared down the hall, and a long couple of minutes later he returned with Downey's computer bag. I got two bottles of Voss out of the vending machine and went back into the interview room.

Downey opened his case and took out the laptop. Then he got up heavily from his chair, plugged the cord into a socket, scraped his chair this way and that, settled in, and booted up. It took a lifetime for him to cue up the video.

He said, "If you see something, say something, OK? Because I have followed this bitch a lot and nothing ever happens."

Downey moved the laptop over to me, saying, "Usually,

after I shoot the videos, I forward them same day to my boss. And then I delete them from my hard drive. Destroy them. I still have this one because it's from the day when I told them my camera failed."

"Gotcha," I said, watching the blank screen expectantly.

"Here she is leaving her office at four-thirty," Downey said. "She drove straight to the Four Seasons."

I watched Ali Muller leave the office building with the Aptec logo over the door. She was wearing the Gucci glasses, the swingy black leather coat, and her spike-heeled boots. She was speaking on her phone as she walked to her car in the underground garage.

Once she was in her car, Downey clicked on the icon for the next video in the playlist. When I saw the opening frames, it appeared to me that it had been shot by a dash cam in a car following Muller's, which was exiting the garage.

Downey said, "Now, here comes one hour and ten minutes of drive time."

"Go ahead and fast-forward," I said.

From my seat in the interrogation room, I watched Muller's BMW negotiate traffic from Silicon Valley to San Francisco, where she got out of the car on Stevenson, a small alley parallel to Market Street.

She gave the valet several bills, and although Jad's camera was out of audio range, I knew she was saying something like "Don't bury my car. I'm going to need it fast."

The video ended—no doubt Downey shutting it down in order to park his own vehicle. As we already knew, bugs had been planted in Chan's room prior to his planned assignation with Muller.

Downey said to me, "That's all. You saw the video from fourteen-twenty. Muller gets naked with Chan and the network goes down. End of story."

"You mind making me a copy of that footage?"

Downey grabbed the laptop away from me and closed the lid.

"Look. I showed you what you asked for. I've put my life in danger for this bullshit. I haven't committed a crime. Now, let me out of here, or I'm getting a serious, no-shit lawyer to sue you in federal court for violating my constitutional rights. Why don't *you* think about *that*?"

There it was. The man had said "lawyer."

"Thanks for your help, Mr. Downey. You're free to go. I'll walk you out."

CHAPTER 84

BACK AT MY desk, I contacted Monterey PD and spoke with the squad commander, asking if he had new information on Muller. I said, "I'm hoping she's been seen."

"No sightings and not a clue," he said. "The husband calls every day, and every day we have to tell him we've got nothing."

I relayed this subzero news to Brady, who told me that a guy from the forensics lab would be at my apartment at eight the next morning to sweep it for bugs.

I said, "Could you get him to come tonight?"

As usual, our lab was overworked and overwhelmed. And now I was pleading for a tech to check my apartment for spy cams. It was just too freaking sad.

"I'll see what I can do," said Brady.

At the end of the day, Conklin drove me home and stood watch as I went inside the building. Mrs. Rose brought me up to the last burp in Julie's day, and after she'd gone home to her apartment across the hall, I ate dinner in front of the TV and had some quality time with my little family.

In the relative quiet, now that I had time to think, something about Jad's recordings of the action in the hotel rooms started to bother me.

What was wrong with those pictures?

Was it something I'd seen or heard? Or was it something I'd missed? I thought about the two tech kids. I thought about Chan and Muller playing on the hotel sheets. I tried to home in on the nagging feeling and get it to come to Mama.

And then, just as *America's Got Talent* was starting, the intercom buzzed and I let Dale Culver, our lab's top bug-buster, into the apartment.

Julie and I sat in Joe's big chair while Dale dismantled my phones and passed wands over the light fixtures and under the furniture. When he had finished and packed away his gear, he said, "Sergeant, you are certifiably bug-free." I thanked the earnest young man for working overtime and put the baby to bed.

I was vigorously scrubbing a pot when my cell phone rang. I stripped off my wet rubber gloves and snatched up the phone without checking the caller ID. I wouldn't have recognized the number anyway.

I just barely recognized the voice that said, "Lindsay. It's me."

"Lindsay's not here," I said.

I jabbed the Decline button and tossed my phone onto the counter, where it bounced and clattered. It rang again. After three rings, just before the call went to voice mail, I grabbed the phone and said, "What do you want?"

"I want you to listen to me. Please."

I walked to the sink and turned off the faucet. "I'm listening," I said with all the warmth of a frozen bag of peas.

"I found Muller. She's hiding out north of Vancouver," Joe said. "I'm flying up there tonight. You should come with me."

"Why, Joe? Why should I do that?"

He said, "We've always worked well together. And I know how much the hotel case means to you."

"I see," I said.

"I thought you'd like to be there."

I called Mrs. Rose. I showered and dressed. I didn't fully understand what I was doing or why, but surely curiosity was prodding me on. Curiosity is both a strength and a weakness.

Same could be said for loving Joe.

CHAPTER 85

A BLACK SEDAN was idling at the curb downstairs. Joe got out of the driver's seat and said, "Lindsay. Hi. If you don't mind, I'd like to take a quick look in on Julie."

I said, "No, Joe. Just—no."

He said, "OK, OK. I understand."

He opened the passenger-side door for me and I got in.

When he was in the driver's seat, I asked again, "Why, Joe? Why do you want me to come with you?"

Joe put the car in gear and said, "I don't want things to be this way between us."

I scrutinized Joe as he made filler talk about traffic and weather conditions. He had shaved and was wearing new jeans and a new shirt. He didn't avoid my gaze. But he did seem removed. Was he remorseful? Ashamed? When he asked me questions, I answered with a similar degree of formality. *Julie is fine. Mrs. Rose is a miracle. We're working some leads on the case, but we're still scratching away at the surface.*

Then I turned on the radio.

We arrived at San Rafael Airport in Marin County, where a Gulfstream jet was warmed up and ready to go. We boarded the plane at just about eleven.

Our seats were separated by an aisle, which seemed appropriate. Joe and I were like strangers. How had such a wide chasm opened between us in only two weeks? I saw him in my mind, having breakfast with Julie. Now I wondered if that sweet domestic scene might have been a little show he'd put on just for me. I slammed the door on the memory.

The pilot made an announcement. An attendant checked our seat belts and overhead compartments. Jets roared, and we were thrown back in our seats as the plane lifted off.

Once we leveled out, I sipped Perrier and watched beads of moisture sliding off the edge of my window. Then I put on a headset, dialed up some jazz, and reclined my seat.

Questions flew up behind my closed eyelids like shorebirds on the beach.

I thought about Joe sitting across the aisle from me, a virtual stranger who had, by the way, shared a significant part of my life. I wondered if a few months from now we'd be divorced and I'd be living in a new place, or if it would be me and Julie in Joe's apartment, surrounded by the memories of happier times.

I thought about Ali Muller: her marriage, her children, her still-undefined role in the hotel murders; and I revisited the images of her with Michael Chan—and that was when those pictures in my mind collided with my experience at the actual crime scene. Something didn't jibe.

And then I grabbed that nagging notion by the toe and didn't let go until it took form.

Michael Chan was shot in the face and chest and he dropped with his feet facing the door. How could Ali Muller have shot him from the doorway when she was behind him in the room?

Had she been working with an accomplice? Had someone else shot the housekeeper, knocked on the door, and shot Chan? Had this unknown killer then shot the two techs in the room next door?

I knew for sure that Joe had told Bud he was coming upstairs. The murders had gone down after that.

Had Joe shot the two kids who'd been expecting him to knock on the door? Was he Alison Muller's partner in these gruesome crimes? After the killings, had it been Joe who had gotten her out of the hotel unseen?

But why? If Joe was partnered with Muller, why would he ask me to come with him to bring her in?

Was I walking into a trap?

My eyelids flew open as my mind violently rejected this idea. No, no, Joe wouldn't, couldn't, set me up in order to kill me. Could he? I turned to look at my husband, who was five feet away, sleeping like a lamb. Who was the real Joe?

It was a short flight. I didn't eat. I didn't sleep. When the FASTEN SEAT BELTS light flickered on, I gripped the armrests and braced myself for violence.

The landing was smooth.

I walked shakily down a flight of metal steps, and Joe took my arm as, with our heads lowered, we crossed the chilly, breeze-whipped tarmac at Vancouver International.

I liked the feel of his hand enclosing my upper arm. Tears slipped out of the corners of my eyes. They were from the wind and so slight that I didn't even have to wipe them away.

We waited inside Avis for the paperwork to chug out of the printer. I tapped my fingers on the counter.

Joe said, "Lindsay. I can't prove it, but I believe that Ali Muller killed those four people in the hotel, and if she did, I have to take her down.

"If you aren't up for this, tell me now, and I'll leave you at a hotel. I don't want you to get hurt again."

"I want to catch her as much as you do," I said, keeping my expression and my tone neutral. Actually, I was telling the truth. "Don't worry," I said. "I can take care of myself. I'm a cop. Job first."

CHAPTER 86

JOE TOLD ME that our route from the airport would take us up the Sea to Sky Highway to Brackendale, about an hour-and-twenty-minute drive.

I strapped in and watched as the lighted roadways took us north through Vancouver's downtown, over the fork of the Fraser River, and north along Granville Street, where the beautifully lit glass skyline unfurled before our car as we crossed the bridge to downtown Vancouver.

We turned left onto Georgia Street and into the tree-lined Stanley Park, and about then, my eyes closed. When I woke up, the dazzling nighttime cityscape was gone and we were driving through the darkest night.

Joe said, "Everything's OK."

He used to say that when I bolted awake, startled by a terrible dream.

"How much longer?" I asked him.

"A while yet," Joe said, and then, as if he'd been bracing himself for whatever would happen next, he inhaled and exhaled loudly. Then he said, "Lindsay, I couldn't tell you where I was or what I was doing. I shouldn't tell you now."

It was a heavy preamble, and although I wanted to know

everything, I was afraid of what he was going to say: that he was in love with Alison Muller, that he had never loved me, that his move to San Francisco was an assignment, that our marriage was a cover story and a sham.

I said, "Look. Don't tell me anything out of obligation."

"I want you to know because you're my wife."

I said, "OK."

Joe said, "I joined the CIA right out of school."

"June Freundorfer told me."

He looked surprised, but after a moment, he said, "I served in Iraq and Afghanistan. I don't talk about that with anyone. It was an omission, Lindsay, but talking about what I did during those wars wouldn't have done either of us any good."

And then Joe began to stitch the pieces of his past together. He talked about working at the FBI, touched on the case we had worked across agency lines three years ago, the intensity of that time we'd spent together having thrown us into crazy-hot feelings and falling in love.

He talked about moving to San Francisco so that we could be together for real. And then he said, "The part I didn't tell you, couldn't tell you, is that around the time Julie was born, the CIA asked me to come back on an 'as-needed basis.' I didn't know they would need me so soon."

We were driving north in the pitch bloody dark. Joe was telling me about his life as if we were on a date. Oh, my God. We'd had so many years between us, a full life, or so I thought. I was struck with memories of the night I gave birth to Julie. Joe was away on "business," a consulting gig, he'd told me.

A ferocious storm had been beating the hell out of San Francisco when major contractions came on in force. From my bedroom windows, I could see trees and electric lines down on the roads. Cars had been wrecked and abandoned; 911 operators told me emergency responders were working without pause, and at last, the fire department answered my call for help. A gang of firefighters in full turnout gear had stood in a semicircle around my bed, telling me to breathe and push. That was the setting for Julie's entrance into the world.

Where had Joe *really* been that night?

"Lindsay?"

"I'm listening. And I want to say that hearing about your secret life makes me feel like a complete idiot."

"I know. I'm sorry. And I still haven't told you everything."

The tension in the car sparked like a downed electric line in the rain. I wanted to grab him and shake him and say, *Come on Joe, cut the crap. It's me. This is* US.

If only.

If only he hadn't kept so much from me.

I looked at him really hard. I wanted to see through the deep lies and casual disinformation. How could I know who he was? The man was a *spy*. Triple threat. Hard-core.

How could I believe anything he told me?

Still, the unasked question shot out of my mouth.

"Where were you the last two and a half weeks, damn it? Why didn't you call me?"

He shook his head. He pounded the steering wheel with his palms. He was strapped into his seat. We were moving at sixty miles an hour. There was no getting away without answering me. I was sitting right there.

"Linds, I've always been committed to doing what needed to be done. For the country and ultimately for us. But you have to believe this."

He stopped talking. We were crossing over a bridge with

the Salish Sea to the left and the cliffs of the highway rising
high on our right. But I didn't know if there was a bridge
strong enough to bridge the gulf between Joe and me.

"What, Joe? What do I have to believe?"

"That I love you. I love you and Julie so much. More than
I ever thought possible. You have every reason to doubt me,
but don't. Because I swear to you, I'm telling you the truth."

CHAPTER 87

I'D ALWAYS FOUND Joe open, accessible, honest—and *real*. My God, it was why I loved him. And now the *truth* was out. He'd lied deliberately and constantly all the time that I'd known him.

So why, when he told me he loved me, did I lean toward him? The answer was as simple as three little words. Despite the lies and deceit, I *wanted* to trust my husband. I loved him.

I said, "Don't stop now, Joe. Tell me about Alison Muller. From the beginning."

There were no other cars on the road at all. It was as if we were in a tunnel chasing two cones of light at high speed toward the edge of the world.

Joe was talking, telling me again that he'd lost touch with Alison until he'd come back to the CIA nine months before. He said it was around that time that the CIA became aware of Michael Chan, a naturalized American citizen who was spying for the Chinese. They'd learned about Chan: that he'd been born in China, had come to the USA as a student, had lived and worked in Palo Alto for the last eight years, and was now teaching history at Stanford.

Joe told me that just a few months ago, Muller volunteered to work a honey trap on Chan to learn what he was passing on to Chinese intelligence and to flip him to our side if she could. And according to Joe, because of his work history with Muller, he was asked to run the operation.

Joe said now, "I told you I thought Chan had fallen hard for Alison. Of course, he didn't know that Ali was CIA and that he was her target. He believed her cover, her job, and the business trips that enabled them to get together. But Chan was going through a stressful time, and finally, he told Muller all about it."

"And she reported this back to you."

"Exactly. About a month ago. Chan told Muller that a Chinese intelligence honcho was about to defect to the United States. He said this defector had powerful and deep information that could take down the Chinese government.

"Muller told me that what was driving Chan crazy was that the defector was his *father*. Chan Senior was planning to come to California to be with his son. He'd gotten false documents using Michael Chan's name and address and so on, and Chan was very worried. He'd heard that some Chinese-American men living in San Francisco had been assigned to kill his father as soon as his plane arrived in the States.

"Chan was just talking to his lover, you know, Linds? He was questioning his own loyalty to the Chinese government. He was desperately concerned for his father. And he had no idea that Muller was feeding this information to us.

"And still, the information was incomplete. Chan didn't know what plane his father would be taking to the States. Muller was going to try to get this critical detail from Chan that evening in the Four Seasons—and then, as you well know, it all hit the fan."

My mind reeled. Chan Senior had been traveling as Michael Chan on WW 888. It was *his* body that had disappeared. Even as I was having this breakthrough, Joe was unwinding the story as he knew it.

Joe said, "Michael Chan was killed. Bud and Chrissy were killed. Muller disappeared, and then, the worst thing imaginable. That passenger jet went down. I'm pretty sure that the men you and your SWAT took down in Chinatown were the ones who were supposed to kill the *defector:* one high-profile government man."

"So what happened?" Joe asked rhetorically. "Were they cocky? Were they stupid? Did they have a shiny new toy? I don't know *why* they decided to hit the plane—with a goddamned missile—but they did it."

"My God. You think they did that on their own?"

Joe said, "I think so. Chinese intelligence was apparently stunned by the crash. They did a slick pivot and tried to blame it on the CIA. And we blamed *ourselves*—for not getting the intel in time to prevent the crash. The head of our internal affairs unit had to find out if I was involved. Who could blame him? After all, I was running the Muller-Chan operation.

"I was locked up and interrogated, *seriously*—that's why I couldn't call you, Linds. I was in an underground location, I don't even know where."

He sighed deeply, then said, "I don't know if I have everything exactly right—but that's pretty much what I know or have reasonable theories about.

"The Chinese made a lot of mistakes. They're amateurs at the intelligence game. Maybe Ali Muller made mistakes as well."

I asked Joe, "Do you think she killed Chan?"

CHAPTER 88

JOE GRIPPED THE wheel and gunned the car along the asphalt straightaway for long minutes before saying, "I've asked myself if Alison was the shooter a couple hundred times. Friendship aside, just bearing down on the facts, I think she's been playing *both* sides—working for us, and working for the Chinese, and doing a pretty seamless job of it."

I heard what Joe had said, but his answer was so off the hook, I had to ask him to say it again.

"Are you telling me that Muller is a *double agent?* That she is actually spying on *us* for the *Chinese?*"

"I'm speculating, Lindsay, but it makes sense. If she's working for MSS, then she's behind the murders in the hotel. Chan was betraying the Chinese by leaking classified information to *her.* He was an enemy and had to be eliminated. It's almost as if they switched loyalties with each other, Chan wanting to get *off* the train that Muller had just gotten *on.*"

"You're saying she would have shot Chan because he was a traitor?"

"So my theory goes. She knew that Chrissy and Bud had

eyes on her from the adjacent room. So if in fact Ali is the shooter, she had to take them out and take their laptops at the same time."

It was as if I were back in that room, looking at those two young people bloodied and dead on the floor, their power cords still plugged to the wall.

Joe said, "Chrissy and Bud hadn't overheard any information about the defector's travel plans. I was on the way up to check in with them, maybe wrap it up for the day—but the elevator took a long time to get down to the lobby floor. When it arrived, everyone standing around piled in. That car must have stopped on every floor."

Joe ran a hand over his face and seemed to be back in the moment when his operation had come crashing down.

"It was all over by the time I got to the fourteenth floor. The kids were dead in 1418. Alison didn't answer the door to 1420. I must've missed her by minutes, or seconds. Otherwise, she probably would have killed me, too. I learned later that Chan was dead. If my theory is right, she was shutting down her undercover job for us and cauterizing loose ends."

"But why would she have changed sides, Joe?"

He shrugged. "I can think of a dozen maybes: payback for some long-held grudge, or she got an offer she couldn't refuse. She's crazy enough to have done it for the thrill."

"She might have killed Shirley Chan," I said.

"OK, yeah. It makes sense if she was mopping up. She wouldn't take the chance that Chan was playing *her* and telling everything to his wife. Another sickening theory."

Joe stopped talking. He turned up the heat, adjusted the airflow, and took a pull from his bottle of water.

My head was throbbing from all this information. I was trying to process it all, thinking that if Muller was a double agent—*if* it was true—then Joe felt responsible for everything Muller had done. Or maybe Joe, too, was readying himself to cauterize loose ends of his own.

Christ. No one knew where I *was.* Was I putting my trust in a man I didn't really know? I shook my head, trying to dislodge that terrifying thought.

Joe said, "I know. It's unbelievable, and I haven't confronted her. Maybe I've got her all wrong."

I said, "So why did she come all the way out here?"

"If she's gone over to the Chinese, BC is not a bad jumping-off point to China. And that's all I've got."

Joe's theory had the ring of truth, but was it *true?*

I asked him—actually, I blurted it out.

"Joe, are you trying to *catch* Muller, or *save* her?"

"What do you think?" he said.

CHAPTER 89

THE SIGN AT the side of the road read SQUAMISH.

What little I knew about this town came from an article I'd read in the *Chron*'s travel section a few years ago about the annual Bald Eagle Festival. I remembered that the area was spread out over a grid of mini-malls and woodsy homes with gorgeous scenery tucked between mountains. Heavily wooded roads connected neighborhoods, and tumbling rivers bisected them, but right now, the scenery was beside the point.

It was lights out in Squamish and there was near zero visibility at oh-dark-hundred.

As we sped through the town, I glanced at Joe's face, lit by the dashboard lights. I wished I could read his mind, but going by what he'd *said*, at the center of the crisscrossing facts, suppositions, and violent deaths was Alison Muller. She was clever, manipulative, and, in my opinion, psychopathic.

Was I finally going to see her for myself? What would happen? Who would still be standing when the sun came up in three hours? Would I see my daughter again?

I had to. I had to stay alive for Julie.

Joe drove the Audi along a two-lane road flanked by

forests of black evergreens. There was a bit of a clearing up ahead on our right, and as we approached, he dropped his high beams down to parking lights. I saw a wood-shingled house with a sagging roof and the flash of our lights reflecting off taillights at the end of the driveway.

Joe said, "She's staying there."

He continued past the house, and fifty yards down the road, I glimpsed two vehicles parked on either side in deep shadow: a metallic Japanese two-door and a rusty Ford pickup.

"Those are ours," he said.

Joe tapped the GPS and a new address popped up on the screen. He took a right turn down a dirt road and another right onto a highway through Brackendale. A half mile later, a lighted VACANCY sign flashed outside a Best Western to our right.

Joe turned into the motor court, pulled the car around to the back, and parked between two cars in front of the rooms.

He switched the engine off and used his phone.

"Slade, it's Molinari. I'm outside."

The suite was on the ground floor and looked modern and fairly new. Three men were sitting around a TV watching CBC News without sound. They were regular-looking guys of medium height and weight, one balding, another with coarse red hair, the third pale with glasses; he looked like a guy with a desk job.

Christopher Knightly, the big straw-haired man I'd met for the first time in my apartment, was in the kitchenette, popping the tab on a beer can.

He was surprised to see me and not in a good way.

Joe said, "Knightly, you've met Lindsay. Everyone else, this is my wife, Sergeant Lindsay Boxer, SFPD, Homicide Squad. I asked her to come because she's intimately involved in the Four Seasons murders. She was at the crime scene. She's also the lead investigator in that takedown op on Stockton. So this is her case, too."

Knightly put the can down hard on the counter and said, "Christ, Joe, talk about breaking protocol. No offense, Sergeant. This isn't San Francisco and this isn't your homicide case. Muller's not just a killer. She could well be a traitor, not just to us, but to the country, for God's sake."

"Chris. It's my decision," Joe told him, "and my ass if things go wrong."

The man wearing the glasses got up to shake my hand, introduced himself as Agent Fred Munder, while the redhead got into Joe's face, saying, "Are you serious? It's not just about you. Our butts are on the line, too."

"It's done, Geary," Joe snapped. "Let's get on with it."

I used the bathroom, and when I came back Agent Munder was saying to the others, "There's been no activity for three hours. Muller is still at the house. Looks like she's in for the night."

"She was always a little too sure of herself," said Knightly. "Smart, yes, I'll give her that. But she's arrogant and, I'm gonna say, twisted. She just loves all the attention she gets from men. Did you ever ask yourself, Joe, why she's so eager to climb into bed with the enemy?"

It was a dig at Joe, and if he was meant to answer this question, he didn't get a chance. Knightly's phone chirped. He grabbed it from his shirt pocket and said, "Yeah?" He listened for a second or two, then said, "Got it. Stay with her."

He clicked off and announced, "Muller's on the move. Something's gone wrong. She's in one of three cars heading north. Was she tipped off? Who did she get to this time?"

Knightly was looking at Joe, and because I was standing next to Joe, he was also staring at *me*.

CHAPTER 90

THERE WAS A quick shorthand discussion between Joe and the other men in the team. Routes and a timetable were roughed out. Then the motel room emptied. Knightly and a partner drove out of the lot first. Munder and his wingman took the second car, and Joe and I took the third position out to the Sea to Sky Highway.

I could imagine that this roadway must be gorgeous in daylight, but the empty two-lane highway was unlit, and the impenetrable woods to the left and the steep, treed cliffs rising a hundred feet straight up on our right seemed menacing.

Joe's phone was in a holder attached to the vents in the dash, and he was in ongoing communication with Knightly. Knightly was also on the phone with the two CIA cars ahead of us, the truck and the sedan that had been following Muller's convoy from the moment they left her safe house.

Word came down the line that Muller's three cars had split up. Knightly's voice crackled over the speaker.

"They made us, goddamn it. We don't know which goddamned car she's in."

New plans were hatched, and Knightly reported to Joe

that our team had now also been split, assigned different routes with hopes that someone would locate Alison Muller's car.

Joe punched coordinates into the GPS and stepped on the gas. The car leapt forward, and Joe drove fearlessly, hugging curves and speeding at eighty through blackness and dark shades of gray.

I was frankly scared out of my mind, watching the needle bounce around the dial as we shot through the wilderness. Joe was gunning it over ninety when our headlights flashed on a sign for Whistler Resort.

Joe spoke over the phone to Knightly. "We're passing Whistler now. On track to that airfield in Pemberton."

More conversation ensued, Knightly saying, "I've notified the Royal Canadian Mounted Police. If we don't catch up with her shortly, we'll see you at the airfield."

Joe slowed to a steady seventy miles per hour, and when an intersection came up on our right, he whipped around to make the turn too fast. The car fishtailed on the empty roadway, then regained traction, and we headed east and picked up speed. Starlight and a sliver of a crescent moon revealed the ghostly shapes of trees looming alongside the road and a glimpse of the Lillooet River.

Joe glanced at the GPS map, said to me, "Hold on," and took the turnoff to Airport Road at near sixty.

I *was* holding on, but the Audi's wheels hit a rut. The steering wheel bucked under Joe's hands and the car slewed hard to one side, then the other. I may have screamed.

Knightly was on speaker and he was saying, "We've lost her."

The word *her* was just out of his mouth when the connection shattered into squawks and static hissing.

Joe yelled, "Knightly! *Knightly,* can you hear me?"

No, he couldn't. We had lost our connection with our lead car and had no idea where in the world Alison Muller was.

"Well, this is just perfect," said Joe.

And then, just ahead of us, another turn branched out under overhead lines. Joe took the turn at way too fast and our tires slid on gravel. The car rocked onto two wheels; then, as before, the tires grabbed and we shot on ahead under an endless, gunmetal-gray sky.

CHAPTER 91

AS WE TURNED onto the airport road, the Coast Mountains, which had formed a forested and impenetrable wall off to our right, were now dead ahead. In front of us and as far as we could see was flat meadowland, rectangular in shape, like five football fields placed side by side and divided by a ten-foot-wide rut of a road.

As we took that dirt road, our headlights hit a cluster of lightweight aluminum sailplane trailers parked haphazardly up ahead and to our left. Peering into the dark, I could just see a small airplane hangar at the far end of the road and off to the right. I could make out several cars to the right side of that hangar, their headlights illuminating a pair of small, stationary airplanes on a landing strip. The runway appeared to be at an angle to the hangar, heading east-west and parallel to the mountains.

Joe doused our lights, eased his foot off the gas, and slowed the car to a crawl.

"That's got to be her," he said. "See if you can raise Knightly."

I reached over to the phone and pressed the Redial button, but as before, there was only static.

I clicked off, then tried again.

I heard bursts of Knightly's voice, and I shouted, "We're at the *airfield.* They're *here.*"

Only crackling came over the speaker.

"You're breaking up. Please *repeat,*" I said, but the connection failed again.

Joe muttered, "It wasn't supposed to go down like this."

As I understood it, the original plan was to surround Muller's safe house, call her out, and bring her in. *This* situation had no boundaries. Not even the sky was the limit.

Joe slowed the Audi, and a handful of people exited the cars parked by the hangar. For a moment, they were frozen in our high beams: four Asian men, a hulking white man, and the woman who had to be Alison Muller. She and the hulk ran toward one of the planes, which looked to be a de Havilland Beaver. I knew it to be a sturdy bush plane.

At the same time, the Asians, now positioned behind their vehicles, opened fire.

Joe wrenched the wheel hard to the left and stepped on the brakes, and the Audi skidded in the grass before coming to a stop in the midst of the small trailers. I had my 9mm Glock in my hand, a solid and dependable service gun but no match for the automatic-weapon fire ripping across the meadow, pinging like a hailstorm into the trailers' aluminum hulls.

It was riskier to turn and run than it was to stand our ground and fight. I'm a good shot, even under pressure.

I was ready.

CHAPTER 92

I FELT UNREASONABLY INVINCIBLE.

Even then, I knew that what felt like courage was an adrenaline surge fueled by present danger and all of the fear, confusion, and rage I'd repressed over the last weeks.

Joe yelled at me, *"Stay in the car!"*

Too late for that. My loaded gun was in my hand and my feet were on the ground. I crouched behind a trailer, which was all that stood between me and the people who were strafing us with automatic-weapon fire.

I didn't have a death wish. I just didn't expect to die. I was rationalizing. We were thirty yards from the shooters. Everyone was firing into the dark.

Joe said, "I don't like our odds."

Then he bounded out of his side of the car and took a position at the butt end of the trailer I was using as a barrier at the front. We aimed and fired on the shooters and reloaded.

When there was a momentary break in the gunfire, Joe yelled, "Alison, give it up! The cops are on the way. No one needs to die. Put down your gun."

Muller laughed. It was a lovely laugh, both throaty and merry.

"You're too funny," she called back.

I saw the flash of Muller's blond hair as she sprang out from behind a car in a crouch. Her bodyguard followed, the two of them running for the open hatch of the closest plane. My attention was on Muller, but there was something about that bodyguard that rang a tinny bell. I knew him, but I couldn't place him at all.

And I didn't have time to think about it.

We had to stop Muller from boarding that plane.

Joe fired into the narrowing space between Muller and the aircraft, and her bodyguard pulled her back into cover behind a car. Joe yelled, "This is a mistake, Alison!"

And then the leading character in this long-running nightmare leaned over the top of her vehicle and fired a long burst of bullets, spraying left, then right across the trailers.

There was a split-second pause in the gunfire, and Muller and the big man made another dash toward the plane. Sighting her, I took aim, followed her with my muzzle, and fired.

Muller jerked and flailed before she fell to the ground.

Her bodyguard called her name and went to her, frantically trying to help her up. But she got to her knees and shook him off as she struggled to her feet.

My shot had gotten her in the back. She could only be alive if she was wearing a vest, and even then, given the angle of my shot, she was lucky to have survived.

Part of me was relieved that I hadn't killed her.

I wanted to talk to her, and I wanted to throw her in jail. But at the moment, Muller was armed and at large and bullets were flying at us again from her direction.

CHAPTER 93

JOE WAS RELOADING his gun when I saw four sets of headlights bumping over the rutted road toward the hangar. The cars drove past us and formed into a rough semicircle twenty-five yards away from the building and Muller's crew. I heard Knightly shouting, ordering people to drop their weapons, and he had plenty of gunpower to back him up.

And then Alison Muller stepped out from between two cars with her hands in the air.

"Hold your fire. I'm *unarmed*!" she shouted.

She was walking toward the headlights in surrender pose, her bodyguard beside her, when one of the Asian men in Muller's crew aimed his gun—at *her*. Her bodyguard yelled, shoved, and threw himself between Muller and the shooter in one movement. They both dropped to the ground.

In that moment, I recognized the bodyguard. But I didn't have even a second to process the thought because the man who had fired on Muller and missed aimed at her again.

Before he could get off his second shot, Knightly fired and dropped him, and in the same moment, Muller got up off the ground.

Seeing Joe, she called, "Joe, Joe! Don't shoot!"

She ran toward him and he lowered his gun.

Just then, I became aware of the waffling sound of helicopters coming in from under the lee of the mountain range, flying across the meadow toward the hangar, two choppers beaming light down on the airfield.

The Royal Canadian Mounted Police had arrived. The odds had decidedly shifted in our favor. My heart lifted as one of the choppers hovered near the de Havilland and landed in front of it, blocking the runway. There was more engine racket as the second helicopter cut off the Cessna's escape path as well.

The din was deafening and the rotor wash swept the field, blowing up dust. I turned away from the choppers, and when I opened my eyes, I saw Joe and Alison in a stunning tableau.

I hadn't heard what Joe had said to her, but clearly Muller had gotten the message. His gun was aimed at her head. And Alison, her blond hair whipping across her face, stood absolutely still with her hands in the air.

CHAPTER 94

DAWN WAS CASTING a cinematic glow over the remains of the firefight. Airplane and chopper pilots were getting out of their aircraft. Munder and Knightly took the three men left standing into custody and stepped around the dead bodyguard. But all of that was in the background.

I was watching Joe, listening as he said to Muller, "It's over, Alison. Turn around. Put your hands behind your back."

She looked at Joe and asked, "How could you do this to me? How in God's name can you humiliate me like this?"

I was standing only ten feet from Ali Muller, and even though she'd been caught moments away from her great escape and had been shot at by her own people, she looked composed. If there was the slightest trace of vulnerability in her face, it was that of hurt feelings. And the way she looked at Joe made me think she was taking her arrest personally.

She said, "Are you kidding me, Joseph? Do you think I don't know what you're doing and why?"

Joseph?

His smile was a grimace. He used Flex-Cuffs to pin her wrists together behind her back, after which he encircled her biceps with his hand. She twisted away, but it was half-hearted. She kept looking up into his face—I have to say, adoringly. I followed them across the grass, between the trailers and toward the shot-up Audi.

I listened as Muller tried to make her point.

"Joseph, have you lost sight of the truth? I'm still working for you. Don't you get that? This was part of our plan."

"What plan? You left the country. You were on the run. You're a traitor, Ali. We'll have plenty of time to talk about this, but not now."

"I'm a *traitor?* You knew I was going to work for us once I got to China. I told you. Didn't you understand that? Weren't you paying attention?"

Joe scoffed, but what I could see of his face was clouded.

Alison kept selling, working hard. Was she working Joe into giving her an alibi? Or was she telling the truth? How could I possibly know?

"You've told me you loved me," she said. "And now, what? You don't love me anymore?"

Joe *loved* her? Hearing that hurt worse than the beating I'd taken on Lake Street. Far worse. The left rear door of the Audi creaked as Joe opened it. He put one hand on Muller's head and angled her into the backseat. He closed the door hard and opened the driver's-side door for me, and I got in.

"I have to talk to Knightly," he said through the open window. "I'll only be about ten minutes. Watch her, Lindsay. And don't believe anything she says. She has an advanced degree in making shit up."

Muller called out, "*Joseph.* Joseph, don't leave me with her. She shot at me." She almost sounded panicky. "She'll kill me. Is that what you want?"

Joe reached into the car and threw the door locks. He

said, "Lindsay, don't shoot her unless you have to. But if you have to, *do* it. Do *not* let her leave."

"Copy that."

Did he *want* me to shoot her?

Would that solve a lot of problems for Joe?

Well, I had my own agenda.

Out on the rosy airfield, Knightly was speaking with the helicopter pilots from the RCMP. Joe said a few words, then headed over to the hangar, joining the agents who were loading the survivors of the shootout into vehicles.

I was alone with Alison Muller, the modern-day Mata Hari who had just sucker-punched my heart, then jumped on it and set it on fire. Oh, yeah, I was throbbing from the pain of that, but I had to push it all aside.

If the City of San Francisco was ever to have the chance to prosecute Muller for the Four Seasons murders, I had to get her to talk to me. I couldn't let my injured feelings compromise a case against her.

This meeting with Muller was why I was here.

I sat with my legs across the length of the front seat, my feet under the steering wheel, my face turned toward the honey-trap beauty. I showed her my gun.

"I'm Lindsay," I said. "Joe is my husband."

CHAPTER 95

MULLER SLID DOWN in the backseat catercorner from me. She stuck the soles of her boots up against the back of the driver's seat and got as comfortable as I imagine she could with her wrists bound behind her back.

I reached up to where Joe's phone was still clamped in its holder, below Ali's line of sight. I pressed the On button. And I pressed Record.

Then I turned around to face her.

I took a good long look at Muller's strong, almost mesmerizing features: her gorgeous skin, the shimmering blond hair with the signature bangs, her large eyes, which were almost all pupils at the moment. No matter the bravado she was exuding with her feet cocked up on the backseat, she'd been through a shit-storm and she was feeling the effects of it.

She spoke. "So you're his wife, huh?"

"That's right. I'm also a cop. SFPD. Just so you know, you don't have to say anything, but anything you *do* say can be used against you in court. Do you understand?"

Her merry laughter filled the car.

Then she said, "You can't touch me, babe. I'm in federal custody and that trumps the SFPD any day, every day. Do you have any idea who I am? Do you have any idea who your husband is? Don't bother to answer. You don't know jack. You don't know Joe."

"You may be right," I said, channeling the benign manner and patience of Rich Conklin. "So fill me in, why don't you?"

"What do you want to know?" she said. "You've got questions about Joe, I suppose. Like, how close are we, exactly? How often do we see each other? How tight are we after knowing each other for twenty-five years? How good we are together in bed? Yeah, I'll bet you'd like to know all that, but why don't you ask your husband? And good luck getting the truth out of him, Lindsay. Lying is one of the top two traits required of a CIA operative. Number two is not giving a shit."

I, too, was still pumping adrenaline. My fight-or-flight instinct had powered my blood into overdrive and my left hand had balled up into a fist. I wanted to lean over the seat back and punch Alison Muller in the mouth. I also wanted to get out of the car and run screaming into the foothills.

I kept it all down. It was the performance of my life.

"Actually, I want to know how you pulled off the killings at the hotel. It seems almost impossible that you got away."

"Hmmm. I had nothing to do with that."

"Well, humor me. Let's just play hypotheticals, OK?"

"Sure, Lindsay. Hypothetically *and* actually, I had nothing to do with whatever you're referring to. I was getting laid. Next thing I know, a masked man shot up the room and killed my boyfriend. I locked myself in the bathroom, and when the shooting stopped, I put on my clothes and got out. Once I was outside, I decided to leave the country and carry on my work for the Agency by pretending to flip to the Chinese side. That way, I could continue to serve my country from China. At great personal sacrifice, I might add. I was going to leave my family, and oh, yeah, stop seeing your husband, my lover, who is also the greatest guy in the world. Is that what you wanted to know?"

"Geez, you're good."

"Thanks. I'd like a cigarette."

"I'll see what I can do for you. But first."

"Aw, Christ."

"The one thing I really admire is how, while you were getting, uh, laid, all the Wi-Fi went down. Your room, the room next door, the common spaces—but not down on Market Street, where a kid who was working for the FBI was remotely taping you and Chan and Bud and Chrissy and everything that went down."

I was watching her closely. Her face stayed composed, but I could see the flash of alarm in her eyes.

She said, "What?"

"Try to keep up, Alison. An FBI surveillance tech had been following you for weeks, and he taped your highly enjoyable tryst in room fourteen-twenty at the Four Seasons from his *car*. He taped all of the passion and the tragedy of Renata and the Prince of Cheese. Every minute. I'll run your whole afternoon for you. Just speak up if I get something wrong, OK?"

I'd rocked her, caught her off guard and planted more than a little doubt in her shady mind. She didn't know the truth: that the FBI kid had also lost his video hookup, and that after their tryst, all we had of Chan and Muller was static and snow.

I might not be as good a liar as she was, but I was dancing on the balls of my feet, jabbing, and sticking to my story.

We were still in the early rounds, and I had to punch above my weight. But I was determined to win the bout.

CHAPTER 96

I WAS HOPING that Joe's phone was charged and recording, but I didn't dare look at it. I didn't blink. Either way, I had Alison's attention. I wanted all of that and more.

I said, "See, here's where it really got interesting for me, Alison. You know what I'm talking about?"

"Not really. And you're not going to get me a cigarette, are you?"

"Not yet," I said. "So, as I was saying, this part fascinates me. Michael Chan didn't know *when* his father was coming over from China…"

Her eyebrows shot up. I kept going.

"But your *partner* in this operation was listening to you and Chan on the coms he'd set up in fourteen-twenty, and he was also listening in on Bud and Chrissy in the next room."

"Maybe in your overheated imagination."

"He heard Joe tell Bud that he was coming up to the room, and that's when your partner pulled the plug on the entire wireless system, as only the hotel's head of security could do."

Alison's face had stiffened.

"Nice story for total bullshit."

"I met him, Alison. I spent almost a day and a half with Liam Dugan watching video of the lobby, the hallway, the elevators. He told me it was a mystery why and how the Internet had gone down, but that's life, right?"

My gun hand was sweating. I switched hands, dried my right hand on my jeans, and switched back again. Muller was watching me like a cat at the window that's spotted a bird. I kept going.

"Honestly, Alison, and this is no bull, I didn't put it together until a half hour ago when I saw Dugan get shot to death. Right. Out. There. He caught a bullet—meant for you."

"Lindsay. You're delusional."

"Am I? I said I'd run the story for you, and look, I'm not done. So, back to the hotel. Liam Dugan was watching the feeds. He hears Joe saying he's coming up to fourteen-eighteen, so Dugan shuts down the Wi-Fi, maybe knocks out a guest elevator at the same time so he can slow Joe down. He takes the service elevator to fourteen, where he kills the housekeeper, a potential witness, and stuffs her body into the supply closet.

"Then he takes the cart and knocks on the door to fourteen-twenty. Maybe he yells 'Maintenance,' something like that, and uses the passkey. Chan gets up to go to the door and Dugan shoots him twice in the face. Gives him another shot in the chest for good measure. And he says to you, 'Get dressed, Alison. Hurry up.'"

"Entertaining, yes, but pure make-believe—"

"And you *do* get dressed. You step over Michael Chan's dead body, and you tell Dugan to let you into the room next door. Again, he uses the key card he took from the dead housekeeper, which is registered with the security system. That was smart."

"Even brilliant."

"I agree," I said. "So now you're in fourteen-eighteen and the two kids are looking up at you, like 'What just happened?' One minute they're watching you party with Michael Chan on their laptops, waiting for Joe to arrive— then the Wi-Fi goes down and now you're inside their room with a gun in your hand.

"Alison, you killed those two unarmed kids and then, I'm thinking, Dugan got you out of the hotel by way of the fire stairs. And then he calls the police, says shots have been heard on the fourteenth floor.

"The Net is back up and hell, I'll bet he wasn't even winded when he showed us cops the crime scene. Very cool guy. I can see why you liked him. So here's a question, Alison."

She said, "Where the hell is Joseph? Oh. You remember I said I'm a federal employee, don't you?"

"Of course. I can't touch you, right? So here's my question. Why would Dugan do that for you? Why would he kill for you? And why would he die for you?"

"This is your story, not mine," said Alison Muller, exhaling like her breath was smoke.

"Well, here's my theory. He did it because he knew you. And as a world-class femme fatale to his former cop turned security chief, I think he would have been an easy score for you. You were beyond his wildest dreams. And—I'll admit this part is hypothetical—I think you told Dugan that you'd run away with him to the People's Republic of China and start a new and exciting life together. Am I warm, Alison?"

She was staring past me through the windshield, considering her options.

I knew it. I wasn't just warm. I was red-smoking-hot.

"Look," she said, "I'm going to get disappeared for a while. I want you to tell my daughters that I'm OK. That I love them. There are a few things I want them to have and there are some things I have to tell Khalid."

I understood what she was saying. She didn't know when she'd see them again. Or *if.*

"Happy to help. Tell me you killed Shirley Chan and it's a deal."

Alison sighed, shook her head, and said, "What a bitch." She was referring to me.

Then she said, "OK. I didn't know if or what Michael had told her about me. She was smart and she could have turned people against me. I went into her house and I put her down. OK? I killed her. Now shut the hell up. I can't stand the sound of your voice."

"Back at you, babe. You kind of make me sick."

I took the phone out of the holder, showed Alison the big icon of a microphone on the faceplate, rewound it a touch, and played back "You kind of make me sick." Then I said, "We're still rolling. Let's have the message for your family."

While she talked to her kids, I was thinking, *Gotcha.* Shirley Chan's death wasn't a government-ordered hit. Killing a mother of two small children was Muller's own personal cover-up to protect herself.

If the CIA spat Muller out, we could charge her for Shirley Chan's murder and do our best to build a case. I thought I could do it starting with her confession.

When Muller finished talking into the recorder, I pressed Stop and said, "That's a wrap."

She smiled—a hat-tip to me for making the deal. And then she started to laugh. Man, it was catching. I laughed, too. This hilarity was more about relief and hysteria than it was about humor, but we were both into it, chortling and giggling like high school girls.

Technically, I laughed last.

And of course, best.

CHAPTER 97

CHRIS KNIGHTLY'S BIG face filled the open car window.

"You girls having fun?" he said.

I didn't like the guy, but screw him. I had what I wanted, on the record. Knightly unlocked and opened the creaking back door and said, "Let me help you out, Ali. Watch your head."

Joe opened the front door, and as Knightly and Muller walked toward a chopper, he got in behind the wheel, reached over, pushed my gun muzzle toward the floor, and peeled my fingers off the butt one by one.

"It's OK, Linds. It's all OK."

He opened his arms and I went into them. He held me and kissed the top of my head, and I just gave myself over to the pleasure of that hug—but not for long. I disengaged, sat back in the passenger seat, and said, "What happens now?"

Joe said, "I'm going with Knightly, taking Muller in for interrogation. Munder is a good guy. He and a few others are taking a chopper to the Vancouver airport. You'll go with them. I'll call you when I can."

I nodded. There was no point asking him, "Where are you

taking her? How long will you be gone?" I took back my gun and holstered it. I let Joe open the door for me and I got out, looking around at this little airfield that had been a shooting gallery a short while ago.

Agent Munder came over and told me there was a bathroom in the hangar if I needed it and that a coffee urn and some rolls had been set out earlier for the crew.

"Help yourself."

A little while later, he gave me a hand up into the helicopter, which was too loud for conversation. I was glad. The flight to the airport was short. I waited in the lounge with Agent Munder for the flight to San Francisco, which was also short.

Conklin and Cindy met me at SFO, and they both hugged me to pieces. I sat in the backseat on the drive into the city, leaning toward them over the seat back so I could tell them about my fifteen hours with the CIA.

I fell asleep while I was talking.

Cindy walked with me upstairs to the apartment and sat with Mrs. Rose and Julie until I'd finished taking the best shower of my entire life. And then everyone left us alone.

I sat in Joe's chair holding our child, and then I sobbed deeply until she started crying, too. Poor Martha was dumbfounded. She barked and yipped and circled until I was all cried out.

We napped. Then we went to the park, my girls and me.

We sat by the lake and watched ducks and people. I made small talk with Martha and Julie. But my mind was working hard.

As usual, I still had questions.

CHAPTER 98

THE PHONE RANG at seven the next morning while I was brushing my teeth. It was Brady.

"Hah-wo," I said.

"Are you all right?"

I spat and rinsed. "Good as new."

"Fine. There's a car downstairs for you. Go to Mission and Cortland. Two officers are at the scene. They'll fill you in. Conklin's on the way."

Brady hung up. I sang to my reflection, "It's gonna be another bright, bright, sunshiny day."

I finished my morning ablutions and welcomed Mrs. Rose, who asked, "How are you?"

Everyone wanted to know how I was. I must look like I'd been dragged up and down Filbert Street behind a garbage truck.

"I'm fine," I said. "How are you?"

"A little tense. My daughter's due anytime. She's packed to go to the hospital. Do you think you'll be home after work?"

"I'll be home by six. Or call me and I will relieve you as speedily as the law allows."

"That's good enough for me," she said.

I kissed Julie, ruffled Martha's ears, tossed her a tennis ball, and grabbed a bottle of tea from the fridge. Then I ran down the stairs.

There was a fire-engine-red Camaro in front of my apartment building with gold hubcaps and matching chains around the plate guards. The envelope taped to the window had my name on it, and there was a set of keys inside, along with a note written in Brady's block-letter handwriting.

"Merry Christmas from the motor pool."

It was not Christmas, and this car's previous owner had clearly been convicted of possession of narcotics with intent to sell. I hated the car on sight. But until Nationwide paid out for my deceased Explorer, it would have to do.

My drive to the Mission would have been a laugh riot if I'd been in a laughing mood. I got suggestive gestures and horn toots and more than one offer to race, but on the positive side, the car went from zero to sixty in a heartbeat, handled beautifully around curves, and braked on a bottle cap. The motor pool had tooled this crass beast into a first-class cop car.

When I got to the intersection of Mission and Cortland, Conklin was waiting outside a cheap variety store near the corner. He was not alone. Three squad cars were at the curb and a load of interested citizens stood behind the yellow tape. Broken glass glittered on the sidewalk.

Conklin met me at the car and took me over to talk to the first officer, saying, "Officer Dow spoke with the lady a few minutes ago. Dow, tell the sergeant what you told me."

The uniformed cop was young and keyed up and clearly wanted to make his report.

He said, "Girl in there says she's had enough of her old

man. She shot him and yelled out to me that she doesn't trust men at all and won't be taken alive."

"Father? Or husband?" I asked.

"Husband."

"SWAT is on the way?"

Dow said, "She says if she sees men in black, she's just going to blow her brains out. But she'll talk to *you*, Sergeant. She saw your picture on the news after the Chinatown bust."

I was back on the job, working a case that didn't involve spies or orphaned children or multiple homicides. It wasn't exactly blue skies with a side of roses, but it wasn't bad. There was even a chance that I could do some good.

My vest was in the back of my Explorer, which was still undergoing a forensic postmortem at the crime lab, but I was wearing my lucky socks.

I asked Officer Dow, "What's her name?"

CHAPTER 99

BY 2 P.M, I was home again with my shoes and cell phone off.

Mrs. Rose was at her daughter's bedside. The victim of the variety store shooting was in stable condition, and the young female shooter had a lawyer and was under suicide watch.

Joe was with Alison Muller at some black site in DC or on foreign soil, and I didn't know when he was coming back or if I would let him into my life again.

I could make a good case for moving on.

I thought of Alison Muller's taunts about the closeness of her relationship with Joe, and although she was a five-star liar, he had an equal number of stars on his chest, maybe more, and they made a pretty good pair.

Mrs. Rose liked to say, "When feeling pathetic, make tea."

I boiled water and took a look at the big pile of mail that had been accumulating for weeks on the kitchen counter. Joe had been paying the bills for a while, but I still knew how to balance a checkbook.

I blew on my tea, switched the radio to Radio Alice, 97.3, for their adult contemporary sound, and put the mail and my computer on the coffee table. I tossed the flyers and catalogs to the floor, separating out the utilities and condo maintenance and the bank statement.

I was going through the statement when I saw a charge for a safe-deposit box that I didn't know we had. I'm not saying it was a secret. Only that I hadn't noticed it before.

The time was now 2:35. Our bank was at Ninth Avenue and Clement, five blocks away. If the baby would cooperate, I could get there before closing time.

I went to the drawer in Joe's office and removed the key I'd found days ago at the bottom of a stationery box. I put on my shoes, strapped Julie into the baby sling, and arrived at the bank five minutes before closing. I told the woman in charge of the vault that I wouldn't take long. I just had to get into the box before the weekend. It was urgent.

Was it urgent? I asked myself, even as she opened the doors. Was I setting myself up for one more hideous disappointment?

"Please, Mrs. Molinari," said the vault keeper. "I have an appointment with the coach at my son's school. I promised."

Joe's key had the number 26 engraved on the shaft. The vault lady put her key into one of the locks and I put my key into the corresponding lock. After the tumblers clicked into place, I slid the long metal box out of the cabinet and took it into the tiny viewing room next to the vault.

I fumbled with the hasp and finally got the box open. I stared in at the contents. There were several unsealed envelopes inside. One of them held our condo lease. I found our marriage license, Julie's birth certificate, and Joe's father's death certificate. Under those envelopes was a long flat candy box with gold edging and a stylized drawing of a bow on top.

As I bridged the lid of the candy box with my fingers, preparing to open it, I reflected on the fact that I was snooping—again, but screw it. I was entitled to whatever truth I could find in this haystack of lies a.k.a. my marriage to Joe.

If there were mementos of Joe's secret life with Alison Muller, I absolutely needed to know.

I removed the lid. Up came the smell of chocolate and cherries, but Alison Muller wasn't inside the candy box.

Julie was there. And so was I.

On top, a sprig of Julie's fine, dark baby hair tied with a slender pink ribbon. There was a photograph a stranger had taken of Joe and me on the ferry to Catalina, both of us grinning, the wake foaming behind us as we stood embracing at the rail. That was the first time we'd told each other, "I love you."

Under that photo was a copy of the marriage vows we'd exchanged in a gazebo lapped by the ocean in Half Moon Bay, and there was a candid snapshot of Joe and me and Cat and the little girls, all of us laughing and walking barefoot down the beach in our wedding clothes. And there was a printout of an e-mail from me to Joe telling him that I missed him so much, asking, "When are you coming home?"

I was struck by the congruence of having similar thoughts now at this very different place and time in our lives.

My musings were interrupted by the vault lady tapping on the glass, pointing to her watch.

"I'm coming," I said.

I put everything back in the box and returned it to its sleeve in the cabinet behind the locked doors, and Julie and I left the bank.

"What now?" I said to my precious little girl as we crossed Lake Street toward the Molinari family home.

"What's going to happen now?"

EPILOGUE

CHAPTER 100

ALISON MULLER KNEW every inch of the cell where she'd been held for a month or more—she wasn't sure how long. It was impossible to grasp even the difference between day and night in the artificial gray light of this underground box, which had been designed by a crazy person.

The walls leaned in and the ceiling sloped and even the stones in the wall were different shapes, laid without pattern or sense.

She was grateful for the crazy stones because each had a personality. Like the one shaped like a kidney next to her bed. And the one next to it, shaped like Ohio. Looking at the stones gave her a place to put her mind.

There were no fellow prisoners, no exercise yard. She had a narrow bunk, a flush toilet, and a recessed shower head over the toilet that dispensed only cold water.

Her one meal and a change of paper clothes were delivered by her interrogator.

He came to the chair outside her cell at regular intervals to question her. He was very formal. His clothes were neutral and boring, but pressed, and he always wore a tie. Alison didn't know him and he wouldn't tell her his name.

"What do people call you?" she would ask. "Just say any name."

"My name is unimportant."

She had called him Unimportant for a while, but it was clumsy. So she tried other names: Bert, Voldemort, Condor. But the name that stuck was Secret Agent Man, or Sam.

Sam was middle-aged, paunchy, and humorless but a fine interrogator. He never hurt her physically, but he knew how to get to her, how to worry her and make her desperate for news of her kids.

He also brought incentives with him: a box of food and a clean, blue, one-piece flushable garment.

These items remained under his chair while he tried to break her. Most of the time when he was ready to leave, he slid the parcels under the lowest bar of her cell. Sometimes he took the food and clothes away with him.

Today, as usual, he'd said, "Hello, Ms. Muller. Are you comfortable?"

"Fabulous accommodations, dahling," she'd said. "If you could have fresh flowers delivered. And a change of linens."

The interrogator smiled, if you could call the thin stretch of his thin lips a smile. He asked the same questions every day. "Who gave the order to blow up the plane?"

And every time, she said the same thing.

"Like I told you, Secret Agent Man. What I heard is that they were rogue Chinese operatives. I didn't know them. I don't know who they were working for. I heard they're all dead. Now. If you don't mind telling me, who do I have to blow to get out of this joint?"

"What information have you passed to the Chinese?"

"None. None at all."

One time, after the questions were done, Secret Agent Man said, "I've seen Caroline."

He pulled his phone out of his shirt pocket and showed her a photo of her daughter coming out of her middle school building. He said, "She has a bruise on her left arm. See there. I think she may be getting into fights. Or maybe Khalid did this to her."

Then he'd asked her another of the everyday questions. "Who is your contact in China? Who were you going to meet when you got there?"

"I didn't have a contact. I was going to be met at the airport. That's the truth. That's the *truth*. It all happened very fast. Remember, please. I am still CIA. I was only going to work over there for *us*. Molinari knows this. Please. I've told you everything. What do I have to do to get out of here?"

Today, after the usual bull, Secret Agent Man had said, "Your meal is a cheese and mushroom frittata. I had one. It's very good. *Bon appétit*. I'll see you soon, Ms. Muller."

And then he'd left.

Alison had thought of killing herself. She had run headfirst at the wall, but she really couldn't get any momentum going and had only given herself a headache. A hidden camera watched her. The one time she'd tried to hang herself on the bars, Sam had appeared and said, "No, Ms. Muller. Don't do that unless you'd like us to take away your clothes. Keep you here in the nude."

She wasn't yet desperate enough to drown herself in the toilet. But she was close.

She was going to be here for life.

She was going to die in this underground stone box.

The sooner the better. There was no way out and nothing left to live for. She couldn't even fantasize anymore. She just couldn't fool herself into believing in happiness.

She went to the cot, which was chained to the wall, and lay down. She pulled out strands of hair, one at a time, and she started the countdown to the one thing she had to look forward to.

The next meeting with Sam.

He was all she had.

CHAPTER 101

ALISON THOUGHT SHE'D finally gone insane.

She heard men's voices out of sight in the corridor beyond her cell. She knew both voices. One was Sam, her tormentor. She knew for sure she was crazy, because the other man—was Joe.

First the muffled voices, then the shadows falling across the stone floor. And then they were both at the bars.

Secret Agent Man said, "You have a visitor, Ms. Muller."

He put the box with her dinner and her one-piece outfit under the chair and then said to Joe, "Take your time. When you're ready, you know where to find me."

Alison rushed to the bars and grabbed them.

"Joseph. Have you come to get me out?"

"I could only arrange a visit," he said.

He brushed her hand with his, then sat in the chair outside the cell. She sat on the floor right against the bars so that she could be close to him.

"Why are you here, then?"

"I wanted to see if you had charmed management into giving you silk sheets and an ocean view."

"Oh, yes, it's just like the Ritz. And no one even asked me to put out."

She grinned but couldn't hold the pose. Her smile crumpled. She put her hands into her ragged hair and pulled it away from her eyes. She looked up at Joe. His expression was cool. But still, she could read that he felt sorry for her. That he still cared.

"I look terrible, I know. I never wanted you to see me like this. How are you, Joseph? What's it like for you now?"

"I'd like to say it's like nothing ever happened, but there's been fallout, of course. Professional and personal."

"You want to talk about it?" she asked.

He shook his head.

"I understand. But to the point of all this, Joseph," she said, making a gesture with her hand that took in all twenty square feet of her cell. "I have to get out of here."

"I know."

"I've answered all their questions. I've been tortured, Joe. I'm not holding anything back. They're not giving me anything off for my time and service in the Agency. They just keep hammering me with the same questions, and I've told them I don't know anything more."

"OK. Well, they're not convinced, I guess."

"But you can help me. You can speak for me. You know what I've done and what I've sacrificed."

"I'm not considered a clean source on you, Ali."

"Joe, please, please. I've got kids. I have more to give to the Agency. I'm a valuable person. You can save me, Joe. I know you can save me."

"Is there anything you can tell me that I can pass on?"

"I've given up everything."

"I was told we only had five minutes," he said.

"Will you be back?"

"I don't know."

He patted her hands and left her.

CHAPTER 102

SECRET AGENT MAN was at the bars of her stone cage at what seemed to be his usual time. Alison noticed that he was dressed as was his style, in a khaki-colored jacket with a white shirt, a blue-striped tie, and a pair of dun-colored pants. His hair was neatly combed and he was clean-shaven. But he hadn't brought her fresh paper jumpsuit and the boxed meal, her only food for the day.

He said, "Ms. Muller. My name is Anderson."

"First or last?"

"Just Anderson," he said. "We have to clean your cell. And I thought maybe you'd like a hot shower before we bring you back."

"Are you kidding?"

The idea of standing under hot water was just tremendous. "Not at all. I have a Taser," he said. "Need I say any more?"

"No. I'll behave. Where would I go, anyway?"

"Exactly," said Anderson.

Alison thought Joe had arranged this. At least he had done this much. Maybe this shower was incentive for her to be more cooperative. Maybe that would work.

Anderson opened the cell door and stepped away, out of Alison's reach. He patted the waistband of his pants under his jacket so that she could see the bulge of the Taser gun.

"Straight ahead, Ms. Muller. You'll see an opening on your left at the end of the corridor. There's a short flight of stairs, and the staff bathroom is up there. There's soap and shampoo and a clean towel on a hook. Your dinner is being prepared now. Pork loin and boiled new potatoes. Chocolate brownies."

"Wow," Alison said, giving him a big grin. "Must be my birthday."

She had walked about ten paces down the hallway when Anderson fired a .44-caliber bullet into the back of her skull. He fired again into her back as she fell. He stooped next to her, flipped his tie over his shoulder, and felt for a pulse.

There was none.

He sighed. Then he walked around her body on his way to the office to make his report.

CHAPTER 103

I WAS HAVING a dinner party. This was the first time in maybe a year since I'd had people over, and I was up for it. Julie was in a sparkly party dress, and she had a new word.

"Mommy."

It was the best word in every language all over the world.

Mrs. Rose had spent the day helping me cook, and my buds were all in my house: Claire and her adorable husband, Edmund. Yuki and my boss and idol, Jackson Brady. Richie and Cindy, of course, and Jacobi had come with a date.

Her name was Miranda and she played "Dora" on a daytime TV show I had never seen, but Mrs. Rose had almost fainted when Miranda walked in the door.

We were all having cocktails. Mrs. Rose had refused the invitation to be my date. She had a new grandchild and was glad to get out of my house.

I gave her a hug and a check and she patted my arm and said, "Have fun. I'll be here in the morning."

Brady came into the open kitchen looking for the corkscrew. He opened a bottle of wine and said, "Whatever is cooking is making me slobber."

I laughed. "Ten more minutes. That's all. Just ten."

Yuki followed Brady in, put her arms around his waist, and kissed his back. God, it had been a long time coming, but these two were just made for each other.

"Do you need help with the salad dressing?" she asked me.

"Of course I do," I said.

Out in the living room, Edmund was roaring with laughter; Claire was, too, at something Miranda had said, and Jacobi was flushed in a very good way. Cindy was in the big chair, holding Julie on her lap. If or when to have babies had been the big logjam in her otherwise wonderful relationship with Richie, and I think every time she comes to my house, she's trying Julie on to see if she can imagine herself as a mom.

I saw Richie standing behind the sofa, looking at Cindy holding Julie. Wow. He was in love.

As for me, I ached more than a little.

Joe had been over a few times to see Julie, and it was a meltingly beautiful thing to see them together. But I had never let him stay the night or even for a meal.

I just wasn't ready. And I didn't know how I would ever be ready. He had lied. He was mysterious. I didn't know where he was living, what he was doing, or how I could ever fit in with a man I no longer trusted.

It was Brady, of all people, who helped me take the roast out of the oven. Claire got the vegetables onto the table and Edmund poured the wine.

Richie was clinking his glass with a spoon, saying, "Lindsay, it's wonderful to be here. I'm personally so glad you had help with the cooking, since we all know you can't even make coffee."

Everyone laughed, even Julie and me.

The buzzer rang from downstairs.

Claire said, "That's the dessert. I'm not telling you from

where. Just get away from the door so I can still make it a surprise."

Claire is a chocoholic, and I say that's a good thing.

I said, "OK, surprise me."

I went back to the table and Claire pressed the buzzer. A minute later, I heard the door latch open and Claire say, "You're not the cake."

So what *was* this?

I got halfway to the door and saw my husband standing there in the hallway.

He said, "Geez, Lindsay, I didn't mean to interrupt."

I said to my bosom buddy, "Claire. You set this up."

"Me? No. Not me. No way. I would never do anything like this. Nuh-uh."

And she melted away from the door.

Joe had a bunch of roses in his hand. He looked like the prince who woke up Sleeping Beauty with a kiss. Handsome. Expectant. And like, maybe, his steed was tethered down at the curb. I stared into his face and saw the lines in his forehead, which were deeper than they had been a couple of months ago. He had some gray at his temples that I hadn't noticed before.

I stood at the door, feet firmly planted, blocking the entrance.

He said, "Lindsay?"

I honestly didn't know what to do or say.

Let him in?

Or say, "Not now. Maybe some other time."

ACKNOWLEDGMENTS

Our thanks to Captain Richard Conklin, BCI Commander, Stamford, Connecticut, PD, and Humphrey Germaniuk, Medical Examiner and Coroner, Trumbull County, Ohio, for generously sharing their time and expertise. We also wish to thank our excellent researchers, Ingrid Taylar, Renee Paradis, Lynn Colomello, and Pete Colomello, and give a high five to Mary Jordan, who keeps it all on track.

ABOUT THE AUTHORS

JAMES PATTERSON received the Literarian Award for Outstanding Service to the American Literary Community at the 2015 National Book Awards. He holds the Guinness World Record for the most #1 *New York Times* bestsellers, and his books have sold more than 325 million copies worldwide. He has donated more than one million books to students and soldiers and funds over four hundred Teacher Education Scholarships at twenty-four colleges and universities. He has also donated millions to independent bookstores and school libraries.

MAXINE PAETRO is the author of three novels and two works of nonfiction, and she is the coauthor of the Women's Murder Club series with James Patterson. She lives in New York with her husband.

BOOKS BY JAMES PATTERSON

FEATURING ALEX CROSS

Cross the Line • *Cross Justice* • *Hope to Die* • *Cross My Heart* • *Alex Cross, Run* • *Merry Christmas, Alex Cross* • *Kill Alex Cross* • *Cross Fire* • *I, Alex Cross* • *Alex Cross's* Trial (with Richard DiLallo) • *Cross Country* • *Double Cross* • *Cross* (also published as *Alex Cross*) • *Mary, Mary* • *London Bridges* • *The Big Bad Wolf* • *Four Blind Mice* • *Violets Are Blue* • *Roses Are Red* • *Pop Goes the Weasel* • *Cat & Mouse* • *Jack & Jill* • *Kiss the Girls* • *Along Came a Spider*

THE WOMEN'S MURDER CLUB

15th Affair (with Maxine Paetro) • *14th Deadly Sin* (with Maxine Paetro) • *Unlucky 13* (with Maxine Paetro) • *12th of Never* (with Maxine Paetro) • *11th Hour* (with Maxine Paetro) • *10th Anniversary* (with Maxine Paetro) • *The 9th Judgment* (with Maxine Paetro) • *The 8th Confession* (with Maxine Paetro) • *7th Heaven* (with Maxine Paetro) • *The 6th Target* (with Maxine Paetro) • *The 5th Horseman* (with Maxine Paetro) • *4th of July* (with Maxine Paetro) • *3rd Degree* (with Andrew Gross) • *2nd Chance* (with Andrew Gross) • *1st to Die*

FEATURING MICHAEL BENNETT

Bullseye (with Michael Ledwidge) • *Alert* (with Michael Ledwidge) • *Burn* (with Michael Ledwidge) • *Gone* (with Michael Ledwidge) • *I, Michael Bennett* (with Michael Ledwidge) • *Tick Tock* (with Michael Ledwidge) • *Worst Case* (with Michael Ledwidge) • *Run for Your Life* (with Michael Ledwidge) • *Step on a Crack* (with Michael Ledwidge)

THE PRIVATE NOVELS

The Games (with Mark Sullivan) • *Private Paris* (with Mark Sullivan) • *Private Vegas* (with Maxine Paetro) • *Private India: City on Fire* (with Ashwin Sanghi) • *Private Down Under* (with Michael White) • *Private*

L.A. (with Mark Sullivan) • *Private Berlin* (with Mark Sullivan) • *Private London* (with Mark Pearson) • *Private Games* (with Mark Sullivan) • *Private: #1 Suspect* (with Maxine Paetro) • *Private* (with Maxine Paetro)

NYPD RED NOVELS

NYPD Red 4 (with Marshall Karp) • *NYPD Red 3* (with Marshall Karp) • *NYPD Red 2* (with Marshall Karp) • *NYPD Red* (with Marshall Karp)

SUMMER NOVELS

Second Honeymoon (with Howard Roughan) • *Now You See Her* (with Michael Ledwidge) • *Swimsuit* (with Maxine Paetro) • *Sail* (with Howard Roughan) • *Beach Road* (with Peter de Jonge) • *Lifeguard* (with Andrew Gross) • *Honeymoon* (with Howard Roughan) • *The Beach House* (with Peter de Jonge)

STAND-ALONE BOOKS

Woman of God (with Maxine Paetro) • *Filthy Rich* (with John Connolly and Timothy Malloy) • *The Murder House* (with David Ellis) • *Truth or Die* (with Howard Roughan) • *Miracle at Augusta* (with Peter de Jonge) • *Invisible* (with David Ellis) • *First Love* (with Emily Raymond) • *Mistress* (with David Ellis) • *Zoo* (with Michael Ledwidge) • *Guilty Wives* (with David Ellis) • *The Christmas Wedding* (with Richard DiLallo) • *Kill Me If You Can* (with Marshall Karp) • *Toys* (with Neil McMahon) • *Don't Blink* (with Howard Roughan) • *The Postcard Killers* (with Liza Marklund) • *The Murder of King Tut* (with Martin Dugard) • *Against Medical Advice* (with Hal Friedman) • *Sundays at Tiffany's* (with Gabrielle Charbonnet) • *You've Been Warned* (with Howard Roughan) • *The Quickie* (with Michael Ledwidge) • *Judge & Jury* (with Andrew Gross) • *Sam's Letters to Jennifer* • *The Lake House* • *The Jester* (with Andrew Gross) • *Suzanne's Diary for Nicholas* • *Cradle and All* • *When the Wind Blows* • *Miracle on the 17th Green* (with Peter de Jonge) • *Hide & Seek* • *The Midnight Club* • *Black Friday* (originally published as *Black Market*) • *See How They Run* • *Season of the Machete* • *The Thomas Berryman Number*

BOOK**SHOTS**

FOR READERS OF ALL AGES

MAXIMUM RIDE

DANIEL X

WITCH & WIZARD

The Kiss (with Jill Dembowski) • *Witch & Wizard: The Fire* (with Jill Dembowski) • *Witch & Wizard: The Gift* (with Ned Rust) • *Witch & Wizard* (with Gabrielle Charbonnet)

CONFESSIONS
Confessions: The Murder of an Angel (with Maxine Paetro) • *Confessions: The Paris Mysteries* (with Maxine Paetro) • *Confessions: The Private School Murders* (with Maxine Paetro) • *Confessions of a Murder Suspect* (with Maxine Paetro)

MIDDLE SCHOOL
Middle School: Dog's Best Friend (with Chris Tebbetts, illustrated by Jomike Tejido) • *Middle School: Just My Rotten Luck* (with Chris Tebbetts, illustrated by Laura Park) • *Middle School: Save Rafe!* (with Chris Tebbetts, illustrated by Laura Park) • *Middle School: Ultimate Showdown* (with Julia Bergen, illustrated by Alec Longstreth) • *Middle School: How I Survived Bullies, Broccoli, and Snake Hill* (with Chris Tebbetts, illustrated by Laura Park) • *Middle School: My Brother Is a Big, Fat Liar* (with Lisa Papademetriou, illustrated by Neil Swaab) • *Middle School: Get Me Out of Here!* (with Chris Tebbetts, illustrated by Laura Park) • *Middle School, The Worst Years of My Life* (with Chris Tebbetts, illustrated by Laura Park)

I FUNNY
I Funny TV (with Chris Grabenstein, illustrated by Laura Park) • *I Totally Funniest: A Middle School Story* (with Chris Grabenstein, illustrated by Laura Park) • *I Even Funnier: A Middle School Story* (with Chris Grabenstein, illustrated by Laura Park) • *I Funny: A Middle School Story* (with Chris Grabenstein, illustrated by Laura Park)

TREASURE HUNTERS
Treasure Hunters: Peril at the Top of the World (with Chris Grabenstein, illustrated by Juliana Neufeld) • *Treasure Hunters: Secret of the Forbidden City* (with Chris Grabenstein, illustrated by Juliana Neufeld) • *Treasure Hunters: Danger Down the Nile* (with Chris Grabenstein, illustrated by Juliana Neufeld) • *Treasure Hunters* (with Chris Grabenstein, illustrated by Juliana Neufeld)

OTHER BOOKS FOR READERS OF ALL AGES

For previews and information about the author, visit JamesPatterson.com or find him on Facebook or at your app store.